Noirlathotep
Tales of Lovecraftian Crime

**Edited by
Paul Brian McCoy and Jennifer King**

for

Psycho Drive-In Press

Contents

Introduction.. 1

Let Sleeping Gods Lie 9
    by Dan Lee

A Stutter in the Infinite 45
    by Alex Wolfe

The Lurker in the Dark 83
    by John E. Meredith

Dan Shadduk's Bad Luck Day............................. 155
    by R. Mike Burr

In the Shadow of Reality.. 171
    by Dan Johnson

Into the Valley of San Fernando 193
    by Rick Shingler

The Shadow Over Braxton County........................ 239
    by Paul Brian McCoy

Who We Be.. 309

Introduction

by
Paul Brian McCoy

If it wasn't for HBO, this book probably wouldn't exist.

The year was 1991.

The year of Desert Storm and the breakup of the U.S.S.R.; Mike Tyson was arrested and charged with rape, while Jeffrey Dahmer was arrested for killing and eating eleven men and boys; the phrase "going postal" was coined after Joseph Harris killed his former girlfriend, her fiancé, and two former co-workers at the post office in Ridgewood, New Jersey; Freddie Mercury confirmed he had AIDS and died the following day of complications (that year we also lost Frederick J. Pohl, Serge Gainsbourg, David Lean, Don Siegel, Johnny Thunders, Frank Capra, Dr. Seuss, Miles Davis, Redd Foxx, and Gene Roddenberry); the 911 Emergency Number was launched in the American northwest, and the internet was finally available and reached its first 1 million users; Nirvana released *Nevermind*, James Cameron released *Terminator 2: Judgment Day*, while Anthony Hopkins played Hannibal Lecter for the first time, and Paul Reubens was caught masturbating in an adult theater; Mariah Carey had three number one hits, *Seinfeld* debuted on NBC, the Super Nintendo invaded homes, and Patrick Swayze was *People Magazine*'s Sexiest Man Alive!

All in all, it was an eventful year. But one night

in early September, something happened that made this book possible. It was Saturday, September 7, 1991, to be exact.

I was 23 years old - there's that mysterious and magical number William S. Burroughs and Robert Anton Wilson alerted us to - and instead of being out gallivanting around town, I was at home watching HBO. Because that night was the premiere of *Cast a Deadly Spell*, written by Joseph Dougherty, directed by Martin Campbell, and starring Clancy Brown, David Warner, Julianne Moore, and most importantly, Fred Ward as hardboiled gumshoe Phil Lovecraft.

It was silly and funny, filled with one-liners, fast talk and faster women, hard drinks and harder knocks. And oh yeah, a search for the Necronomicon and the threat of the world ending with the awakening of great Cthulhu in 1948 Los Angeles. In this alternate America, magic was real and everybody used it every day. Except for our man Phil, that is. Which is why he was hired to track down the book. As the search goes on, he interacts with pretty much every cliché from noir played fast and loose, tongue-in-cheek, and with a loopy respect to both Film Noir and Cosmic Horror.

Now, fighting magic and the occult in fiction wasn't a new thing. The Occult Detective is a tradition going back in literature at least as far as Algernon Blackwood's John Silence (1908) and William Hope Hodgson's Carnacki (1910-12) - although there is an argument to be made for Poe's Chevalier Auguste Dupin (1841), Seridan Le Fanu's Dr. Martin Hesselius (1872), or even Bram Stoker's iconic Dr. Abraham Van Helsing (1897). In film

2

and television we had *The Night of the Demon* (1957), *The Devil Rides Out* (1968), and *The Night Stalker* (1972). But in these examples, the detection is done by scientists, aristocrats, and investigative reporters rather than actual hardboiled detectives. In fact, it may not have been until the introduction of Clive Barker's Harry D'Amour - in the short story "The Last Illusion" (1985) - that the connection was made in print. And despite not really playing the role of Occult Detective so much as Agent Provocateur, 1985 also saw the first appearance of Alan Moore's John Constantine in *The Saga of the Swamp Thing* #37 (June 1985). Then, the release of Alan Parker's 1987 satanic noir, *Angel Heart*, brought the genre mashup to film in all its sleazy, sweaty goodness.

These agents struggled against devils, angels, and things in between, though. None of it was Lovecraftian.

While having a huge following and inspiring countless other horror and science fiction writers from the early 1920s to today, H.P. Lovecraft's influence on film was decidedly lacking until around that same time in the mid-80s. Sure, there was Corman's *The Haunted Palace* in 1963 (cleverly disguised as another Poe adaptation), *Die, Monster, Die!* In 1965, and the 1970s-riffic *The Dunwich Horror*, but none of them were all that faithful to the tone and philosophies of Lovecraft's work.

1985 is the year that Lovecraft film really came into its own, with Stuart Gordon's gonzo splatter-fest *Re-Animator*, followed quickly in 1986 by his equally audacious *From Beyond*. Both films starred

Jeffrey Combs and Barbara Crampton who would essentially become the King and Queen of Lovecraft on Film. None of the other Lovecraftian adaptations that followed really hit as high a benchmark as those first two 80s extravaganzas, but by 1991, Lovecraft was decidedly in the horror public's consciousness and Joseph Dougherty saw the opportunity to mix up a cocktail of his affections for Raymond Chandler and Lovecraft over at HBO.

Cast a Deadly Spell was the first time Lovecraft and the Occult Detective motif came together (not counting the failed 1965 television pilot, *Dark Intruder* - which I'm not counting because Lovecraft's Elder Gods are really only mentioned in passing during a more traditional, but still very entertaining, Victorian mystery) and the magic of watching *The Big Sleep* channeled through the Mythos became, for a young, aspiring writer like me, a touchstone going forward.

But I never really got around to writing a story - or stories - in that milieu. I don't know if I just didn't think the audience was there or if I was just lazy. Probably the latter.

It wouldn't really be until this past decade (give or take a couple of years) that mixing Eldritch Horror with Hardboiled Crime in literature really became a thing, with novels and anthologies like *The Tales of Inspector Legrasse* (2005), *The Midnight Eye Files: The Amulet* (2005), *Hard Boiled Cthulhu: Two Fisted Tales of Tentacled Terror* (2006), *Deadstock* (2007), *Looking for Darla* (2008), *Cthulhu Unbound 1 & 2* (2009), and *Dance of the Damned* (2011). Most recently, Peter

4

Rawlik has dipped his toes into the waters with *Reanimators* (2013) and its sequel *Reanimatrix* (2016), Victor LaValle revisited "The Horror at Red Hook" with his novella *The Ballad of Black Tom* (2016), and Matt Ruff's *Lovecraft Country: A Novel* (2016) is a book everyone should read.

To be honest, *Black Tom* and *Lovecraft Country* aren't straight noir, but share enough elements to be included here.

The book you hold in your hand (or are reading on your tablet or future phone) was an idea that started out years ago as a play on words, as my friend and super-awesome manga translator/comic writer, Zack Davisson and I were throwing around some ideas that would make good mashup anthologies for comics or prose and the name Noir-lathotep came up as a Lovecraftian Hard Boiled Crime combo. We both loved the name and filed it away for a rainy day when we could collaborate on something, stories, comics, we had no clue.

That rainy day never came.

Then, on Valentine's Day 2014, Psycho Drive-In launched, carrying over the TV and Movie coverage of Comics Bulletin (comicsbulletin.com) so they could continue to focus on comics while we could flood the internet with our ramblings about horror, sci-fi, and cult film and television. I've been the Publisher and Editor-in-Chief since Day One, funding the site out-of-pocket, originally hoping to build up enough of an audience to bring in enough ad revenue to pay our hard-working and multi-talented writers. While we've built up a decent, but still small following, that's still just a pipe dream (and my day job barely pays a living wage).

So to offset the costs of running the site, I decided to launch PDI Press, repurposing columns as e-books, with *Marvel at the Movies: 1977-1998*, *Marvel at the Movies: Marvel Studios from Iron Man to Ultron*, and *Spoiler Alert: Hannibal Season One - An Unauthorized Critical Guide* helping to ease the financial pain a little. But not enough, so I dug deep into my past inspirations and pitched an idea to my writers that I wasn't sure anyone would agree to. But they're all not only excellent critics, but extraordinarily talented fiction writers hungry to get eyes on their work.

The idea was *Noirlathotep: Tales of Lovecraftian Crime*.

And people agreed to it.

R. Mike Burr, Dan Johnson, Dan Lee, John E. Meredith, Rick Shingler, and Alex Wolfe all stepped up and volunteered to write crime stories with a Lovecraftian flair to help fundraise for Psycho Drive-In, and it isn't possible for me to love these people more. We've got classic noir, bizarre murder mysteries, humor, existential dread, and a touch of neo-noir, all with a nod and a wink to the masters of crime fiction and cosmic horror, old and new. Whatever your particular tastes when it comes to Lovecraft homage, I think we've got you covered.

This is the good stuff, folks.

And the best part is that all the authors own the rights to their work. We're publishing *Noirlathotep* as an e-book and a paperback, then everybody's free to do what they like with their stories; adapt them into comics, screenplays, write more adventures in the worlds they've built, etc., all while helping to keep Psycho Drive-In up and running for as long as we still feel that need to write about weird shit on film.

So come check out everybody's work at psychodrivein.com, share your thoughts and opinions with us, and keep an eye out for another fiction anthology in the near future.

Let Sleeping Gods Lie

by
Dan Lee

It was another gun barrel birthday, sitting alone in an empty apartment with nothing but half a handle of cheap whiskey and an old .38 special I'd carried in another life. In the one hand was the poison that had ruined my career, destroyed my marriage, and left me lying on the cheap tan Berber of a low-rent one-room apartment in the middle of nowhere. In the other hand was a permanent solution to the ongoing run of bad decisions that I'd spent an entire lifetime making for myself. Either way, the room would still smell like shit and there'd likely be a mess to clean up come tomorrow morning. Looking up at my reflection in the broken screen of an old television, I couldn't see much reason to keep going. My hair was receding into a salt and pepper widow's peak as my skin slowly continued to wrinkle at the eyes and lips. At thirty-eight I was hardly the man I'd been when I was a police detective. Virile, handsome, with a razor-sharp wit and the highest number of solved cases in the entire department, I'd been something, all right. That was before the wreck, before I'd put my car around that willow tree down the street from the bar and nearly killed myself in the process. Before my wife had decided that my drinking meant more to me than she did and took our daughter and all my money. It was long before I'd become some cut rate P.I. who didn't have a pot to piss in, who hadn't seen so much as a workman's comp case come my way in months.

I took another belt of whiskey and cocked the hammer back on the revolver. Bottle still to my lips, I pressed the muzzle to my temple and gently squeezed the trigger.

Click.

I dropped the gun to the ground, followed by the whiskey, and leaned back until I was lying completely on the floor. Leave it to me to carry an empty gun to my own suicide.

"Having a bad day, Mister Mitchell?" a man asked from behind me. I was drunk, but not drunk enough to be hearing things. *Not yet, at least.* I jumped to my feet, staggered around as the room rotated on a tilted axis, and righted myself in time to stare at the figure framed in the soft fluorescent light of my bedroom door. He was tall, broad at the shoulders but tapering oddly the further down from his head you looked. He almost seemed to float, some vaporous apparition brought on by alcohol and what I could only assume was my own rapid descent into madness. He was shaded in ways that made it impossible to make out any of his finer features. In an almost form-fitting pinstripe suit, soft white with a blue aura caused by the lighting, he moved across the floor with a foggy swiftness.

"Who are you?" I slurred the question.

"My name is…well, unimportant at the moment. I'd like to speak to you about a business proposition."

"As you can see," I told him, slapping my hand down on top of the broken television, "I've got a very busy schedule. I don't think I'll be able to

10

pencil in any creepy fuckers before the first of next month."

From the shadowed darkness around me, a hand gripped my throat and lifted me off the floor. Strangling, face burning, eyes bulging in their sockets, I looked down to find my uninvited guest dangling me in the air like a meat piñata about to burst. His fingers were cold, clammy like a corpse's, and his sallow skin reeked of death and foulness. His eyes were faint but I could just barely make them out inside the shadowed contours of his face. They were cold, emotionless eyes that had all the compassion and concern a cat gives a cornered mouse.

"Let me reiterate," he said evenly. "I've come to talk business. The surge of adrenaline dumping into your veins right now should be more than enough to sober you. Time is of the essence, though, as you're fast running out of oxygen and will soon be unconscious. I've left a business card on your nightstand. You'll also find a credit card beneath it. The credit card will only be activated after you have called the number on the business card and accepted the job offer."

I dug my fingers into his hand, started kicking and flailing wildly. I couldn't breathe. My lungs were on fire, begging desperately for that one inhalation that would alleviate my pain and save my life. Darkness began to creep in from the sides of my vision.

"Also, I've placed the bullets from your revolver by your lamp and the cards. You'll be needing them sooner than you may have thought."

My body began to spasm as I continued to

11

struggle and fight. I could feel consciousness slipping away from me.

"Good night, detective," he said. "We'll talk again soon."

He lowered me onto the floor as the lights faded and darkness swallowed me whole.

I woke up with the worst hangover I'd ever had in my life. Daggers stabbing me in the eyes, skull throbbing, I managed to stagger into the bathroom, wash my face, and wonder if I'd drunk to the point of hallucinating the night before. It was, after all, a birthday ritual to become so completely blackout drunk that I could almost forget about the terrible choices I'd made over the years. It was that special little gift I gave myself once a year. I downed a handful of aspirin, found my whiskey, and obliged in just one more belt before flopping onto my bed. The force of my dive shook the nightstand and sent bullets tinkling off onto the floor, clattering against each other before rolling away. I sat up and immediately found a pair of cards sitting by my lamp. The first was a plain white business card with only a number on it. The second was a solid black credit card. It was flat, no bank logos or raised numbers. There was a magnetic strip and a silver chip but otherwise nothing to suggest that it was legitimate.

"Why not?" I asked myself as I fumbled for my phone. I dialed the number on the white card and listened as it rang.

"Mister Glenn Mitchell?" a woman asked.

"Yes," I told her.

"Your black card has been activated. Your PIN

12

is four zeros. There's a car waiting in front of your apartment that will bring you to the office for a brief conversation with Mister West. Please, be sure to dress professionally."

The line disconnected.

At least I have a name, now, I thought wryly.

I wandered over to my bedroom window and looked out into the parking lot. There was a black sedan, no make or model markings anywhere in sight, idling in front of the beat-up red Toyota Celica I normally drove. I could make out the faint outline of a man in a chauffeur's hat sitting behind the wheel. Closing the blinds, I opened the closet and dug out the only decent suit I still owned. Black jacket, white shirt, black slacks and a black tie combined with the slight paunch I'd grown over the last few years and I looked like the worst *Blues Brothers* impersonator of all time. Still, I got dressed and, almost as an afterthought, found my revolver and loaded it. Slipping it into a holster on my belt, I went out into the parking lot and climbed in the passenger seat of the car.

The driver wasn't the talkative sort. Or the friendly sort. His face was hard, square jawed, with leather skin the color of mahogany and curving scars that looped and swirled from the corners of his eyes to the side of his neck in an almost rhythmic pattern. Big and small, raised and dimpled, they seemed to move with every pulse through his veins. His hands were firm on the steering wheel, his gaze absolute as we wound through the backroads and narrows, until we found ourselves in the deep country outside of town. Trees and power lines bowed under the thick, snaking growth of kudzu slowly choking them into submission. The asphalt gave way to cement, further into gravel, and then dirt as we finally came across an old antebellum home in a far-off and slightly overgrown field. Fog had risen up over the verdant earth as dew melted away in the first bit of early morning heat.

The home itself was ancient and looked the part, with the fading white paint of its wood plank walls chipping away from the Greek columns on the front porch in a fine, powdery ash that littered the ground. The roof was sagging as kudzu and other vines slowly crept up along the frame of the old mansion and constricted the aging wood beams. The car grumbled to a stop at a moss covered stone archway about a hundred yards from the home.

"He's waiting for you inside," the driver growled. "I will be here when you return."

With that, I stepped out into the muggy air and trudged up the cobbled, weed-infested path leading to the front porch. The first few steps were hellish, the humidity so thick I could barely bring myself to put one foot in front of the other. As I crossed the stone threshold, a cool breeze blew across my face and took with it the oppressive southern heat that had bogged me down. My next few steps were into a well-manicured, lush garden of purple iris and honeysuckle swelling to life between stone statues and looming willow trees swaying in the wind. The decrepit house sinking into the overgrowth was suddenly as beautiful and stately as it had been a hundred years ago. Sitting on the front porch in a rocking chair was a small man in a white suit, with hair that had begun the transition from blazing red to a muted gold. His eyes were small, almost pinpoint, inside the creased, tan folds of a face covered in a thick beard of the same strawberry fur.

"Welcome, Mister Mitchell," he called from the porch with a thick, southern drawl. "Come on up and have some lemonade. You look parched."

I climbed the short set of steps onto the porch and lowered myself into the rocker beside him.

"Quite a place you've got here," I said as he handed me a cold glass of lemonade. "Looks a lot nicer up close than it does from the road."

He laughed.

"Yes indeed," he said. "Old magic. Sorry for the bit of trouble my man caused you last night. He isn't quite a people person, but he does his job well."

I nodded. "So what can I do for you, since you've been so gracious to invite me here?"

"All business; I like that," he said, chuckling. "Tell me, do you know why there's so much limestone in Tennessee, Mister Mitchell?"

I shook my head.

"Well, that's because the entire southeast portion of North America was once in the middle of the Atlantic Ocean. Millions of years ago, in fact. Why, we have some of the most amazing fossils of ancient sea creatures you could ever hope to find."

"I don't know that I'm following you."

"No matter. Just a little trivia I suppose. I tend to ramble on sometimes."

"You had a business proposal for me, Mister West?"

He nodded his head gravely. "Yes, I'm afraid I do. You see, I have a rather extensive archive of old, even *ancient* items that I've collected over the

15

years. Fossils and tools and trinkets, that sort of thing; but the most prized possession in my little collection is a grimoire of sorts, a journal belonging to a medical doctor named Jonas Mills from the early 1800s. It details strange stone formations and fossils that he encountered trekking through the region before settling here in the mid-state. Two days ago, that book was stolen. I'd like for you to get it back for me."

"Sounds more like a matter for the police than a P.I.," I said.

"You haven't asked me how I did it."

"How you did what?"

"How I changed the entire makeup of the world around my little house. It looks like a rotten old hovel from the other side of that stone wall, but clearly it's quite a spectacular little place."

"All due respect, you had some guy *vampire* his way into my apartment last night and put me in a sleeper hold. I've seen some weird shit, and the one thing I try not to do is get myself in over my head. You've clearly got some kind of science or hoodoo or something on this place. All I want to know is where should I start looking and how much am I getting paid."

The old man smiled.

"You're straightforward and to the point. That's admirable. Money's no object so long as I get my book back. I believe the person who stole it was a young woman in my employ who was cataloging my more…*peculiar* artifacts. I don't care what happens to her, but I must have that book back as soon as possible."

"Any reason for the urgency?" I asked.

16

"Yes."

He handed me an envelope from inside his jacket pocket, then poured himself another glass of lemonade.

"There are some who might kill for this book, Mister Mitchell," West said, looking at the statues in his garden. "I'd like for you find her before such people become necessary."

After leaving the plantation I did what any responsible man would do if he'd just been handed a credit card with no limit by an eccentric billionaire: I went to the bar. *The Hangman* had earned a reputation over the years as the most notorious dive in town. It was a doublewide trailer butted up to the edge of a cliff overlooking the railroad tracks running through town. There were constantly beat-up cars and motorcycles parked in the grass and gravel surrounding it, and a heavy odor of marijuana coming from a hidden underground cellar that, try as they might, the local cops had never been able to access or even prove existed. It was the sort of place a respectable person wouldn't have thought about as they drove by. It blended in well with the overlapping kudzu and vegetation growing up around it, trying so desperately to swallow it into nothingness.

Inside, the place stank of skunk weed and cheap beer, with a permanent atmosphere of cigarette smoke heavily filtering the already dim lights. At two in the afternoon, the place was pretty much empty. Aside from me, there was a burned-out cowboy with an overgrown beard and a filthy leather vest tending bar, and some two-bit lot lizard loitering by the taps with her caked-on makeup and Virginia Slims, ready to spread love and syphilis to whatever punch-drunk want-to-be biker was dumb enough to take her out back. With Doctor Hook and the Medicine Show playing from the jukebox in the back of the bar, I drowned my troubles in beer and chased them with whatever turpentine-laced hooch they were passing for whiskey at the time.

The envelope that West had given me was filled with useful information. It practically lit a sign over the girl's head showing me where to look. I learned everywhere she had ever lived, every place she frequented, and everyone she'd ever known, all from the crumpled sheets of paper inside. Hell, short of her blood type and the date she lost her virginity, I knew everything about her. And that was a problem. West had known exactly where to look if he wanted his book back, and he clearly had the resources to get it -- between his giant chauffeur and his shadowy, unusually strong messenger. I didn't feel like he really needed or even wanted a detective at all.

He'd *hired* me as a detective. He was hoping, though, to find a hitman.

It was all laid out in single-spaced, plain black font. He was hoping for a confrontation, for a fight with the girl that would end tragically. Strange as he was, rich as he was, there was no doubt in my mind that he hadn't been able to prevent her from witnessing things on his farms. Things he'd rather have kept quiet. He wanted more than just a book, all right. The credit card was clearly cloned. It was just a blank card with a strip that had no bank markings or insignia, not even an account number attached to it. People did it all the time – the right equipment and know how, any lowlife could clone a card and rob a man blind without ever opening their wallet. I'd worked dozens of cases like that when I'd been on the force, which could easily implicate me in the theft. He'd no doubt create some dubious online relationship between the girl and me, maybe even a combined plot to steal his fortune and run away together. Sure, a lovers' spat when she changed her mind, a moment of passion, and then murder.

There'd be no hard evidence to connect him to any of it, just loose threads easily explained away by bad decision-making and genuine-looking corroboration. I'd go to jail, she'd be in the morgue, and he'd have his book and his secrets.

I ordered another round.

Cash advances. I could take out thousands of dollars, maybe even hundreds of thousands without him noticing. Ditch the card, fake my death, and be living large in the Caribbean until I was a little old man tanned like a leather wallet, lying out on some white sand beach.

I was so wrapped up in my thoughts – the blatant trap and the poorly executed escape plan – I failed to notice the man who had sat down next to me until he spoke.

"Rough day?" he asked. His voice was deep, gruff. It was an otherwise innocuous question whose tone carried so much danger I almost didn't answer.

"It's been interesting, I'll say that much."

He put a piece of paper on the bar in front of me. There were numbers on it, the sort that start out small but then have lots of commas and zeros that follow. I looked from his rough, calloused hand up along the tailored red suit to a black silk shirt and red tie that blazed like the fires of hell. Further up I found an equally gruff scarred face that went with the man's voice, and dark, piercing eyes that were so bright blue they seemed to glow in their sockets.

"Who are you?"

"Randolph Jermyn," he said, offering a smile. "I'm a collector of sorts. I believe you may have met a former colleague of mine today, a Mister West?"

"I'm going to be honest. As much as all you people seem to know, I don't know why the hell you even bother talking to me."

Puzzled, he looked at me.

"Not your fault," I continued. "Just wondering how it is so many people who know so much seem so desperate to talk to *me* all of a sudden."

The bar stopped. The music was silenced; the flickering of the lights steadied. Even the smoke flowing through the air in great currents and eddies was suddenly still. The bartender and the working girl were frozen in place.

"Allow me to start again," Randolph Jermyn said. His voice was cold, monotonous. "This figure is a reward. Consider it a bounty. The book belonged to me long before West ever managed to place his filthy hands on it."

"Then go get it," I told him. I pulled the envelope with the girl's information out of my jacket pocket and slapped it on the bar over his offer. "Christ knows I'd rather not be stuck in the middle of this shit."

"Would that it were it so simple, detective."

"It's either at her apartment uptown or her family's cabin out in BFE at the county line. Take your pick."

"You misunderstand. I know where to find the book; it's simply a matter of being able to lay hands on it. If you haven't noticed by now, West and I have a certain set of skills about us – skills that can make directly taking such an artifact into our possession impossible. We both need a medium, a go-between who is otherwise indifferent to our abilities and our cause. You are just such a person. I'm here to negotiate a price."

I held up the credit card.

"Right now, the going rate is apparently his entire fortune versus the cocktail napkin with a number written on it."

Without another word he disappeared.

And when I say *disappeared*, I mean his entire body went up like an old celluloid movie reel burning on a bulb. He vanished like so much smoke as the room came to life once more. From the jukebox, "Freaker's Ball." From the bartender, an emphysemic cough. From the hooker by the taps, a come hither stare.

I finished my beer and dreamed of the Caribbean.

Emily Vance was twenty-six years old, a grad student with a master's in archeology and a number of minors in mythology, theology, and ancient cultures. The picture included with her credentials looked more like a model's headshot than a work I.D. With her big brown eyes, freckled cheeks, pouting lips, and shoulder-length strawberry hair, I almost couldn't believe a woman so gorgeous had stolen something so strange and dangerous. Her apartment had been empty when I went by to look for her, not that I'd really thought I'd find her on the first go around. She'd packed in a hurry, leaving her dresser drawers hanging open and her closet in shambles. She'd taken a laptop but forgotten the power cord, left a note for someone named Jan to take care of her cat while she was out of town. Her neighbors told me she had planned a weekend getaway at her father's cabin in the woods just outside of town. I'd hoped to avoid a hike through the middle of nowhere, but life is full of unpleasant compromises. It felt like the plot to some terrible horror movie and smelled more like a set-up than anything else. I didn't like it one bit. Still, it was a paying job, and I needed the cash more than anything right now, so I decided to roll the dice. I had a fallback plan or two in mind if things went south, but I found myself clinging to a faint hope that it wouldn't come to that.

West had explained that money was not an object to him so long as I recovered his book, and had authorized me to spend whatever I needed in the way of expenses. First order of business, after getting sufficiently drunk enough to even accept the job, was to buy a decent shotgun to supplement the old revolver I kept on my hip. Between my new benefactor and his spurned lover – or whatever the hell Mister Jermyn had been – I decided I'd rather be well armed instead of trusting. Besides, the Vance family's cabin was five miles off the road and up a winding trail into the woods. There was no telling what I'd find up there.

An old girlfriend of mine who had spent years in every New Age movement and weird, occult group that would take her had been kind enough to research the book and its author for me... for a price. Parting with some of my newfound fortune had been hard, but listening to her drone on and on about chakras, past life experiences, and magic crystals had been an almost painful two hours of my life. She'd spoken of ancient gods, primordial creatures existing between worlds in hidden enclaves disguised as normal looking places in our own world, and shuddered as I told her about West's plantation. In spite of all her hoodoo and hippie conversation, what she'd managed to find for me had been the least promising of all.

The book itself was originally a record of strange rock formations and odd bones found by Jonas Mills and his family as they moved west from the Carolinas through Tennessee and settled in a region to the south of what would become Nashville. But, as the doctor had grown older, the journal descended from scholarly observation into a hallucination-fueled nightmare, complete with strange dreams of ancient monsters that had ruled the land when it was several miles below the ocean. He'd become increasingly paranoid of black men – "shadow men" he called them – stalking his every movement, and, by the time he took his own life in the 1840s, the book had reputedly become a Satanic tome meant to conjure and control these ancient beasts that he was certain still lived and existed deep beneath the layers of limestone and bedrock under his own home. Coupled with the strangeness of my houseguest and the plantation where my new employer lived, I was absolutely certain that I wanted nothing to do with this book, and the sooner I could get it back to Mister West the better I'd feel.

The summer heat was oppressive as I locked up my Toyota and slung the shotgun over my shoulder. With a canteen full of ice water on my hip, I started up the narrow, rocky foot trail that would lead me to the Vance family's cabin and, hopefully, the book. The humidity was thick and sticky, an invisible weight pulling me even harder toward the ground as I struggled up the hill. The thick canopy of tree branches overhead did little against the heat, and only seemed to worsen the already unbearable mugginess and block the slight breeze that might have otherwise offered a moment of relief. The family had nailed signs to the trees along the path: mile markers and slogans of encouragement that did little to actually help me feel any better about being so horribly out of shape as I slogged through the woods on what might have been a ten-mile round-trip goose chase. My lungs were on fire, muscles aching with every labored step. I'd have killed for a cigarette and some air conditioning.

Every so often I would stop and look over my shoulder. Since I'd left the car, I felt like someone was watching me, following me step for step along the narrow path. I wrote it off as animals at first and pressed on. There had been a few squirrels and a distant, curious little fox when I first started the hike, and they'd probably been interested in seeing if I'd dropped any food along the way. Still, visions of a man in a suit in the dim light of my apartment haunted me, even here on the trail. I could see him out of the corner of my eye, behind every tree, in every outcropping. Sure, I could ignore it, but it didn't change the fact that whatever it was had decided to follow me here.

Around the third mile marker, the atmosphere began to change. The sun was a bit lower, a bit darker, and the heat and humidity seemed to ease up with each step. The trees were all a bit sickly, their bark turning gray as autumn colored leaves struggled to hold on to any branch they could and moss sloughed off the edge of rocks like flesh stripped from the bone. There were strange symbols carved into the bark. Some were fish with rows of legs and eyes looking up through pyramid gaps with long, rippling tentacles hanging down in place of lashes. Some were more runic, claw marks almost, with patterns seeded between symbols. The trees themselves had bled dark amber sap that had hardened from the wounds and left a blood red residue. I swung the shotgun around into my hands as an unsettling feeling came over me. In the distance, the little cabin sat with warm firelight flickering through the windows and smoke billowing up from the chimney.

The door and all the window frames had been covered in the same runes and symbols as the trees surrounding the tiny home, all of them written in deep shades of maroon. There was an unfortunately familiar odor of copper and bile that hung nauseatingly in the air and took me back to my own past as I walked up to the door. Whatever waited for me on the other side would no doubt be unpleasant. I could hear her long before I opened the door and saw her. She had a sweet, melodic voice that seemed to be singing a single verse over and over again in different languages. Carefully, I pushed open the door and looked inside. She was standing in front of the fireplace, completely naked with her hair cascading over her shoulders and back in a strawberry waterfall. There was a tattoo at the small of her back, another runic glyph like the ones on the cabin and the trees. Everything about her body was perfect, from the rows of freckles that ran from her shoulders down her back to the firm, pert butt and gorgeous legs rooting her to the ground.

"Are you the assassin or the acolyte?" she asked without turning to face me.

"Neither," I answered. "I'm just here to collect a book for my client."

"Das ist nicht tot, das ewige Lüge. Und mit merkwürdigen Äonen kann sogar Tod sterben." She continued with her chanting as if I wasn't there. "Que no está muerto lo que yace eternamente. Y con eones extraños incluso la muerte puede morir."

"What's that, you say?" I asked.

She turned around and in that moment ruined every perverse sexual fantasy that had filled my mind since I'd walked in and found her. Her eyes were gone, scooped out by her own fingers, and her face was covered in gashes that mimicked the runes and symbols I'd been introduced to along my hike. Her pale skin was beginning to marble in the front, black veins rippling like dark lightning across the sickly alabaster of her stomach and breasts, where the skin had become loose and begun to sag. Her pouting lips were parted wide, split with most of her jaw, as black fingers groped out from inside her mouth. Each finger moved independently of its kin

26

and looked like the legs of a crab or some giant spider scuttling in the air.

"Quae aeterna quae exstincta non est mendacium. Et morte morietur Aeonum alienis." The voice came from deep inside her throat as she walked slowly towards me. "That is not dead which can eternal lie. And with strange aeons even death may die."

Without a thought I raised the shotgun and fired into her chest. Her body collapsed backwards, her skull cracking in a thunderclap as ash and bits of burning wood flew out into the cabin. The book was on a table by the door. I grabbed it and slowly began to back out of the room.

"Sa se pa mouri sa ki ka manti p'ap janm fini an. Se avèk aeons etranj menm lanmò ka mouri." She continued to babble as the smell of burning flesh assaulted my nostrils. "Ce n'est pas mort qui peut mensonge éternel. Et avec des éons étranges même la mort peut mourir."

The wind began to howl, leaves and branches crashing and violently trembling as they fell to the ground. Fleeing from their perches, the birds began their fluttering frenzy of feathers and wings as they tried to escape. The cabin was burning now, the walls smoking as flames lapped out along the eaves of the roof. In the noise and commotion I could hear a voice echoing from inside the small piece of hell that I had stumbled across.

That is not dead which can eternal lie. And with strange aeons even death may die.

Randolph Jermyn was sitting on the trunk of my car as I slogged my way out of the woods. Even with the smell of seared skin and ash stuck in my nostrils, I could smell the cheap cologne he had bathed in. He was still wearing the same black silk shirt and red suit he'd been wearing back at the bar, though the tie had been loosened and the top button undone. It had to be a hundred degrees in the shade with that thick wall of humidity steaming up from the ground, but he hadn't broken a sweat. Reclined though he was, he was still a large, intimidating figure to find waiting for me as I escaped the utter insanity smoldering in the darkness of those woods.

"Get a bit more than you bargained for, detective?" he asked, sliding off the trunk of my car.

"What the hell is going on?"

"Nothing that concerns you," he said. "Just give me the book and I'll see to it that you're substantially rewarded for your time and trouble."

"Suppose you tell me what it is that everyone really wants with this first," I said.

He shook his head.

"You want no part of this," he told me. "You've made it clear that your involvement is more out of desperation than an actual quest for knowledge."

"Maybe I've changed my mind."

"That could be a dangerous thing."

I nodded and thought about it for a moment.

"I just killed a woman back there," I said. "Never once had to shoot anyone in all my years as a cop, but tonight I shot a twenty-six-year-old woman in the face with a twelve gauge. But she wasn't really a woman, was she? Not anymore, at least? Something was inside her, something insane and alien and horrific, and it came from this book.

28

Now, you can answer me, or I can march back into those woods and burn it up in the same fire that's baking her body to ash right now. Your choice."

"This world is not our own," Randolph Jermyn said gravely. "It belonged once to creatures more terrible and powerful than anything you could ever hope to imagine. They lived in the darkness of the ocean, used it as a conduit for dark magics that allowed them to traverse time and reality in ways our greatest minds are only now beginning to comprehend. As the oceans receded from the land, they were driven further into the depths, down into the earth where men cannot go. It was only after their retreat that mankind flourished in this world."

"So, if they're so far gone, what does this book matter?"

"Their acolytes and disciples remain," he told me. "From ancient monsters in myth and lore to the magicians and alchemists of antiquity, they all sought wisdom and power from these old gods. In exchange for their arcane knowledge, the old ones asked that these followers work to bring about their resurrection. They opened Doctor Mills' eyes and used him to pen the single most powerful tome ever written."

He looked from the shotgun in my hands to the backpack slung over my shoulders, then into my eyes.

"I'd lock the book away in my archive; bury it so deep that none would ever find it again."

"Why not just burn it?"

"That is not dead which…"

"Stop," I interrupted him as he began to recite the chant from the cabin. "I've heard enough of

29

that. It doesn't answer anything."

"The book was bound in immortal flesh, inked in blood from sacrifices of the heart and soul of the author. The magic that binds it will never let it be destroyed."

"You've got lots of magic too, as I recall. Why not just give it to West and be done with it?"

Grabbing me by the scruff of my shirt, he pulled me eye level with him. It was only after being so uncomfortably close to him that I noticed his eyes. They weren't normal. The colors were all wrong, shades of indigo and neon fluid spiraling around narrow black pupils. As they spun deeper into the black vortex I could feel myself falling into that darkness, passing scenes and moments that made no sense at all. I saw people, people like Emily, their bodies scarred and mutilated, their faces erupted into gruesome flowers as those crustacean appendages writhed inside the carnage. I saw bodies floating through midnight seas red with blood and viscera. In the darkness, from the edge of my own field of vision, I could see hulking monstrosities swimming weightlessly through a black starscape stretching out into an eternal, maddening void.

And then I was back, standing in the weeds and gravel on the side of the road beside my beat up old Toyota. In my hand was a business card. It was matte black with raised, metallic lettering and a single phone number stamped on it.

"Why don't you think about what you've seen, what I've said, and then give me a call?" I could hear Jermyn saying from somewhere inside my mind. Like the magician he was, though, as I blinked he was already gone.

I went home with the book. After what I'd been through, I couldn't let it go. That shadowy messenger who had vampired his way into my home in the middle of the night might have remained a strange sort of phantom in my memories, a bad dream that I just couldn't shake. I could have written off West's homestead as a magician's trick – mirrors and facades and diversion, all designed to warp my sense of perspective and keep me off my game as we spoke. I could have even dealth with that creepy bastard Jermyn appearing out of the blue around every corner to try and buy me off and intimidate me to get his hands on this book. But I'd killed a woman, a creature clawing its way desperately out of her body, and then burned her in a little cabin in the middle of a dead and desolate patch of forest. *All for the sake of some old book.* Before I turned it over to its owner, or even decided who that owner might truly be, I was going to find some answers.

The binding was leather, very well worn but well taken care of. There was grit to it, a rough texture across the front cover like it had been scraped with sandpaper or something equally abrasive. My fingers came away from it with a thin film of oil, the way they'd feel after grabbing someone by the arm. It almost felt like the leather was alive, still attached to a living body. The pages themselves were a thick parchment; starched linens pressed into pages and bound inside the animal-hide shell. They seemed normal at first, black ink in cursive script with the occasional sketch of stone pillars or some kind of animal bones. The writing was neat, evenly spaced, and easy enough to read and comprehend despite the archaic phrases and dialect. It was a nature journal detailing the woods and wildlife of a strange new land being explored for the first time by a young doctor and his family. But the further I read, the stranger it became.

Excavating for a root cellar had led to the discovery of a strange animal skull, some marine mammal that would have been millions of years old by the time it was found. The skull was like a whale's, but had numerous openings for eyes. Around the jaw were long appendages like arachnid legs that would have acted as mandibles to pull prey into its gaping mouth. He had detailed everything painstakingly, and offered sketches of his discovery as well as his assumptions on how it might have looked when it was alive. That's where things started to go downhill. The next few pages were incoherent ramblings of dreams in which he saw the creature in the depths of a black ocean. He described the grace of it, floating through the water, propelled by fins that stretched out across its back like the wings of some giant bat, while tentacles swooped down from under the curve of its body and snatched large crustaceans up from the wet sand and into its horrifying maw. The stone pillars he'd seen as he journeyed through the woods, the ones he had previously attributed to natural weathering, were in fact the foundation of giant, megalithic statues carved from underwater mountains in tribute to terrible, ancient gods; primordial beings who had existed in the chaos long before mankind had ever been imagined. He detailed the history of how the receding oceans had robbed the beasts of their ancestral home, had driven them into the Atlantic and the Gulf of Mexico until such a time when the tides would bring them home. He spoke of a race of specters, too – creatures born out of the old ones – and their desire to return. They were little more than shadows who would spend the aeons preparing for their masters to return, influencing the other races born from the absence of the old gods to facilitate that end.

The last pages detailed rituals that had been shown to him by his monster, incantations and sacrifices to return them from their exile and bring the ocean back once more to Tennessee along the Mississippi River. He warned that the oceans would swell, that the river would "drink deep those dark Stygian waves," and would wipe out all life in the southeast before they could return and reclaim their place as the rulers of the world. He then detailed the ritual sacrifice in which he slaughtered his wife and daughters and planned his own suicide as a means of waking the first of several old gods who would make his dreams a reality.

Throughout the entire ritual, he repeated one phrase again and again.

That is not dead which can eternal lie. And with strange aeons even death may die.

I closed the book as the words circled inside my mind. I could still hear her voice echoing through the night, telling me in so many languages before a shotgun blast had ended her suffering. Securing the book in a small safe I kept in my bedroom, I lay down on my bed and stared at the ceiling fan chopping slowly away at the air.

"What the hell have I gotten myself into?"

33

I was drowning, water crushing around me, filling my lungs as I sank deeper and deeper below the waves. The pressure was incredible around my throat, invisible hands strangling me, pressing me further and further into the abyss. Light, blue-white and rippling through the filter of the water's surface, gave a sickly glow to the strange land slowly consuming me. Enormous statues emerged from the darkness below me, mountains of slime-covered stone with arms outstretched towards the sky as if they were trying desperately to reach the world above them. None were human, even remotely, in their design. One was a large lobster-tailed monster with two crab-arms on either side reaching up above a head not unlike the creature that had been described in the book. Another was a squid covered in a hard armor shell with rows of eyes climbing up along a head that ended in a flowering, open beak. Swimming in and out of these and other monuments too far off to see was the whale creature with the giant fin wings and tentacles that had been described in depth in the book. It was massive – hundreds of feet long –but moved with an elegance, a grace that seemed hypnotic.

It grabbed me in its clawed mandibles and dragged me as deep into the valley of monuments as it could, until my limp and lifeless feet began to drag along cobbled rocks. Hands reached out and took hold of my arms and legs, held me so that I was looking up at the megalithic structures that loomed over us. They were pale, familiar hands; hands that belonged to the man who had broken into my home and held me by the neck – the one who had placed the card on my nightstand, who had started this entire surreal odyssey. They were his hands pulling me to the ground, holding me so that I could only watch as the sunken city rose up from the waves.

Bodies began to sink into the water as the monuments climbed – first a few, then hundreds. Men and women and children, all screaming in agony as plumes of red erupted from their faces and gave the water a murderous hue. I watched as their bodies were torn apart from the inside, as arachnid arms ripped open their torsos, as their skulls split open into mandibles with rows of dark red eyes running along the crustacean forms growing within.

That is not dead which can eternal lie, it whispered through the water. *We are risen.*

The ocean began to tremble, an artificial sunlight shining up from the crust of the earth through the edges of the city of stone pillars. The strange, horrifying whale creature was joined by others, larger and smaller versions of itself. The shadowed creatures that held my drowning body began to cheer, their voices a high-pitched warble joining the deep whale song that the other monsters had begun. From the edges, the places where the light was brightest, tentacles and spider legs the size of freighters began to claw upwards to the surface.

That is not dead which can eternal lie, the creatures sang their refrain again and again. *We are risen.*

I woke up soaking in sweat as the first rays of sunlight came through my bedroom window. Sitting up, I choked, gagged, and then vomited onto the floor. Salt and bile filled my mouth as seawater splattered onto the carpet. Grabbing the revolver from my nightstand, I looked at the safe near my bed. No matter what it meant for me, I had to destroy that book and anyone who wanted it.

Mister West clapped his liver-spotted hands together like an amused child and chuckled as I walked through the stone archway into his hidden home. He bounded down the front porch steps and met me halfway between the wall and the mansion. The look of unbridled joy creasing his face betrayed none of the madness, the malevolent insanity of the man himself, as he took the book from my hands and clutched it tightly to his chest.

"I was worried you wouldn't find it in time!" he shouted excitedly. "There's still so much preparation to be done. Thank you, Mister Mitchell."

He turned to walk back into the house. I reached out and grabbed him gently by the shoulder. He stopped suddenly, staring straight ahead.

"If it's all right with you, I'd like to stay and watch."

He turned cautiously and looked up at me.

"You've seen, then?" he asked. "They've shown you the glory?"

"They have," I told him. "That is not dead which can eternal lie."

He smiled even wider and ushered me into the home. Racing through the foyer, down the long hallway and into the kitchen, we turned sharply and descended into the cellar. The air was musty, thick with the scent of wet dirt and roots, of mildew and age. Pushing to the back of the cellar, he ducked quickly into a small arch that climbed about halfway up the wall that led to an ancient stone staircase and yet another narrow corridor. Electric lights gave way to gas lanterns, then to torches and candles, lit and hung along the moldering wet walls. Eventually, the stairs ended in a sloping, well-worn walkway on a slick sheet of limestone. There were footsteps worn into the stone, imprints of boots and loafers, of bare feet, and of appendages that belonged to nothing I'd ever seen. Cold air roared up from the darkness ahead, carrying with it the crashing of waves and a cool dampness.

"This cave system…" West said without looking back, "…it runs from here into Alabama and Mississippi, and ends in the Gulf of Mexico. Here is where the old ones have slept, where they have rested, waiting for the day that their servants might call them again to rule this world. You see, the entire south was once a part of the Great Shallow Sea that divided the continent. It was their kingdom. In their absence, their acolytes and disciples have come to the children of man and taught them the ancient ways. Even now, they wait in the shadows for the offering."

I looked around. Faint shapes moved in the darkness, man-sized shapes that were anything but human, with glowing eyes that cut through the darkness and into my heart. From their shadowed warrens I could smell cold death, the perfume of the uninvited visitor who had ushered me into this odyssey. A chill ran along my spine as I felt them watching me.

"Are they like the one who came to my

apartment?" I asked.

"Yes," West said. "We have worked in tandem for this day. Were it not for the girl's meddling, the invocation would have commenced days ago, and the ceremony could already be complete."

In the distance, orange light flickered across the walls. Figures danced around the fire, men and women bared of everything but the scarred flesh covering their bones. Like Emily Vance in her cabin in the woods, their faces were mutilated, crawling mandibles gripping at the air and at the fire as they danced and chanted. The stench of rot, of blood and bile and open decay, mingled with the musty wetness of the cave and made a sickening air so thick it was almost unbearable. Their voices were a quavering mixture of rhythmic humming and insect trills. My hand slid to my waistband, to the holster beneath my jacket.

"Don't be afraid," West told me as we approached the fire. "They volunteered to carry the divine seed within them. They are children of the great old gods, a *rebirth*, if you will. They have allowed the great ones to merge their new flesh with the old magics from the dark, chaotic times before men existed. We will share this gift with the world tonight, Mister Mitchell. We will bring humanity into a glorious new dawn."

He opened the book and leaned over the fire, allowing the light of the flickering flame to dance with the words of the ritual. Whispering, he began to recite words that had not been heard in centuries. Creatures from the shadows brushed past me and into the darkness beyond the fire. I drew my gun.

"You're amongst friends here," West said

reassuringly. "Besides, that won't do much of anything now, will it?" He laughed.

From the shadows, the hulking mass of West's chauffeur stepped forward and took the book. Lumbering wordlessly toward the flames, he approached a podium overlooking the large fire and stood at attention. The podium itself was onyx, painstakingly carved and polished until even in the darkness it seemed to shimmer like a window into some strange, alien void. The legs were tentacles that curled around the solid base – a familiar base, like those I had seen in my dreams the night before. It was a window, an eye looking into our world, watching for a sign that the time had come to return, for those primordial gods to rise up from whatever hidden sanctuary in which they existed. West stepped up to the podium and shed his clothes onto the cold, damp stone floor. He was disturbingly emaciated, barely a memory of a man, with pale, sagging flesh clinging desperately to his bones. Through shadows and the creases of his aged skin I could make out tattoos and scars, the runic glyphs I'd seen in the woods the night before.

Opening the book, he raised his arms and began to speak in croaking, lisping verses.

I cocked the hammer on the revolver.

"I've seen their world," I offered quietly. "And I'm sorry, but I can't let you do this."

He laughed. It wasn't that light-hearted, joyful laugh that he'd offered when first we met. It was a maniacal, evil sound that made the blood run cold and sent shivers down my spine.

"You don't understand anything," he scolded. "The invocation is over, the ritual is complete. With this sacrifice I bring forth the great old ones again into the waking world. *That is not dead that sleeping lies...*"

I pulled the trigger. With a loud crack his skull erupted, spraying into the flames with a sizzle as his body collapsed onto the podium, then further into the fire, along with his precious book. The acolytes' song became a scream, their voices a high-pitched hiss. The chauffeur turned, his bulging arms reaching out towards me. Another shot left him curled up near the flames with his master. I didn't wait to see what happened next. I just ran. I ran back along the slick limestone, upstairs and through the cavernous corridor. Wet footsteps slapped angrily, quickly along the stone behind me, bare feet and chitinous nails plodding and clacking in pursuit. I smashed the pistol into the gas lamps, shattering the glass and snuffing the flame as the gas continued to hiss through the spigot. Reaching into my pocket with my free hand, I grabbed my cigarette lighter and struck it. It flickered to life. I turned long enough to toss it into the tunnel behind me before I continued my escape. Climbing up the cellar stairs, I bolted down the hallway, through the foyer, and out onto the porch just as the flame and the gas met. A rumble of thunder quaked below my feet as I slipped in the lush green grass and rolled through the stone archway, out into the summer heat. The façade of the decrepit plantation home remained the same even as the fire swallowed the mansion whole. Wheezing and coughing, lungs burning from the full-on sprint I'd made to escape, I lay down in the grass and looked up at the sky.

I glanced through the stone archway in the

fence, looking at the carnage as flames licked up from inside the remains of the old plantation house. A looming, familiar figure in a dark suit stood in the fire, staring at me. His eyes were gray, emotionless, and his pallid and implacable face glared at me from the hellfire consuming him. The specter who had threatened me in my home, the acolyte of those ancient gods, had chosen to use the last of his strength to try to destroy me. He wove through the stone statues, across the verdant grass, moving like the smoke puffing steadily into the sky. The ground began to tremble as he approached. The arch collapsed just as one gnarled, slender hand reached through to grab at me, closing the bridge between the façade and reality. In the distance, I could hear a faint echo, a deep moaning like a whale song on some *Discovery Channel* special. It bellowed once and then faded into nothing.

I've been sober now for eight months, medicated for depression and focused on my work. Realizing that your life – that everyone's lives – are so utterly meaningless in the eyes of the universe is a painful revelation. Realizing that there was some educated moron out there playing at games conceived by gods an eternity before I was born, jeopardizing that tragically short existence I've struggled to enjoy, was even worse.

I called Jermyn and told him what had happened. He sounded disappointed, but told me not to worry. Said something about a pocket dimension where West had resided, how the collapse of the archway had sealed it entirely and trapped anything he might have summoned inside.

He tried to sound reassuring as he told me not to worry and hung up the phone.

I was still plenty worried.

The black credit card maxed out at around five hundred thousand dollars. With cash advances and purchases, I'd made it work to my advantage. I left my apartment, my tiny little pit in the middle-of-nowhere, and entered into a deeper self-imposed exile. The ex-wife wasn't thrilled to see me, but the hundred grand in cash I gave her to move herself and our child as far away from the water as possible had been enough to soften her expression and make her receptive to what I was saying. With everything that was left, I found a little shack up in the Appalachians and started back to work, doing what I do best. Sifting through the fictions and fantasies of the internet, through musty books in poorly-lit rooms of museums and libraries, I started to piece together a puzzle. What West had shown me had only been the tip of the iceberg. Sitting alone at night as the fog that gives the Smokies their name rises from the canopy of trees below, as that ethereal cloud surrounds the peaks, I can still hear those alien voices, feel the water slowly pulling me from this life into the immaterial realm of my dreams.

That is not dead which can eternal lie. I can only hope that no one else tries to wake them before my time is over.

A Stutter in the Infinite

by
Alex Wolfe

8:19am

Yeah, he's dead all right.

I had coffee with Warwick two weeks ago. While I don't feel the pang of shock that I probably should, I can't help but be a little surprised at being called in to ID his corpse.

The kill looks like it was simple. Three bullets; one in the chest, one near the throat, and one between and just below his eyes, making a complete mess of what was once a perfectly acceptable face. Panicked attacker, maybe? Definitely not someone familiar with guns – each shot was higher than the last. Someone who hadn't expected the recoil of the weapon they were using.

I look up from his body, surrounded in an outline of marking tape and soaking in a pool of blood that's mostly dry. This kill may not be hot off the press, but I'd wager it happened this morning, or late last night. If I were a betting woman, anyway. I'm not.

"I'm sorry to call you in on this, Lindsay. You knew him, right?" Lisowski's voice jars me from my own head, bringing me back to the real world, back to the interior of the run-down little inner city pawn shop where Warwick was killed. Back to the rain pounding down on the metal roofing, muffling the detective's voice just enough for me to wish I

45

could ignore it outright. Not because I need time to grieve, but because I want time to think. Time to chew on the information I have before I get any more thrown at me. Time to digest the grisly death of someone who had known me as a friend.

"I did, yeah," I mumble back, inhaling deeply through my nostrils and immediately wishing I hadn't. The smell is truly fucking repugnant, both from the native scent of motor oil and sawdust that I assume the pawn shop started out with, and from the slowly leaking post-mortem gasses of Warwick's bloating body. "He was..." Not really a friend, not exactly. "I knew him, yeah."

Lisowski nods. He's a decent guy, as far as I've ever been able to tell when he calls me in for consults. Minds his business. I like that. Knows his limits, too; knows when to ask for help. Making him everything his partner isn't.

Henley's dark-haired and rail-thin, a one man army in his quest to dispel the myth of the fat, stupid, asshole cop by being a skinny, stupid, asshole cop. I'd commend him on the effort if I didn't have to deal with him. "Alright, so we got a reliable ID," he grunts from the other side of the body, jotting something down on his notepad. "Can we get rid of the weirdo now?"

"Not yet," Lisowski sighs, shooting an apologetic glance at me for his partner's sake. "Lindsay, we've got an...a, um, an issue...with the case."

"In that you have absolutely no clue where to even start, since both doors were heavily locked and all the windows have bars in them?" I ask, finally pulling my eyes from Warwick's body to look up at

Lisowski, doing my best to ignore his partner for the moment. This is my job, more or less. Despite a lot of official detectives not wanting to take in outside help, there are enough without raging egos that I can make a living – cops who don't mind having a "weirdo" take a look at a case that doesn't make sense.

"How'd you know?"

"A murder takes place in a pawn shop in downtown Detroit in the itsy-bitsy hours of the night. I can safely assume that the owner wasn't here when it happened, or you'd be questioning the fuck out of him right now instead of me. Nighttime security in this place has to be tighter than a Shaolin monk's jerk-off grip, and none of the ways in or out are visibly damaged. Am I warm?" I glance at Henley, who makes no effort to hide an annoyed scowl.

"The Vulcan speaks," Henley grumbles, not wanting to openly admit that I'm right – which I'm quite certain that I am. "Aren't you just cool as a cucumber, too? Thought your friend just died, and yet you still have enough steam to come in here and tell us how to do our jobs. Such a goddamn genius."

"The analytical power should not be confounded with simple ingenuity; for while the analyst is necessarily ingenious, the ingenious man is often remarkably incapable of analysis," I intone, knowing Henley won't know where it's from. He doesn't.

"That's clever; you make that up?" he counters, venom dripping from his Boston accent.

"Not remotely. Edgar Allan Poe, *Murders in the Rue Morgue*. Give it a read sometime, it might come in handy for cases like this."

"I'll bite," Lisowski says, flicking open a pack of cigarettes and withdrawing one, looking from me back down to the corpse. "What kinda case is this?"

"A locked room mystery – a case where there's no way for the person who committed the crime to get in or out, yet they seemingly did anyway." I find myself fixating on the cigarette dangling between Lisowski's lips, briefly distracted as he fumbles around for a lighter. I considered smoking myself, once, but after weighing how cool it would make me look against the health hazards, I eventually decided against it. "Most of the stories that came after Poe's all involved secret doors or key replicas. Since I find myself doubting that there were any sub-tropical arboreal apes involved, those are what you should probably start looking for. Did the victim have any enemies?"

"He was your friend, not that you seem too beat up about him dying," Henley grunts. "Shouldn't you know?"

"We weren't that close." I exhale and force myself to look away from the body, away from Warwick's gray, frozen gasp of terror and agony. Another sign that he took the bullet to the chest first – he was clearly in pain before he was killed. I start to pace around the rest of the pawn shop, careful not to touch anything as I look for something out of place – something on the floor that could cover a trapdoor, something on the walls that might conceal a secret door in the wall. As much as I like the idea of a fake key, it doesn't work in this scenario; the

48

doors weren't just locked, they were *barred* from the inside. There was no way anyone could have gotten out once they were inside, not unless Warwick set the bars himself before shooting himself three times. I think it goes without saying that I don't find that explanation to be particularly feasible.

"Doesn't fucking fit," I whisper under my breath, drawing my brows together as if it will grant me some kind of boost of cognitive capacity. It doesn't. Help, that is. It doesn't fit either, though. Nothing's doing anything I want it to.

Behind me, I can hear Lisowski and Henley talking to each other, seemingly disappointed with my insight, though Henley more vocally so. Can't blame them. My insight isn't even helping me, and that makes me deeply frustrated. Lindsay Alexander, police consultant and resident expert on puzzles and patterns, completely stumped as to how a killer managed to get out of a room with absolutely no viable means of exit.

"We don't actually *pay* her for this, do we?"

"Technically the city does, so, no, not really."

"I hope a positive ID and some bullshit about a horror novel is gonna be worth those taxpayer dollars." That stings a little. Not in a deep-set, hurt feelings kind of way, but it does challenge me to consider what I'm actually worth to the world around me. Not every consult's gonna result in an arrest, after all. Not every consult's even gonna result in a worthwhile lead.

I run my tongue along the front of my teeth in annoyance, wracking my brain for something that works, something that might help. "Why was he even here in the first place?" I think out loud, causing the two detectives behind me to stop talking and turn their gazes my way.

"What was that, Mr. Spock?" Henley calls back mockingly. "Think of something the least bit helpful?"

"Firstly, I don't find your *Star Trek* references the least bit offensive. Please come up with something less desirable to compare me to if you're going to keep on doing it," I mumble, stalking back over to where the two of them are standing, looking down at Warwick's glassy, screaming stare into oblivion. "Secondly, why was he here? Warwick was a normal guy, single dad, no real habits I knew of. He was a 'beer with dinner' kinda guy, not a 'dead in a pawn shop in the middle of the night for no goddamn reason' kinda guy. It doesn't fit. None of this does."

"Lindsay, I hate to sound like a dick, but that really doesn't help us," Lisowski says, frowning. "Listen, I'll get the forensic guys in here and we'll look around for, um...hidden doors, or whatever. If we find anything new, we'll call you, okay?"

"Please do," I nod to him, pulling my smartphone from my front pocket and sending a text, waiting to see if I get a response. "I'm going to do some more digging of my own. You have my number."

"Wait, this an official police investigation, you can't just--" I'm already out the door. My phone buzzes with a reply. She's where I want her to be.

"Let her go, Dan," Henley says, though I barely hear him as I make my way out into the driving rain. "Let her hang herself with her own rope."

Dipshit. Doesn't matter, though. I have leads of my own to follow, contacts that are too afraid to talk to the police, but will talk to me.

Okay, so by "contacts" I mean "contact." But it's a good one. I dry my phone off on my shirt and draw my jacket tighter around my shoulders, popping the collar and rushing out to my car, putting the key in and first turning on the lights, then the windshield wipers.

I like to think my heart doesn't start racing when I suddenly see what looks like a rush of movement behind the sheet of rain, blurred from the water and the shadow of dawn. The wipers cleanse it away along with the layer of liquid from my windshield, giving me a moment to catch my breath and try to dismiss it. Probably a squatter or something – if it was the killer, there's no way they'd come back to the scene of the crime when the cops are still there. Can't trust my eyes. But I can always trust my mind.

I let out a slow, deep breath and put my pitiful little sedan into drive, taking off into the deeper, more desolate areas of Detroit. I have a favor to call in from Moonlyte.

10:25am

Since Detroit went downhill, squatting in the threadbare urban ruins has become a way of life for some people, but today I'm looking for one person in particular. I'm looking for a woman living in the burnt-out husk of a White Castle, a woman who has the best chance of giving me the information I'm looking for.

51

Old cans and bits of debris crunch under my tires as I pull into the parking lot. This place hasn't been cleaned in what could very well be years, and Moonlyte sure as fuck doesn't have any interest in making the place look like someone lives in it. Her strength is her anonymity, which is why I'm deeply pleased that she happens to like me. Hopping out, I make my way carefully to the shattered glass of the front door, taking a brief moment to admire the excessive tagging on the side of the building. Most of it's familiar, but some of it appears to be new. I can't help but wonder if Moonlyte did that herself to create the illusion that the place was in a more dangerous area of Detroit than this one.

"I know you're in here..." I say loudly as my feet crush old hamburger boxes beneath them, wandering into the desolate restaurant and making my way towards the kitchen. "It's not like you ever leave..." I mumble under my breath, looking over my shoulder as I invade a little more deeply, past the open front area and into the manager's back office. Here I see the familiar setup of about twenty monitors, each of them rigged to cameras around the city and linked to an underground generator.

In the middle of them all, hastily typing at a keyboard and seeming not to notice me, is Moonlyte herself, shoveling a rusty spoonful of pork and beans past her full, soft lips. She could have been a movie star if she weren't – for lack of a more accurate psychiatric diagnosis – cracked in the fucking head. Paralyzed by her paranoia, the knockout blonde that was once known as Katelyn Webb was transformed into the all-knowing, all-seeing, filth-encrusted inner-city hacker hermit known by the code-name of Moonlyte. It's like she thinks she's a video game character or something. Then again, with the hookup she has here, she may as well be.

"Moonlyte, I need your…" I pause, blinking as I look up from her to the screens themselves, and what they're displaying. Of the two dozen or so monitors, only one of them is functioning. The others are sporting a matching snow pattern that scrolls vaguely downward. "…help."

"Wrong day. Wish I could. Busy. Sorry. You're fucked." Moonlyte chatters back around a mouthful of scavenged canned food, her fingers never stopping for a moment as she scans through the coding of her setup. I can only assume she's trying to find the element that isn't working, the glitch preventing her monitors from being operational. "Bring me a present?"

"You just told me I was fucked," I reply coolly, reaching into the front pocket of my jacket and wrapping my hands around the bottle of Dr. Pepper I brought her. It's still cold, wet with condensation. I slip it out just enough for her to see the cap. "So it seems like you don't want any of this ice cold cola beverage."

Those deep, marbled green eyes of hers narrow, and finally her fingers stop moving, hands motionless at her sides as she stares longingly at the bottle in my jacket pocket. "Give me it."

"I need to know where Warwick Hayes was last night – specifically, how he got to the pawn shop on the east side. It should have been very early, maybe three or four in the morning, maybe earlier." I tuck the bottle carefully back out of sight, waiting for Moonlyte to make her move.

"Don't know him. Who's he to you?"

"He's dead is what he is. And he was a friend."

"No cops on it?"

I tighten my brows together, frowning. "Katelyn, I expected a lot better of you. Putting your faith in the police now?"

"Yeah, yeah, fuck you," she growls, looking back to the smaller monitor in front of her and sighing, lazily typing in a few more lines before squeezing her eyes shut, visibly frustrated by something. "My shit's been fucked for the past two days. Can't help. Only one cam active."

I run my tongue over my teeth in annoyance. Of course it would be the day of an unsolvable murder that Moonlyte's entire system would go down. But that seems a bit too convenient to be an accident, doesn't it? The one person who might have been able to put a face to a place is out of commission exactly when I need her? I don't believe in coincidence. "What's on the one cam?"

"Nothing. Like literally nothing," Moonlyte grunts, rolling her chair backwards and pointing to the only active monitor, giving me enough room to squeeze into the little nook where she hides herself away. She's telling the truth. The monitor shows the dimly lit interior of an empty building, dark and grimy and littered with graffiti. Maybe an abandoned car dealership? It's certainly spacious enough inside to be one. "That doin' anything for ya?"

"No. But that doesn't mean I'm not going there," I sigh through my nostrils, backing out of

54

the little room and withdrawing the bottle of cola, tossing it into Moonlyte's lap.

"Don't *fucking* throw it! You'll make all the fizzy disappear," she yelps, scrambling to catch it and then holding the twenty-ouncer close, lightly running her tongue along the side of the clean plastic. Yeah, she's more than just paranoid, she's nuts. Probably why we get along. "Sweet chilly baby..."

It may not have been the info I wanted, but it's a lead, even if it's a shitty lead. I make my way back to my car, checking my phone's GPS for any dealerships nearby, finding one on the other side of town. It's not much, but it's something. I get moving, not expecting to find anything, but hoping against all logic that I'll reach some clue, any clue; anything at all.

11:03am

There's no doubt in my mind that I'm at the right place. The image on Moonlyte's camera was dark and blurry, but so is this place, now that I'm here. Sunlight peeks weakly through the heavy cloud cover of the still-drizzling sky, creating a fittingly apocalyptic haze over Detroit's deserted, waste-littered streets.

As I thought, it's a used car dealership; or it was, before whatever the fuck happened here... well, *happened*. Now, it's more just a mess than anything else. Broken glass crunches beneath my boots as I make my way inside and fuck, it stinks. Not just stinks like everything else; it isn't that normal smell of dust, grease, and decay -- it's something I can't even begin to put my finger on, a deep-set reek that's so strong I can fucking taste it.

Tucking my head down into my jacket, I press on, wincing as the stench permeates through the leather to assault me. I can't help but think that maybe, just maybe, I've stumbled onto something bigger than I thought – that maybe Warwick was part of some greater plan, something that involved taking Moonlyte's cameras down. It didn't answer everything, of course: it didn't explain why a single camera would be left unblocked, or why whoever killed Warwick had seemed so surprised to be doing it. But those are the answers I'm trying to find now.

A sound like a great yawn draws me deeper in, my curiosity piqued as I make my way through the abandoned dealership and toward the back offices, over the broken-down platforms where cars used to be displayed. Still that smell, but now that sound starts to grow louder, more layered, and it's nearly as sickening as the smell – like wet flesh pressing and sliding against something, slithering and shifting; like an orgy of sweaty, reeking lovers just out of sight, their soaked, sticky meat slapping and grinding into one another. My stomach turns at the thought, and the reek that inhabits this place doesn't help in the slightest, growing stronger as I continue to make my way toward the back of the building.

I stop dead in my tracks, blinking as I'm finally confronted with something that doesn't seem possible, considering the exterior layout of the building: a hole in the wall, cracked and splintering around the edges like it was formed from a single, massive impact, leading only into darkness. The sound and the smell come from in there. That much is instantly obvious to me the moment I wind around the husk of an old customers-only popcorn machine and see the hole, nearly as tall as I am and echoing those revolting sounds from the endless blackness within.

...Within...

The chasm attracts me like a magnet, my pupils going wide as I stare into its depths; captivated yet empty, my mind is completely blank now as I take another step towards it. I know I shouldn't, but I do anyway, peering into that yawning, slurping abyss, trying to see what's inside of it.

Nothing. Just squirming darkness, a perverse endlessness that strengthens its grip on my faculties as I take another step nearer to it. If I'm careful, I might be able to make it inside...

7:44am

I'm jarred awake by the sound of rain. The bleak, pale white sky has been replaced once again by the hungry gray of early morning, and I'm back in my car.

Blinking weakly, I do my best to get my bearings. The latte that I got this morning is right where I left it, in its cup holder. Warm.

Warm?

I blink again and straighten my back, looking around and quickly recognizing where I am. I'm outside of the pawn shop where Warwick was killed. Lisowski and Henley's squad car is still parked out front, right next to mine. If déjà vu had a cruel older sister who liked to beat him up and pour soda on his pants before he got to school, she'd be the exact sensation that I'm feeling right now – absolute, impossible displacement in a day that I'd already been in the middle of *enduring*.

Had it all been a dream? Is it even possible for a dream to feel that real? Warwick's death, the locked building, the visit to Moonlyte, that hole in the wall, that smell, that sound...

Yes. That was the only answer, and it explained everything with a pretty little ribbon on top. I'd gotten up too early and I'd fallen asleep in my car as soon as I arrived. There was no hole in the wall, and I sure as fuck didn't time travel. Maybe if I'm lucky, Warwick won't even be dead.

"Hey, lady, you gonna come check this out or what?"

The sharp rap at my window reminds me very clearly that, despite all the uncertainties in my life right now, Henley is still very much an asshole. Praise be to Odin.

Swigging from my coffee cup, I get out of the car and head inside, taking note of the scuffed doorbar propped against the side of the building. The police had experienced some difficulty getting inside the building at all, I understood. That is, I'd understood it this morning, the first time I was here, before the...dream?

"Alright, what are we dealing with?" I say as I make my way into the pawn shop. Lisowski's already inside, standing over the body. A body in a pool of warm, drying blood, surrounded by marking tape and in a very familiar position. A very familiar body.

"We were hoping you could tell us," Lisowski sighs. "He was a friend of yours, right?"

Fucking Warwick.

"Yeah, he..." I swallow hard, blinking. Everything's fucked. This whole thing is fucked. How did this happen, how am I here? Where have I been all this time?

My mind races for alternatives to the unacceptable obvious, anything that seems logical. A drug maybe? Maybe *this*, not everything else, is the illusion. Some drug that has me reliving what I've already been through. Some kind of mental...something. Fuck. I don't know.

"I have to go," I finally say, turning and shouldering past Henley on my way out, who shouts something back after me. I don't hear him, don't hear Lisowski. I'm in my own head now, churning through possibilities and not coming up with many. If I'm right, and I did already meet with Moonlyte, then retracing those steps will be pointless. I need to start a new angle of investigation, and find out what the fuck is going on.

Fortunately, I happen to know where Warwick keeps his spare key. If the police are already on the scene, then it seems pretty likely that someone's already looking after his kid, so his apartment should be empty. Searching his house feels desperate and pointless, but it's the only play I have at this point. I need more information. I need to fill in these blanks that just keep piling up – it feels like I started doing a five hundred piece puzzle only to find out that it's a two thousand piece puzzle, but I didn't know that because the other fifteen hundred were fucking gone.

I hear more talking from the two detectives behind me as I get into my car. I've gotten everything I can out of them for now. This is now, unofficially, *my* case, and the next stop is Warwick's apartment.

8:31am

As fun as the grime and the litter and the emptiness can be, there's something peaceful about being in a noisier, more populated area of the city. Something a little less depressingly apocalyptic. I finish my coffee and can feel its creamy, caffeinated influence taking hold of me as I arrive at Warwick's apartment, head inside the complex and up the stairs, and find the spare key taped to the top of the little light beside his door.

Reaching for it, however, I notice something at the frame of the door leading inside – something I did not expect, in that it might be the slightest bit relevant to the case. Around the frame, barely noticeable, is a very thin edging of solid matte red, something I definitely don't recall ever being there before. Blinking, I lick my lips and very carefully touch my finger to it, throwing caution to the wind as I investigate its texture: somewhat waxy, yet somewhat rough, almost like a mold or a very thick paint. It gives me no information of use, but it's something.

Turning the key, I open the door and stop before I take a single step inside the apartment. That redness litters the inside of the house, forming long, jagged letters across every wall, every flat surface, some longer strings of words even stretching to the

60

ceiling. I think it goes without saying that someone's been here in the time since Warwick was murdered.

More disturbing is the content of the words that are scrawled across the apartment in such excess. They vary slightly from word to word and phrase to phrase, but whoever wrote them was very focused on a specific message.

DONT LOOK

NEVER LOOK

PLEASE

CANT SEE

DONT SEE

STOP LOOKING

CANT BE SEEN

CANT LET THEM SEE

GO

A normal person probably would have left the building then and there and never turned back, washed their hands of the entire fucking thing and done their best to forget what had happened, and live out the rest of their life in peace, minus one Warwick. For better or for worse, I'm not a normal person. Creepy words on the walls can't do me any harm; I'll save my fear for when I come across someone or something that can.

For caution's sake, though, I do draw a kitchen knife from the rack on the table, staying alert and leaving the door open as I start to explore the apartment. The writing on the walls is pretty consistent; though it does seem to grow denser the closer I get to the master bedroom, coating the walls so thickly that the words begin to overlap each other. I stop cold in the hallway, my hand tightening around the knife as I hear a sound, something so soft and so rhythmic I hadn't noticed it at first: Breathing. Shallow, rapid breathing, coming from the bedroom.

The master bedroom is solid red from floor to ceiling. Everything is covered in that gritty, dusty substance – everything from the bed to the window, which floods the room with weak ruby light. A small, semi-humanoid frame is huddled, stationary, in the far corner of the room, and above him are emblazoned three words, these ones seemingly cut or clawed into the wall with big thick ruts. *DONT SEE ME.*

The person – I don't know if I can call it a person or not, but I can't fathom another word I'd use – is small and sickly, the size of a child or young teenager; its pallid, peeling gray skin fully exposed and showing off the frail, bony frame underneath. It faces away from me, huddled in the corner, that breathing almost deafening now as I hold my own. On the back of its misshapen little head is a white porcelain mask, staring blankly at me with cut-out eyes providing windows to a hairless gray scalp, and wearing a wide, close-lipped smile.

I stand still there for a long moment, staring at the creature as its mask stares back at me, its tiny body visibly rocking with each fast, gasping breath, crouched in the corner and not moving, not even acknowledging that I'm in the room. In that moment, I'm frozen. No course of action seems reasonable, and while something in the back of my brain still struggles to make sense of what I'm seeing, the rest of me is quite focused – get out of this room without it knowing I'm here. Leave this place. Call the police. Could I even call the police? Won't they call me crazy if I say there's some kind of gremlin lurking in the corner of a dead man's apartment?

Letting out a slow, careful breath, I take one step backwards, my heel creaking against the floor. The creature, whatever it is, still doesn't move – there's just that rapid breathing, still echoing off the walls, a nightmarish percussion for my every rushing thought.

I almost don't hear it when it speaks, the muffled creak from my second step back almost, but not quite, obscuring its voice. "Please." It's a gasped whisper; quiet, yet harsh like sandpaper. I freeze again, my throat filling with saliva that I have to struggle not to swallow.

"Please." Its voice grows a little stronger. "Don't look."

I hold my breath. Its head starts to tilt a little, resting on its shoulder for a moment before continuing, rolling back to a sickening angle. I can see a ragged, pointed nub at the edge of its mask that looks like it might be an ear, and the creature's breath slows as it sits and listens. Listens for me. "Don't ever look," it says again.

A slow, nearly silent exhalation leaves my lips, and I take another step backward. This one's quiet, no creak like the others. I'm out of the bedroom now, back into the hallway, still staring at that mask and the impossible angle that the creature has fused its neck into. Another step back, slowly, carefully.

A loud creak.

"Wraaaaaaaauuuuggghhhhh..." the little gray thing lets out a long, low sound, a blend between a frog's croak and the scream of a hawk, slowed way, way down. A fight or flight instinct seizes me but I resist it – *stay in control*. I'm not a slave to the will of my body, and the creature hasn't moved yet. It might still not know I'm here.

"Told...you..." its voice lowers again, quieter, as it begins to shift its stance from its awkward crouch. It doesn't stand, however. Not quite. Its legs seem to bend and tilt, folding around and arching the way its neck had. Its legs were positioned at its sides now like that of a crab, though still keeping its frail-looking body low to the ground. "It doesn't listen. It wants to see. Can't let it see. Can't let it look!"

Retaining my dignity in a state of panic, however justified, is a monumental task that I am currently not up for attempting. I turn, scrambling, running, almost falling as I head for the door, storming across the apartment's living room and toward the only escape. I see its movement, vomitous and spider-like, only peripherally as I dash away from the creature. But I can hear it. Hear the awful pops and scrapes of its thin bones battling against each other to propel the thing forward. Hear its constant droning whispers as it comes after me. Hear it getting closer.

"Don't look don't look don't look don't look don't look--" it doesn't stop, never seems to stop as I feel my weight shift and drop down to the floor, legs and arms wrapping around me from behind, the thin, bony appendages clutching tight. Legs wind up under my armpits and hook upward, its pallid, mottled feet in front of me all I can see as I feel its arms wind around my throat, elbows sticking out at awful angles as its entire body squeezes around me. It's small, but strong, its grip like steel and its skin cold as ice, stinging my skin as it crushes my windpipe. I claw desperately at the stretchy, creaking limbs around my throat, trying to pry them away, but I may as well be trying to peel the door off of a titanium safe with my bare hands.

"--Don't look don't look DON'T LOOK DON'T LOOK NEVER EVER LOOK--" Blurry white patterns kaleidoscope across my field of vision and my head starts to feel swollen and heavy, circulation to my brain cut off entirely as the creature punishes me. I claw frantically at its arms, feeling one fingernail chip against its wrist. Then there's nothing. No sound but the pulsing of blood in my own head. Then silence.

6:51am

My eyes open to the hollow darkness inside of my room. I'm in bed. Exhausted, like I've gone through a full day already, but in bed.

65

I already went over the dream theory, but dreams have been known to be very persistent, right? Could I have gone through everything earlier, woken up within the dream, and only just now woken up for real?

My cell phone is buzzing beside me, and I sit up, reaching over to sharply tap my finger against the front of the screen. It lights up, showing my still-bleary eyes an incoming text from Det. Dan Lisowski.

Need an ID on a vic from last night. Think you might have known him. Forwarding the address now. It's the same exact text I got last...*this*...morning. Before everything else. Part of me still refuses to accept what's happening to me, thinks that the things that are going on around Warwick's death are not, and *can* not, be real.

A glance down at my hand proves otherwise. My fingernail is chipped in exactly the place it was when I was trying to pull the masked creature off of me. It stings to touch my neck, and looking down I can see deep, fresh bruises around my armpits and shoulders where the thing held me. Everything that happened had *happened*. I'm facing the reality that attempting to disbelieve something that is so clearly real is exactly as conceited as putting faith in something which cannot, likewise, be proven.

Logic demands that I accept what's happening – either I'm in the middle of some kind of supernatural murder case, entering time loops that are spiraling me further and further backward into the same day, or I have finally become what everyone said I was. That my "personality disorder" was actually something sinister, foul, and uncontrollable, just as I'd always claimed it wasn't. That I was fucking insane.

But if I'm going to go insane, I'll do it on my own terms. I ignore the text for now -- I'm not interested in meeting with the detectives for a third time in the same day, and I have work to do. If I'm gonna go crazy, let's go crazy, and look at the information we have without trying to sugar-coat it: Warwick died in the middle of the night, in a room that was barred from the inside. Moonlyte's entire network of cameras went down two days ago, according to her, so I'm still not early enough to check in with her, and the only lead she gave me was the dealership, containing the yawning pit of doom. Warwick's apartment has become the lair of the masked creature, who doesn't appreciate visitors in the slightest. And Henley is still an asshole.

It doesn't give me a lot to work with, honestly, except for leading me to a single murky conclusion: This entire thing was planned. I'd been following a trail of breadcrumbs, and whoever was leaving it seemed to know what I was going to do before I did it. But what was the motive? And more importantly, why did I keep going backward? If any part of this plan was to kill me the way they'd killed Warwick, they'd had their chance and elected to leave me alive.

"Are you sure you want to do this, Lindsay?"

I startle, drawing the covers around me and closing my eyes for a moment as a voice appears not from behind me, but in front of me. A voice I know. A voice that I'm not entirely surprised to hear despite knowing that hearing it should be impossible. I take a deep breath, looking up to see

67

Warwick standing in front of me in my bedroom, unharmed and looking as alive as he had ever been. His expression is somber and concerned, something I'd seen on his face many times before – whenever he'd fret or worry about something I was doing.

"You know I'm not going to stop until I figure it out," I reply, offering a small smile, though I'm not sure why. I've never smiled genuinely in my life, and while I'm not above smiling to comfort someone, Warwick's dead. I can't imagine a smile bringing him comfort about that.

"It might not be too late to turn away from all of this. You can't bring me back."

"You think I don't know that?"

"I think you're too stubborn to care about it, yes."

"Then quit beating your head against a wall. Go back to being dead."

Warwick smiles. "I never stopped being dead, Lindsay. But you're dealing with things you don't understand. Things you couldn't possibly understand."

"Why don't you actually give me something useful? Tell me where to go next. I'll take anything, at this point."

"You're already on the right track," he says, his smile growing a little sadder now, sympathetic. "Just keep going back. Keep slipping."

"I was hoping you were going to say something that didn't resemble, in any way, the thing that you just sa--" He's gone. Faded away like too little butter on a slice of hot toast, leaving only an oily concept in his wake.

I don't particularly care for the events that lead to me going backwards, and I'm not looking forward to experiencing any more of them. But whether it's my mind that's spiraling out of control, or I've actually entered some vicious loop of temporal belches, I'm fucked, and I may as well find out what's at the bottom of the rabbit hole.

I try to consider what's been happening so far. Each time I've "slipped" back, things have seemed different, worse, darker, like the color and light is being slowly leeched from the world around me each time I spiral backwards. It's not much of a theory, but I'm starting to suspect that things are changing when I go back, that the world I'm dropped off in isn't necessarily exactly the same as the one I left.

Like I said, it's not much of a theory, but if I'm going to try to prove it I need to go back to something I already understand, something I know well. Something I've already experienced in its completion. It means I'm going back to the pawn shop.

For the third time.

7:31am

This drive is all too familiar to me now. I skip my trip to the coffee shop this time; caffeine isn't gonna help the kind of deep-set weariness I'm starting to feel. All I need to get past that, now, is the adrenaline that's persistently pumping through me on my way to the shop. I make it there almost fifteen minutes earlier than I did last time, and already I'm starting to suspect that my theory was

69

right – that each slip isn't just taking me back, but altering the world around me. I don't remember it being quite this dark out, though the driving rain still plays its part in that.

"What's your plan?"

"See what's different. Get a gun, maybe," I say to Warwick, who's sitting beside me. It feels like he's always next to me, now, though looking for him only yields results about 20% of the time. "Not expecting either of the detectives to give theirs up, but then again, I'm really not sure what to expect at all at this point."

"You think a gun will help?"

"No. But it'll make me feel better."

"You know there are so many America jokes I could make right now, Lindsay," Warwick says with a little smile.

"I know. But I'd prefer you didn't."

I park and get out, heading inside. Warwick disappears, like his corpse can't exist alongside his...spirit, or my vision of him, or whatever it is that's been talking to me. The blood surrounding his body should be fresher, and it looks wetter, but it's also darker – nearly completely black now as the two detectives stand over him, Lisowski holding a cigarette between his fingers while Henley remains a safe distance away from the cancerous plumes of smoke.

The second thing I notice is that both detectives are wearing wide grins, the kind of grin someone wears to frighten a small child, paired with appropriately wild, staring eyes. Something tells me my new nightmare is about to begin, but I steady myself, breathing in deeply and nodding to the two of them. "I'm here, Dan." I nod towards Lisowski, then Henley. "Mike. What do you need?" Exactly what I said when I got here the first time.

Lisowski doesn't reply the same way. "That's great. That's so great," he says, his voice quiet and even. "I need your advice on something. Something important." Still he stares down at Warwick's body, his gaze never even flickering toward me. Henley's eyes are transfixed on the corpse as well.

"What's that?" I know it's a mistake as soon as I say it.

Slowly, Dan raises his gaze to look at me, his chest heaving and twitching with laughter that he's visibly trying to hold back. "Do we eat him first, or fuck him?"

"I say we eat some," Mike says, his grin widening impossibly, stretching his cheeks until the corners of his mouth begin to bleed. "Get a nice snack before we have our fun."

"What do you think, Lindsay?" Dan whispers.

This is a question I have no desire to answer directly. My eyes flicker from Warwick's body to both detectives' belts – they're both carrying, and both pistols are secured pretty firmly in their holsters. Getting a hold of one is going to be tricky, and if I thought getting one of these two to give up a weapon willingly was gonna be hard, it was gonna be even harder now that they're talking about fucking-slash-eating a dead body...unless I use that to my advantage.

I look up at the two of them, stretching my lips into a grin to match theirs as well as I can. "We fuck him first. There's no way I can wait," I say, slipping my jacket down my shoulders, then off, tossing it aside. They're convinced, something I never had any doubt of. I've been lying to people since I was a little girl, and even in their...*state*...they're just humans, as far as I can tell. And I can manipulate humans.

"I was hoping you'd say that," Dan almost squeals, biting his lower lip as he starts to undo his belt. Henley's undoing his too, but taking his time – amidst the sudden cannibalistic insanity, he retains enough of a seed of his true self to be distrustful of me. I don't have time to wait for that, though – crazy or not, I'm not going to let them fuck Warwick's corpse. That's just a matter of principle.

As Lisowski fusses with his underthings, I dash for the gun belt, grabbing and unclasping it, drawing it from its holster. I couldn't say for the life of me what the make or model is, or how many bullets it holds, but I know to look for the safety, and I find a little black slider on the side that I assume is what I'm looking for. I push it to the side, exposing the red underneath as Henley reaches for his own gun; I'm already pointing my weapon at him as he stoops back down to pick up his pants.

"Don't...fucking...do anything, alright!" I raise my voice, my breathing steady but my heart racing.

"Lindsaaaaayyyy," Dan whimpers, though the smile hasn't faded from his face, like his bleeding rictus grin is fused to his skull. "Don't be like this. Don't make us sad."

"Shut up. I'll shoot both of you and sleep like a baby; you know that." The gun's handle is a little bit big for my hand, but I clench my fingers around it anyway, cocking back the hammer and keeping my finger firmly on the trigger, tight enough that an accident could easily happen. But my hand doesn't shake. I'm telling the truth, and somewhere in his mind, Lisowski knows it.

"Fucking do it then, bitch," Henley growls, his eyes going dry and bloodshot after so long without blinking. He's still holding his gun belt in his hands, his own pistol fastened into its holster, but he's touching the handle. I don't approve.

Actually, now that I think about it, I'm never gonna get a better opportunity in my life to fatally shoot Detective Mike Henley. And I really wasn't lying about that sleep thing.

I pull the trigger three times, not taking any risks. The first bullet goes into Henley's breastbone, a gush of blood bursting free of him as the structural linchpin of his ribcage explodes. The second goes through his cheek, and the third goes straight into his nose, bursting out the back of his skull. He lets out an awkward, sputtering laugh as he sinks to his knees, one hand going to his chest as if trying to push the blood and chunks of bone back into his body. He fails. Then he dies.

Dan rushes towards me as I shoot his partner, his fixed grin widening, mouth opening like he's going to bite me as his arms reach out for me. I stumble backwards, aiming the gun and firing off a shot just a little too late – hitting him, but not fatally. His body slams into me, pinning me to the concrete floor of the pawn shop, and he slowly drags his warm, dry tongue across the side of my face, fingers digging into my shoulders, pinning my arms – and the gun – to my sides.

"Can't give it to me any harder than that, Mommy?" Dan whispers, his bloodshot eyes staring into mine as he snarls and lunges forward and to my side, digging his teeth into my ear and biting down hard, tearing a piece of it away. His wail of delight is only barely eclipsed by my shriek of pain as I push back with every ounce of strength I have left, relying as much on sheer determination as I am on Dan's distraction in his cannibalistic ecstasy. In a rough shove and roll I manage to shift him onto his side, blood streaming down my face and neck as I press the gun against his face.

I'd never really considered Lisowski to be a friend, not even as much of a friend as Warwick had been, but he'd been a decent man, a decent cop, and he'd been decent to me. I'd say I feel sorry that he went the way he did, regardless of how he was affected by the stark, sucking insanity of the darkness that our world was being swallowed by. I'd say I feel sorry but I don't. I don't feel things like that.

When I said I wouldn't lose a night of sleep, I really wasn't kidding.

I pull the trigger three times, bullet after bullet screaming through Lisowski's temple and out the back of his face at various different angles, the majority of his skull ceasing to exist as fragments of it are blown across the room amidst a sea of blood and brain and eye and spine.

"Harder...Mommy..." he rasps, his lips seeming to move on their own as his neck flops to the side, the half a skull he still retains falling limply backwards and his body going still. His dead weight is heavier than before, but not so heavy that I can't get out from under him, staggering to my feet and looking around for something, anything, that can be used to stop the fairly substantial bleeding from my ear.

I am, of course, in a pawn shop. It takes mere seconds before I find a spool of half-used duct tape and haphazardly bind my wound with it; my breathing hard and fast now as I look down at the three corpses on the floor – two killed by my hand – making the entirety of the pawn shop's cold, gray slab of a floor slick with blood and various chunks of meat and organs. For the first time I pray that the world really is dissolving around me, because if I'm crazy, it means I'm spending the rest of my life in a padded room. Not high on my wish list.

Lisowski's belt is a little too big for me, but I adjust it as best I can and holster the pistol, scavenging Henley's clip as well after a bit of trial and error to eject it. That goes in my pocket, and I've gotten what I came for. I had to kill two people to get it, but I have it – I'm armed. Exhaling slowly, I make my way for the front door, opening it and finding only chaos as the world dissolves.

3:82am

The sky screams in a vibrant vortex absent of color, glistening and coalescing like soapy water in shades of piercing white and the empty black of the void. I try to avert my eyes, but there is nowhere to look – the pawn shop has vanished and I now stand in an empty field of withered flowers, a place I feel that I have never been.

But the dried, brown husks don't stay that way for long their petals flying away and drifting up to join the maelstrom above me, their stalks

75

disintegrating and their seeds scattering to the cracked ground, which I now see appears to be concrete. I take a few slow steps, forward, though unsure which direction to travel as winds whip and blur around me, growing strong for only a second at a time before fading again, changing course on a dime, whipping my hair to and fro before I have time to turn my head.

The seeds begin to sprout, fresh green stalks growing upward from the shattered gray floor beneath me, then blooming, vibrant red flowers reaching up to embrace the sky. Flowers the same bright matte red of the writing on the walls in Warwick's home. Before I have time to dwell on them any longer, they, too, begin to wither and turn brown.

It starts to make sense in the way that only a madman can make sense of something that can't possibly be real. In this dead world I've stumbled into, reality seems to be in fast-forward. The cycles of life and death are faster than a mayfly's. Only I am constant. Only me, and the gnawing, yawning nexus of the sky. Now, time itself twists and cavorts in its hellish waltz across the fabric of what I once knew as reality.

For the first time, I am truly afraid.

Creatures I can deal with. Even the...glitches...in the way I perceive reality, can be explained by the fact that I was never right in the head to begin with. Any amount of emotional or primal sensation I can endure, because I am not subject to those things. What is happening now, however, is like being forced to watch *The Fountain* on a global scale, assaulting my senses on a level that is not only emotional, but intellectual, taking firm hold of each finger of my grip on reality and peeling them back. The world is gone, life is gone, death is meaningless, time doesn't exist, and I remain alone in the center of it all. The nexus of the spiraling sky is centered on me, and I have no way of explaining why.

Why me, why Warwick, why anything? As if the universe – or whatever hateful, writhing entity chose me from behind the starry barrier that separates us from the gut-clenching terror of the beyond – hand-picked my desire to understand, and chose to deny it to me on a fundamental level. As far as I can tell, it succeeded.

I don't give up, though. Whether or not I am mad, my stubbornness comes first. I start to move forward, even if it feels like I'm struggling through a wall of aspic as the air tries to force me backwards. I may be afraid and confused, and at this point I have no idea whether or not I've gone completely insane, but I'm not going to sit down and let that madness claim me.

I keep moving, foot after foot, step after step, my body exhausted and my ear burning from the bite I suffered. I try to anchor myself to a single question – the simplest question, the one thing I might be able to find an answer to: Who killed Warwick? I don't know what direction I'm going in, but I'm determined to find that answer.

From behind me comes a great bellow, a sort of droning, thunderous yawn not unlike the one that had come from the hole in the wall. Once again I can hear that slurping and slapping and shifting, though it transcends mere sound, penetrating my mind and lingering within it, unshakeable, inescapable. I tense my muscles and start to run – as best as I can, anyway – gasping for breath as I push against the thick, hungry air around me, charging forward regardless of where forward leads me. I can hear that sound starting to grow louder behind me, advancing, my blood pounding in my head. I can feel my ear start to bleed again, the warm liquid streaming down over that which has already encrusted my neck. I don't give up.

It's far away, but it's a goal: a door. Not attached to anything, but standing alone in the middle of the vast expanse of concrete. A foggy shimmer is descending on me that nearly obscures it. This fog is the same oily monochrome as the sky and nearly blinds me, stinging my eyes, slowing me down. I need to get to the door. It's all I have. The bellow from behind me grows louder, seeming to envelop me. I don't dare look back. Need to stay focused.

My fingers close around the handle of the door and I open it, run inside, slam it shut behind me without turning around. Next to me is a heavy metal bar, and I slam it into place along its rack in front of the door. I don't know if it will help, but it's worth a shot. A last, desperate effort to protect myself from whatever is outside.

000:000ys

I suck in a deep breath of air, closing my eyes and trying to get my bearings. That sound is gone, and I'm inside again. It may not be safe, but it's

78

something I can pretend to know, rather than the vast, inky planetoid where I'd just been.

I turn away from the door and open my eyes. I'm in the pawn shop again, the place where this all started. Two things are different, my eyes quickly catch – first, Warwick's body is not here. Second is the writing on the walls. That same deep red, those same long, scrawled letters. The message, however, is different this time.

WATCH HIM RISE

WATCH HIM RISE

WATCH HIM RISE

WATCH HIM RISE

WATCH HIM RISE

WATCH HIM RISE

WATCH HIM RISE

The hair on my arms raises, and I unclasp the holster on my scavenged belt, drawing out the gun. I don't know if it will help me or not – the empty pit of hopelessness in my gut certainly doesn't seem to think so. My grip around it grants me no comfort.

"Please," I finally whisper, pressing my back against the door and waiting for inevitable escalation. It feels like weakness when the word leaves my lips but it comes out of its own accord. A desperate gasp for help, mercy, anything.

"Please what?"

I can tell from his voice, from the dark skin of his arms, that the speaker is Warwick. He wears a mask now, the same mask that the creature had worn, though it's on the front of his face rather than the back, staring at me with that wide plastic smile. The eyes are hollow, and lead nowhere. Only ink.

"Please stop," I say softly.

"Stop?" he says. I raise the pistol, aiming it at him. This time, my hands do shake. "But you're just in time."

I fire three times, the kick of the gun sending my arms upward. One shot in his chest, the next bursting through his throat. The last enters the oblivion where his face should be, the white mask exploding, taking the world with it.

119392:28491949ys

The crack in the world opens, and the sky opens to meet it. The Gate not only unlocks, but shatters, belching forth darkness and emptiness and starving, squirming rage, twisted and shrieking from being so long hidden beneath what is real. I'll never know whether it swallowed everything or only me. I'll never know why any of this happened, why I was chosen, how they continued from here.

But I did finally learn who killed Warwick.

I did.

The Lurker in the Dark

by

John E. Meredith

She wouldn't meet with him until after dark. That was the second thing that made him wary of the voice on the phone. The first thing to ring hinky was someone like her wanting to hire someone like him at all. He had only been doing this gig since the end of the war, just a black private dick who barely got any business from his own people. He could already tell that she wasn't from his side of town.

He had trouble sleeping anyway, always had, so he told her to meet him at his office on Lich Street. They set the meeting for midnight. He knew she'd be there early, so he showed up at 11:30. She'd already been there for an hour. The lights of his old '40 Plymouth sliced into the alley, cutting her face in half. He killed the engine, and once again she was lurking in the shadows, looking like she *belonged* there.

"I'm guessing you're Theda Lang," he said.

"Detective," she said, and nothing else. He noticed that she didn't extend her hand.

Without another word he turned into the alley, leaving his back to her. His office was the second door down, the one with *August Winfield, Private Investigation* in cheap stencils on the glass. Winfield opened the door without producing a key and stepped inside, leaving it open like an invitation. He was almost surprised when she followed him, a white woman alone in the middle of the night with a black man. That's when he knew that he had more to fear from her than she did from him.

"I see why you don't bother to keep the place locked."

The office was almost the size of a closet. It was dark and it stank, but everything inside was neatly ordered, like his mind. There were books and case files and not much else. Winfield draped his overcoat on the chair behind the desk and went to the radio in the corner, tuning the Philco in to WESX Channel 1230 out of Salem. Jimmy Dorsey filled the tiny space with the mellow, melancholy sounds of "Tangerine."

"Anybody who wants what I got doesn't know where the place is, and anybody who knows where it is doesn't want what I got. Besides," he said, "someone tries something funny, I start squirtin' lead."

Theda Lang was a large woman, tall and thin, with a smile that didn't reach her eyes. They were as dark as her skin was light, framed by hair that looked like ravens perched on her shoulders. The coat she wore, from the flesh of some unfortunate animal, hung on her frame like she had only moments ago acquired it. Like she frequently didn't wear clothes at all. Winfield knew that in those deep pockets she was probably packing some heat too.

And there was a scent about her. Sweet, but probably deadly.

She closed the door and sidled into the chair in front of his desk, like she wasn't worried about a thing in the world. Yeah, she came across calm, but there was something twitchy under it all, and she passed it on to him like a virus. Even in the confined space, he began a measured stroll back and forth behind the desk. Radio voices in the room crooned, *and I've seen times where Tangerine had the bourgeois believing she were queen.*

She lit a cigarette without asking. "You don't trust me," she said.

"I don't trust anyone."

The hand not holding a Virginia Slim crept down the front of her coat. Toward one of those big pockets. Her long fingers slipped inside, then she slapped a wad of green on the desk. "How about that? Think you could learn to trust that?"

Money was just a piece of paper crawling with germs, but everybody was looking to get sick on it. Winfield was no better and no worse. "So what's the grift?" he asked.

"No grift. I hear that you're a bloodhound."

"I've been called worse."

He reached under the desk for a glass and the bottle of Blue Bird. Gin poured like blood from the open neck of the bottle. Winfield took a swig, then slid it across the desk to Lang. She promptly tapped the ashes of her cigarette into the costly alcohol. Of course it was like that. She shifted in the chair, slowly, purposely opening the fur coat. She was built like a bridge and liked her dresses low. It was hard not to notice, even though Winfield tried.

"Look, ace, I've been picked up so many times I ought to have handles. Say what you will about that, but I've had my reasons. There's something I've been after."

"You shouldn't have any trouble getting it," he said. He reached for the gin, slamming it down, ashes and all.

"That's not what I'm talking about, detective. I'm not saying I'm not willing, if that's what it'll take. But I can see that I make you nervous. Hell, maybe *any* woman makes you nervous. There's a change coming, more than you know. We're coming out of the kitchen, Mr. Winfield."

"And the fields," he said. "But none of that matters. Are we going to sit here beating up our gums all night, or are you going to throw me a motive?"

Suddenly she wanted to play coy. Her eyes were all over the room, like there was that much to see. She stubbed out the cigarette in the empty glass, lit another. Then she fastened onto a spear of moonlight piercing the blinds behind her, making strange shapes on the age-worn carpet. They seemed to change even as she watched them.

"You got a mother, detective?"

"I'd like to think I was hatched from an egg."

Her eyes latched onto his. There was something darker in them now. "We've all got a mother," she said, "whether she's underground, or we don't know *where* she is. I'd like you to find mine."

"You think she'll be proud?"

"I think she'll give me some answers."

"That's a pretty long bet," he said.

"You see them all the time, in the market and in the park. Mothers and their children. They look happy, like they don't know any better. What do I know, maybe they don't." It looked like she was going to go weeping-willow for a moment, but the moment passed. "It's too late for me to be on the one end of that, but maybe I can still be on the other. That's what I've been trying to do."

Winfield sat down, heavily. "To find her?"

"No, detective, to *be* her. I've been trying to have a child."

"Sounds like you need a doctor more than a detective. Or maybe a few more boyfriends."

"What I need is to fix something, and she's the only one who can tell me how."

Winfield said nothing for a long time, but he was thinking plenty. He knew that you could live your whole life a good man, but trouble was still going to find you. That's what she was, nothing but trouble in a low-cut dress. He reached out for the stack of cash. She put her hand on his, white on black, and he resisted flinching.

"Wisteria," he said.

Her eyebrows arched like the back of a cat. "Detective?"

"Your perfume. I've been trying to place it, and now I know. It's wisteria. You talk about mothers, and mine always smelled like that."

Her hand was still on his. "Last I heard, she was talking to some professor up at Miskatonic, someone named Meursault. That was years ago."

"I've heard of the guy. Any other useful knowledge you care to share?"

"She was very interested in some cult, and not very interested in being a mother."

He was looking at their hands and thinking about wisteria. It could gracefully climb the trunk of a tree, but eventually choke even the mighty oak to death. It looked beautiful even while it killed everything around it. "I'll start in the morning," he said.

Her lips twitched a smile. "If you need anything else, detective..."

"I'll settle for the lettuce. Hate to be the one that gives you that miracle child."

She stood up, allowing time for him to get another look at her. He kept his eyes on the money. "Don't worry about contacting me," she said. "If you figure anything out, I'm going to know. Then I'm going to be there when you find her."

"So, Ms. Lang, why not knock on my door in the daylight?"

"Things are different in the dark," she said.

He tried not to watch her walk away. Before she stepped out, she turned to look back at him, nodding at the radio that was busy squeezing out Stan Kenton. "You're a moldy fig," she said with a wink. "You know, they're coming up with new music all the time. Maybe you should try some Mingus or something."

"I like this music because it's simple," he said. "There are no bumps."

"Life is nothing but bumps, detective, and the real players don't try to pretend it's any other way."

"I'll consider myself educated," he said.

Then she was swallowed up by the night, leaving nothing but an open door. Winfield reached into his pocket for a handkerchief, wiping out the glass and depositing it back under the desk. He cut Kenton off mid-phrase and retrieved his coat.

From across Parsonage Street, where it crossed Lich, the burial ground looked bigger than usual. Like it was already making room for an active season. He wondered if that explained the movement he caught, for just a moment. Something only half seen. Something dark lurching against an even darker background. A graveyard worker with a bad leg and implements for digging, maybe. Toiling away for a few bucks in the middle of the night. But Winfield didn't really believe that.

He didn't know it yet, but we were already there with him. We were watching and we were waiting.

The Miskatonic University looked like a vibrant spook-house even in the sunlight, of which there was not much in Arkham. An immense series of ivy-covered brick buildings crouching in a fertile campus, it was the most colorful location in all of Essex County. Some believed that the not-so-secret tunnels beneath the quadrangle formed a kind of water duct from the nearby Miskatonic River, but that didn't explain the monochromatic tone of the warehouse district on River Street, or how the remaining city cast the impression of life dimly remembered. Nor was there anyone left who could recall stories of when the school was built, leaving the notion that it had sprung from the feral woods that once haunted this area, birthing the city and its people around itself.

Whatever the reason, Winfield had always been partial to the university. Maybe it was the vast library and all the secrets buried in those rare and obscure old pages, secrets being half his business. Most likely it was the absence of any women on the grounds. Theda Lang was still banging around in his head that morning, and he knew it was no place for a woman. You want to swim in them, but they'll watch you drown and count your screams as music.

The first person he saw when he pushed through

the wide front doors was Jupiter Lucius, the only other man of color within a mile of the place. The hunched old figure looked up from polishing the oakwood floor.

"Mistuh Winfield, that you?"

"In the flesh, Jupiter. What's the rumpus?"

"Well, Lordy be. These ol' eyes ain't so good n'more, sir. No wonder I ain't seen you 'round a while."

With gnarled hands, he reached up for Winfield, who pulled the old man to his feet. Jupiter chuckled and shook his head. "Man, I could tell ya some stories 'bout gettin' old," he said, and then proceeded to do just that.

Winfield listened and nodded along, trying to beat Theda out of his thoughts.

"How is Charlotta?"

"Oh, she's good, Mistuh Winfield, real good. Ain't a day goes by we don't thank the Almighty for you, sir. What you done, trackin' her baby sister down like that, well, it meant the world. It truly did. And then to be gettin' me this work." On cue, the old man reached down to rub his twisted knees.

Winfield always wanted him to knock off with all the misters and sirs, but had to admit they felt better than a gut-punch. "And the sister?"

"Naw, sir. She ain't good at all. It's like I said, we 'preciate what you done, but Biddy, she wa'n't right when she got back home. It was like she brought somethin' else back with 'er. She done run off one more time."

He didn't know how he found the girl in the first place, more luck than anything else. She had been over a hundred miles south of Arkham. Looked like she'd dragged herself through the mud getting there too, making haste for the woods past Aylesbury. Couldn't remember a thing and willing to say even less. Winfield wasn't sure now, but at the time he thought she might have been with child.

"If you need her tracked down again, Jupiter..."

"Naw, Mistuh Winfield, she dead."

Those words were no surprise to Winfield. He could see the girl's face, older than it should have been. There was something in her eyes that was older still. If he could have found her years before anyone asked him to, it still would have been too late.

"We found 'er out on Hangman's Hill," Jupiter said. "It was a couple days later. The dogs or somethin' been at 'er, but there was still 'nuff-a her left to know it was Biddy. I tell ya, I di'n't think Charlotta was gonna make it through. Seein' somethin' like that. It was *bad*, sir."

"What do you think happened to her out there?"

The old man looked left and right, then quietly said, "We thought it mighta been one-a them white boys from down on High Street, Lord forgive me. You know we had some triflin' with them. But they done seem just as surprised as we was. Then one-a they own end up the same, and I jus' got to feelin' like they got bigger troubles than some ol' Negro girl."

"Well, dammit, Jupiter."

"It's alright, sir. Charlotta, she startin' to get on now, and...well, you *seen* how that girl was when she got back. Sometimes bein' dead is jus' the best way out."

The old man was right, but she was as good as

dead when he found her. He took her back to her family that night. They lived in nothing more than a shack, with no electricity, barely running water, but they still found a way to celebrate. Charlotta had rationed food for the big return, inviting Winfield in for a feast of fatback and red peas. He raced home to bring back his old Admiral battery-operated tube radio. Jupiter searched the airwaves for some spirituals and everyone spent the night eating, singing, and praising the Lord.

Except for Winfield. He was too distracted by the dead eyes on the guest of honor. Jupiter and Charlotta raised their voices right along with Blind Willie Johnson. *Won't somebody tell me, answer if you can. Won't somebody tell me, just what is the soul of man?* But Biddy, she was silent, just waiting for whatever took her soul to come back for the rest.

The past was nothing more than a long hall with too many doors. All you wanted to do was get to the end without opening too many of them. Winfield had started to take an unwanted stroll down that hall when his thoughts were dashed by the clack-clack-clack of hard-heeled shoes on oak. A suit with a pinched face had just lain eyes on him and was making a predictable beeline. He knew that it would happen sooner or later.

Winfield was gaunt, with a shaven head and dark eyes set into a pale face, at least pale for a black man. Sometimes it worked in his favor that he was lighter than most of his people. Sometimes it didn't.

"Good morning, *sir*." The last word was strained, the sound of decorum preventing the use of another. "This is the Miskatonic University. Is there something I could help you with?"

Winfield opened his mouth for a retort, but it wasn't his voice that rang out.

"This man is my guest, doctor."

It was Meursault.

He had appeared without a sound from behind the detective. For such a big man, he was one of the stealthiest bastards Winfield knew. And one of the kindest. "Go on now, Herbert, back to the lab. Mister Winfield and I have some stories to share."

"Yeah, pal, dangle. It's business."

A cold front moved through the doctor's blue eyes, but he didn't say a word. When he slunk off, Meursault faced the detective. "I assume it's true," he said. "There are stories to share?"

"Something like that."

Jupiter greeted the professor, then, "Mistuh Winfield, sir, I got the business of this floor to tend. It be a good thing seein' you again. Don't be no stranger to us now, hear."

Winfield extended his hand, surprising the old man. He shook it eagerly. "Can't get rid of me that easily, Jupiter. You go ahead and give Charlotta my regards."

"Will do, sir."

As he walked away from Jupiter Lucius, already going to work on the university's floor, he kept turning the old man's words over and over in his head: *sometimes being dead is just the best way out.*

Something in the Miskatonic's library always smelled like the sodden fur of a very large beast. Not that Meursault would have noticed. He hadn't stopped flapping his lips all the way across campus, past the sports field, the School of Languages, and Science Hall; nor upon passing the colossal ornate octopus that marked the library entrance. Ascending the staircase to the upper floor, then back to the most remote corner of the library, still he talked.

He spoke faster and faster, eyes flashing, a man in love with arcane tales. About the curious manuscript delivered to the college last week, bearing a few words that resembled the Arabic used in Mesopotamia, but otherwise unknown by any authority. About non-Euclidian geometry and sleeping gods, and about poor Delapore, who returned to his ancestral home, and how something there drove him to feast on his own kind. About the failed expedition to find the great horrible city of R'lyeh, fabled resting place of the terrible Cthulhu. "Those men never returned," he said, nearly giddy with horror. "They are said to have gone completely *mad* with what they saw."

"We all go a little crazy, professor."

"Indeed, indeed, but can you imagine the sights they beheld? *Indubitably stupendous*. Oh, well look, it seems we've reached our destination. I think we can finally talk now."

Winfield gazed down upon wall after wall of relentless books from a kind of upper-deck proscenium arch. Ancient tomes rose nearly twenty feet in every direction, like bodies in an endless mausoleum of knowledge. Here was the last bastion of studies that had fallen out of vogue: ritual necromancy, alchemy, medieval metaphysics. There was even a rumor that, somewhere, this very building housed one of the last remaining copies of the dread *Necronomicon*. It was said as well that

Tesla once attended the university under another name, taking something back with him that helped provide the world with light.

Merely the thought of these things, with only the barest understanding of what they meant, made Winfield realize that there were more mysterious things in the world than missing girls.

Meursault was a large man, due mostly to his profound love of food, though he claimed that he had to be so big in order to fill himself up with stories. He always had room for just one more. "Forgive me, detective, but I've always wanted to ask. With a mind like yours, how on earth have you come to do the work that you do?"

"When the war really got going and all the boys started getting killed, they were taking anyone stupid enough to join. Didn't want to miss their chance to get a few Negroes killed too. I was getting a little old, but not too old to die for Uncle Sam."

"He does seem particularly interested in seeing his boys die."

"That he does. All that I learned in the 92nd was how to fix things and how to hold a gun," Winfield said. "Turns out, even up here in the land of the free, holding a gun was the only one that mattered."

Meursault nodded. "Not to everyone, my friend. But where on earth did you ever develop your interest in matters more supernatural?"

"My mother," he said, recalling a much smaller wall of books, but it was as if uttering the word hurt him. "Speaking of which, I've got a dame looking for hers. A possible grift named Theda Lang. Thinks the old lady might've talked to you a few years back."

"Well, I don't get many dames."

"Says she was really keen on one of the local cults. Can't tell you much about the mother, but her baby girl has a big chest full of cash. She claims to want to reproduce and only dear ol' Mom can tell her how."

Meursault reached up to twist his eyebrow. "*Maybe*."

"I don't know why, but this one feels kind of important."

"There *was* a woman, I believe it was in the final year of the war. Yes, that was it. She must have followed me for a while, because she knew where I lived. It was late in October, like now, and she apparently tracked me from here to Sentinel Street. Because, you know, they don't like to allow just anyone into the university."

"Yeah, I noticed."

"Though I insisted, she never graced me with her name. This was truly ironic, for she unleashed almost every other ragged nugget of information about herself that I never wanted to know. She was quite troubled. One might even say that she was *haunted*. It seems that she had precisely the opposite problem that her daughter did."

"Well, she managed to have a child."

"*Mon ami*, she gave birth to over a *dozen* children. She would give them away, leave them on the doorstep of the Baptist church, and, I suspect, she may have even *killed* a few of them. She was an older woman; there's no way to know how many progeny she actually left behind. There was something she was looking for with each new child that she produced, but I could not ascertain if it was something extra or the *absence* of that something extra that she was seeking."

Winfield pushed his fingers across his scalp. Maybe he needed to lay off the gin, because he didn't feel right. He turned his back to the rows of books below. He breathed in slowly, wiping his face with his hand.

"So what'd she want from you?"

"I'll be damned if I know. She provided so much information with so little clarity. She even offered me money, though I could not understand for what purpose. I think the poor thing was out of her mind, or nearly so. However, she did mention having *done right*, as she said, at least once."

"The daughter."

"Possibly. However, as her increasingly nonsensical soliloquy progressed, she grew ever more..."

"Cock-eyed."

"Yes, but fearful as well. She had begun talking about such esoteric matters that not even I could understand her. I don't know if she even understood *herself*. What she seemed most concerned with was a means of resetting the clock. Whether the inquiry was in regards to herself or something larger, I do not know."

"Haven't you ever wanted to cut away a piece of your memory, professor?"

"Me? Oh, heavens, no. If I could acquire memories beyond my own, I would be unstoppable." He laughed. "This was when she inquired about a specific cult. Not surprisingly, I had known about them. They were active at the turn of the century, going so far as to get involved with the local politics, but they had fallen silent as the First World War started brewing. They called themselves 'the Believers.'"

"What did they believe in?"

"The usual apocalyptic themes, but with a more cosmic tone. The end, they claimed, would come from the shadow-haunted 'Outside.' That's how it was described, which most likely meant a cold and distant star. The extinction of humanity would arrive in the form of some kind of slowly crawling chaos that would engulf us all."

"Well, if the war didn't do that, I don't know what else could."

"Now, detective, I *know* you have more of an imagination than that. The only constant is change, but none of us alone can really determine the direction of that change. There will be bright and shining moments in our future, for races of every kind. There always are."

Winfield eyed him skeptically.

Meursault waved him off and continued. "But it's a universal law that the light is an anomaly amidst the darkness. Neither can exist without the other, of course, and yet we are nonetheless in a perpetual struggle for the victory of one over the other. But it's not a victory that can truly be won, and even if one side *were* victorious...well, what are darkness and light without each other?"

"Thanks for the pep talk, professor. As it turns out, you're not the first person to preach about change lately."

"Your mystery girl?"

"Yeah, she's convinced that something big is

coming."

Meursault seemed to have even heavier thoughts hanging over him, but wasn't sure how much he wanted to share. "*Change*, yes. You know, I have a rented room where I've lived for over twenty years now," he said. "Each night I watch the parade of pedestrians on the street below my window. I once knew them all, but, in recent years, only gradually, I have begun to see something...*different* among them. Some of them do not seem to be like us, detective."

"The end of war brings a lot of immigrants."

The professor looked like a man who knew he was going to have to shoot his favorite dog. "Some of these immigrants are from much further away than you could possibly imagine," he said.

Winfield decided that what he needed was probably more gin, rather than less. Then he felt like he could lie down for a nap lasting approximately a hundred years. Something about this conversation had made him decidedly uneasy.

"Any idea where I can dig up some of these Believers?"

"Many years ago, they were said to have dwelled somewhere across the river, though I never passed that rumor on to your girl's mother. The last thing I wanted on my conscience was the body of a drowned woman."

Winfield nodded. "Well," he said.

"Yes, well."

Then, as Winfield began to walk away, Meursault added, "I might urge you to be cautious, August. There are forces far greater and more malignant than either of us out there, and I rather

99

enjoy our conversations."

Winfield smiled and patted his overcoat, indicating that he was armed.

"Perhaps," Meursault said, "but bullets may do you no good."

All this talk about mothers had gotten Winfield thinking about his own. It left him wishing that one of his doomed siblings had made it past their first year, but there wasn't so much as even a tombstone. There were barely any memories. He had nothing but questions as he got older, but there wasn't much point in asking. The woman had been gone for years and had spent most of his childhood getting ready to leave. Nothing but the house remained, just a few walls that had been falling down since before the war, and there was nothing there he hadn't already torn through.

He stopped for a deck of Luckies, then found a record shop that hawked every jazz album he could imagine. With a long-player called *Mingus Sings* under his arm, he stepped back out onto Main Street and found the nearest pub that would serve him. Not even three hours of alcohol could clear his mind. It was raining when he stumbled from the bar. Street lamps made halos in the air. A neon sign advertising a travel agency flashed *The World Is Yours* above his head, making him vanish and then reappear like a crimson phantom, over and over again.

Winfield wasn't too sufficiently sauced to realize he was being tailed. There had been a black-and-white on him since he left the university, trying to make itself invisible from a block away. None of it was much of a surprise. He'd learned that lesson when he got back from the war, expecting to be some kind of hero. He was still just another Negro, and having risked his life for freedom outside these borders meant a lot less back inside of them.

He got the Plymouth for a song, no one figuring on him being able to get it started again. But he knew more than just his place. Then, one night, coming around the corner from his new office, he found the tires slashed. The damn thing had only been running for a few days. He'd never been so ready to snap his cap. And there were the words of the local bull ringing in his ears, *Where you going so late, boy?* Like the car and the office weren't both his own.

Where you going so late?

Trains arrived and departed along the river. They rumbled through the dark, then shrieked to a dead stop. Figures in raincoats moved along the platform, their features obscured by hats and shadows. He was almost certain that they were looking at him.

The bluecoats finally dropped off, but other dark shapes continued to follow in the rain.

Staggering across Boundary Street, he could see the old abandoned graveyard amongst the rain-blurred trees. Beyond that, the rising mound of Hangman's Hill, where over a hundred executions had been carried out. Goody Fowler was lynched there. They said she was a witch, but then they always lied about the ones they wanted to kill.

He stopped to fish for a cigarette in his coat, squeezing Mingus between his legs. Before today, the last time he smoked had been during the war, somewhere in Italy. *Dammit, dammit, dammit.* He

101

lit a match against a dead lamppost, then inhaled deeply. It was only as he lurched to the left at Hill Street, almost home, that he remembered the Plymouth back at the bar. *Well, shit.*

Someone was standing in the street in front of his house.

Theda?

No. The unperfected stroll, a face too dark. And now, as she approached, all those *baby, baby, babies.* This was one of the neighborhood pros. He'd seen too many of them when he got back to the States. Victory girls, but nobody had told them there was nothing to celebrate. *Hey, baby, would you like a date?*

No, no, no. Waving her away.

The hell with you then. What you prefer, white women? Or maybe men.

"I prefer no one."

Then, turning back from the door, he saw that her numbers had grown. She wasn't alone in the street. More of her, of them. Blackish, but moving wrong. Hers, a hopped-up strut, but these, more like slithering. *Goddamn I'm drunk.*

He opened the door.

In the dark of his four walls, fumbling around like a blind idiot god. Maybe some music. The needle goes down on Mingus. Dissonance. Skip, skip, then bass, piano, cello. *Weird nightmare, you haunt my every dream, weird nightmare, tell me what's your scheme, could it be that you're a part of a lonely broken heart?*

He tumbled then, down, down into the darkness, where he dreamt about vines wrapping around limbs and about his mother and about things that

102

wriggled and squirmed and reached for him with tentacled gnashing mouths.

And we watched and we waited.

When he awoke, there was a man without eyes looking at him.

For just an instant he thought that he was hallucinating. Then he was scrambling for his holster, for the Colt that was in a pocket. Still drunk, he stumbled, snagged the barrel of the gun on his coat. But then he had it, locked and loaded, pointed at someone who was somehow pointing back at him.

"What the hell?"

Moonlight poured in through the open front door. The raggedy, sightless wretch held out his finger and thumb like a gun, laughing. He was bobbing from side to side as if he were playing a game of shoot 'em up, draped in some kind of robe that might have been clean when Roosevelt was president. The holes where his eyes should have been were two black pits in his face. It looked like they had been scooped out a long time ago.

The man was giggling like a sick child. "We still live across the water," he said.

Winfield was trying to steady himself, to will his heartbeat to slow down. He was trying to see clearly. "Alright, pal, I've got seven chunks of single-action, semi-automatic molten lead with your name on them. I'm about to introduce you."

"I don't care," the man giggled. He spread his hands like he were doing a magic trick. "For I have seen the great Ahtu, and none of you can make me fear anymore. He is Fear Itself and all other fear must dissolve in his presence."

"I don't know what you're talking about."

"He is the Skinless One, and the Horned Man. He is the Bloody Tongue. He is L'rog'g the glorious. I did not believe, so he came to me. He came to me in a form I did not want to see, but who am I that I would ask *him* to change? It is I who must change for *him*. So I tore out my eyes in order to see him more clearly."

"Dammit, man, *I'm going to shoot you.*"

The eyeless man lifted his gun-finger to his own temple. "You must cross the river," he said. "You must cross the river, and then you, too, will see. Cross the river and look for the fish-man." Then he shot himself in the head with his finger and turned, laughing all the way out the door, back into the night from which he came.

And we watched and we waited.

The old asylum was hidden away like a secret just past the edge of town. It was a place that Winfield knew well.

He told himself he was there to find out about any escaped lunatics that were missing a set of eyes, but he already figured on a dead end. Danvers just confirmed it for him. The doctor also noted that Winfield hadn't been around much lately. There was no one here that he counted as a friend, not like he did at the university, but they had known him since he was a young boy. Familiarity could go a long way toward friendliness.

"Have you gone to see him yet?" Danvers asked.

And then Winfield knew that's why he was

here.

He pulled up a chair in front of an old black man. The man had stopped talking years ago, when they cut away pieces of his brain. If he even knew his own name anymore, no one could say. As they sat face to face, the detective focused on the stream of saliva trailing from the man's mouth. He resisted the urge to reach out and wipe it away.

He didn't remember much, mostly just his mother's talk after the man was gone.

Images came tumbling back to him, words that made no sense. *The Devil's in New England, son, and the Devil's in you and me. But he doesn't look a bit like you think he does.* Winfield always figured it was hard for them, even in the North. Maybe hard enough to drive both of them out of their minds.

But he remembered the river and sitting in front of the man before he was shriveled and silent. Those hands were so much bigger around his own then, showing him how to hold the old cane pole. It was different, depending on what you were trying to catch. *Keep tension in the line for catfish and keep moving for bass. Wade into the water for trout and then move upstream.*

So they moved upstream, water rising to his chest, the man's arm around his shoulder. Stopping him from being swept away. *Drag it out over the surface, gentle now. It takes practice, but it's good to learn.*

You can get into some hard places. The secret is stealth.

He remembered slipping, ever so quietly, down a long hallway that only got longer.

And he remembered those words, from the night

they came to take him away. *Them things come in after you, that's how they do it. Monsters are real and they are right here.* Maybe that's what he had been looking for when he opened up his stomach with a kitchen knife. They got the bleeding stopped and got his guts back inside. But he never spoke another word of sense, and now he would never speak again.

The eyes that gaped back at him were vacant and silent, and he wondered what those eyes might have seen. He wondered what monsters were inside of him right now.

"Goodbye, Father," Winfield said.

Hunched over the Miskatonic, the Garrison Street Bridge looked like a monster even in the light of day. Despite Arkham's occasional bouts of prosperity, due mostly in recent years to the university, the portion that lurked across the river had long been regarded with unspoken terror by the local people. When the first great migration of black people occurred during the Civil War, the predominantly white populace of Arkham had naturally urged them to make this area their home. Most of them, however, would have taken slavery over the gray dread of a place that teemed with unearthly life after dark. There was something just not right about that side of the bridge.

While people of color squeezed instead into the reputedly haunted region just west of Hangman's Hill, the far side of Garrison became a place that few spoke of and fewer still dared to venture. Anyone passing through the murky part of Arkham did it quickly, during the early morning hours, and only on their way to Ipswich or Innsmouth at the northern edge of Massachusetts. The sun had begun to retreat from the late afternoon sky when Winfield finally reached the bridge. His Colt was fully loaded, holstered, and ready for action. The most accurate maps he could find were on the seat beside him, along with additional ammo and several nickel-plated carbide flashlights. He was stone cold sober now and felt like he would be for the rest of his life.

The bridge was narrow, with barely enough space for two automobiles to pass each other, and the dubious barriers on either side seemed to be no more than an afterthought. If anything hit those rails, it would tumble right into the darkly swirling waters below. No one would see you again until you were dumped into the Atlantic several miles away. As the old Plymouth began rumbling across the pockmarked surface of the bridge, he tried not to think about all of the cars that had mysteriously been swept over the side.

Though it was obscured by the dusk, Winfield knew about the small nameless island squatting in the middle of the river somewhere beyond the west side of the bridge. It had long ago been visible from River Street, before the textile plants had thankfully formed a wall between that portion of the Miskatonic and the good people of Arkham. It was said that the Devil once held court there beside a fading stone altar that was older than the local Indians. Winfield had little use for such superstitions, or for the religions they ultimately formed. But it was hard not to wonder if he was wrong, in the eldritch velvet of a night like this.

His first impression of the other side was one of an abyss. While even the deepest night in Arkham proper was dotted with streetlamps, business signs, or the small lights that many kept to ward off the darkness while they slept, here there was nothing but blackness. Without the headlights of his car, Winfield would not have known that a city existed here. Not so much as a candle flickered as the Plymouth crept onto Water Street. Its tires thumped and wobbled on a road that had not been repaved since it was first laid. The sleeping giants on either side had once been a continuation of the warehouse district, a very short-lived attempt at normalcy by the local industries, but now they appeared more like sentinels that even the rodents would fear to enter. But there seemed to be no rodents, nor animals, automobiles, or human life of any kind.

Still, he knew that he was being watched, though he could not have said by what.

He had scarcely anything to go on beyond his hopelessly outdated maps and the words of a blind lunatic urging him to look for a fish-man. This might have been the wrong day to quit drinking. In the deathly silence of the car, he reached up again to make sure the Colt was still in its holster.

An uncertain stretch of time had passed as he tediously explored the darkened streets. Winfield had just turned back onto Water Street at its easternmost edge, with the faint glow of French Hill attempting to reach across the river. As the car veered right at the crossroads, something drew back from the roving light. Something big. The wheels cried out as he wrenched the car to a halt. Throwing it into reverse, he raced as fast as possible toward

108

the area of the movement. The headlamps splashed against the side of another monolithic structure.

Peering up and up, he looked upon the shadow-cast figure of a gigantic man with the head of a fish. Beneath the aged carving that protruded from the side of the building was a simple door, accompanied by a painted and peeling sign declaring that this had long ago been *The Dagon Inn*.

He switched off the car and extinguished the headlights.

"I never wanted to live forever," he said, turning on one of the flashlights, checking the holster for his gun again. Then he started toward the waiting building, the jagged pavement beneath his feet like a walk down the hangman's scaffold.

He did not expect to be greeted at the door.

What opened the door as he approached seemed to be female, given the form beneath the dark floor-length robe. The facial features, however, were still in question. He had seen men who dressed as women, women who dressed as men, and even heard there were operations that could make you into whichever one you weren't. But that wasn't what stood looking at him now. Whatever it was seemed to smile, though in a way that didn't put Winfield one bit at ease. Not a word was given, but he understood, when it turned and proceeded within, that he was meant to follow.

The space he entered was dimly lit by torches on the wall. Goddamn *torches*, he thought. It seemed more like the antechamber for the *biggest damn mausoleum ever* than a lobby, and he wondered distantly what the hell this building had been before Dagon invited everyone inside. Though the figure ahead of him drifted mutely across the room, toward a much larger double-door, he could already hear strange sounds from beyond. They seemed to form a hellish kind of music.

The doors swept aside to reveal a grand ballroom full of elegantly dressed people.

There must have been at least a hundred people here, both black and white, and other races as well, none of them finding it necessary to segregate themselves. They were all mostly dancing together, two by two, as if this were the most high-class society function the world had ever seen. The rest had gathered into groups and clusters, talking, laughing, drinking. The strange alien music filled the air and fairly muffled all other sounds. Somewhere to the left, a band of distinctly normal-looking human beings played instruments that Winfield had never seen before. Despite the size of the crowd, no more than three people bothered to turn and look at the new arrival.

Winfield felt strangely underdressed for the occasion.

His eyes found the thing that had let him in, moving into the thickest part of the crowd. It disappeared, then reemerged when tuxedoed men and finely dressed women began to step aside. When they parted, they revealed a tall, darkly skinned man at the center of everything.

Dressed like a king in yellow silk, nearly shining with baldness, he was obviously the focal point of the room. One long arm held a buxom red-haired woman nearly overflowing her dress, while the other held a brawny, suited man with a long rope of hair trailing down his back. He seemed to be dancing with them both, but stopped to face the doorway where Winfield stood. The way his face twisted around couldn't exactly be called a smile.

He glanced side to side, snakelike, at each of his partners, then proceeded toward the door. Winfield watched him approach but could not consciously see the man's feet moving across the floor. Maybe it was the alcohol leaving his bloodstream. He felt like he needed to splash his face, or maybe lie down for a while. He felt like he was batting way out of his league.

"*August*," the man in yellow said. His voice was like a dried husk blowing across a wooden floor.

For just a moment, Winfield wondered if this was a man at all.

"I'm afraid you've got me at a disadvantage," he said. "I've come all this way, and I have no idea who you are."

The lips pulled back from the teeth, dark eyes glinting, the approximation of another smile. But something in those eyes, in the strange fishlike cologne that clawed at Winfield's senses, made his mind flicker and whirl into a thousand different directions. Images flashed of things he wanted to forget, other things that he didn't want to know.

"My name would be unpronounceable to you, August, and names are not important anyhow. However, I know that you need to call me something. So I will allow you to call me Lord Barlow."

He extended a hand, a studied gesture that could be found in books. The hand was as cold as frost

111

and seemed to wriggle in Winfield's own. He quickly pulled back, to find his only response in that unearthly smile, a rictus grin which froze in place for a few seconds too long.

"Do you like the sound of our music?"

Something wailed like some unidentifiable dying animal. There was a hypnotic, membranous vibration winding through it that was felt more than heard. Other strange sounds wove themselves in and out of this acoustic deluge, while beneath it all a deeply cutting kind of bass line hummed ever louder and louder. Together it all had the effect of a nauseating, growing frenzy.

"I guess I just prefer the classics," Winfield said.

Barlow smacked his hands together, a wet and violent sound that leapt above all others in the room, and unleashed a disarming laugh. "Classics," he exclaimed. "Well, now, you *are* delightful." He draped an arm around the detective, the long fingers coming to rest upon the mound of the Colt beneath his jacket. Winfield realized that the firearm would indeed do him no good here.

Other scents crept out from under the strange odor of Lord Barlow.

Scents like wisteria.

Then Winfield was thinking about his mother again. Wondering how she had managed to keep the house after his father was gone. She was absent for such long stretches that he assumed she had a job. But where would she have worked?

He was thinking about the voices he heard sometimes after dark. The voices, and the other sounds. Something rustling, moaning, like the wind through the trees on an autumn night.

And the night when a scream shattered the darkness, dragging him from the depths of a nightmare-fueled slumber. Heart thudding in his chest, he forced his feet onto the floor. Pushing himself into the darkness, down the hall, ever so silent. The hall that seemed to stretch out and out and...

As they moved deeper into the room, Barlow smiled and nodded at each fancily dressed participant. The gesture was very reptilian. Winfield could clearly imagine his host swallowing a live rat. Some of the crowd, too, had begun to look rather odd; like the thing that had led him into the building. They loped about at the furthest edges of the ballroom, some of them in suits or dresses, but most in shadow-painted robes. Their eyes, pressed into faces that simply didn't look right, watched most eagerly.

"I don't suppose I need to ask, but you are the Believers?"

"Oh, we believe," Barlow said, "but what about you? What do you believe in, *detective*?" The last word was mockingly spit out, as if there were nothing on earth that Winfield could detect, and it didn't matter if he did. Winfield chose not to answer.

In a cavernous alcove just past the musicians, there was a strange array of objects both large and small. This was where Barlow had been leading them. Winfield recognized that these things were all used to make music. Some of them looked vaguely familiar, like the Theremin, and a long snakelike cone that was obviously a kind of wind instrument.

Others looked like contraptions conceived during a hallucination.

"The snakelike item *is* indeed a bass wind instrument," Barlow said. "It's called the Serpent. The triangular body beside it is the contrabass balalaika, a kind of Russian folk guitar from the seventeenth century. Near the back is the American fotoplayer, a player piano which was used to provide sound for your silent movies – an irony in itself, don't you think?"

"I never cared for movies until the gangster pictures," Winfield said.

"Well," Barlow countered, finally removing his arm from Winfield's shoulder in order to gesture at a stilted table upon which rested a human skull. It was brightly painted in colors that Winfield could not entirely classify. "This horn makes the loveliest melody. There is no reason why it should, but the better sound comes from the skull of a virgin..."

He looked at Winfield knowingly.

"Perhaps it's just the awareness of everything missed that makes it so sweet."

The long fingers seemed to stretch even further as Barlow motioned toward a spiraling grayish object stretched out in display upon the furthest wall. "This is another wind instrument, made from the small intestine of a human being. There's another irony – that it's actually longer than the large intestine, reaching as much as twenty-five feet in length. When properly treated, it can be quite pliable, and the sound it makes is stunning. I don't think one could be more of a gangster than that, do you?"

Winfield wanted to run.

114

Barlow continued the musical education. "According to native populations, instruments made from the bodies of human beings possess a greater aptitude for reaching the gods. Savages, my friend, are much closer to supernatural knowledge than civilized men."

He realized that the man had not blinked, not once. Barlow looked like some of the people Winfield had seen on the African continent, possibly Egyptian, but Meursault's words came back to him: *Some of these immigrants are from much further away than you could possibly imagine.*

"We could do this all evening," Barlow said, lips moving out of sync with his voice. "Trying out the sounds of the water phone, the singing saw, or the Aztec death whistle. I have instruments here from nearly all places and times. There are so many delights I could share with you, but I understand that you are here on business."

"I'm not here to dance."

Another rasping roll of laughter. Then Barlow said, "This was once a dancehall, *not* a mausoleum. Long ago, it was frequented by an associate of mine, hence the faded name on the outside of the building. Can you imagine, dancing in a place such as this?"

The lights had begun to dim, almost imperceptibly at first.

"What you see here is but a glimpse of what some people have considered the good days. Except that *your* people are also represented here, whereas they were usually outside, moldering at the end of a rope, while those with a lighter skin tone danced. But you know all about that disparity, now don't you? Oh, I am sorry, I'm still learning how to be a proper host. Would you like to have a drink? We have enough alcohol for you to drown in, if that's what you wish."

Where you going so late, boy? Take your hat off when a white man talks to you.

Winfield knew that he should leave this place, and quickly. The man without eyes had just appeared, then disappeared, between the tuxedoes and dresses. Tenebrous, misshapen things were moving at the furthest edges of his sight, just beyond the well-dressed society crowd. It could have been a trick of his spiraling thoughts, but the shapes seemed to grow more numerous as the lights continued to fade.

"I'm looking for a woman..."

Barlow leaned in close, until his mouth was mere inches from Winfield's. His breath was rot, darkness, and insanity. His eyes appeared to writhe and squirm. "Of course you are," he said, "and you *will* know where to go to find her. But first, you must take part in one of our party games."

Like a joyous funeral procession, men and women in fancy dress filed noisily from the riverfront exit of the building. Winfield was carried along like just another lamb for the slaughter. He thought of waiting until he was outside, then making a play for his vehicle. Filling as many of them as possible with lead. Jumping inside the Plymouth and getting as far from here, as far from Arkham, even the North, as he could. But as soon as he emerged into the putrid fog coming off the Miskatonic, he knew that he wasn't going

116

anywhere.

The crowd emptied into the vacant lot beside the river, gathering around what appeared to be a small pool. Their voices climbed into the voluminous night to be consumed by the waiting stars. Hands still clung to wine glasses and cigarettes, as if this were all just another form of entertainment. But eyes darted among them and laughter slowly faded.

Where there had been only darkness before, a cold gray light now filtered down from the murky sky. It was almost conceivable that aberrant shapes were hunkered down just beyond the edges of sight. The blinking glint of dreary moonlight could easily have been taken for eyes, anxious and watchful. From only twenty feet away, the river could almost be heard to whisper and conspire.

Not until everyone filled the lot did Lord Barlow make his entrance. His robe flowed like a fantastic yellow membrane behind him, moving through the lowing drone of the crowd. The wind murmured a faint but unnatural march as he passed through the gathered masses. Some fanned themselves to be so near to him, while others looked ready to erupt with convulsive applause. Winfield had seen plenty of these kinds of images in newsreels.

Barlow rose upon the closest edge of the pool and lifted his arms into the air, an obscene prophet. "Humanity has learned how to place fire in the sky," he said, his voice gathering dark wings against the night. It seemed to fill up every one of the senses.

Winfield nudged his way through the milling horde of tuxedos and dresses.

"With the clouds you unleashed above the Asian continent, you believe that you have made yourselves secure. You believe that you have smothered something that filled you with fear. You believe that your deadly bloom has brought your wars to an end, but there are many more that have not yet begun."

His eyes dropped to Winfield. "They are already growing in the streets below the rooms in which you sleep."

Barlow's pulpit wasn't so much a pool as a large basin, and something was moving within it.

"It is a time of great political and social upheaval. People are going about with pale and worried faces, for they know that something savage roams among them."

Winfield glanced about the crowd and many of the pale faces glanced back at him.

"They know, in their true hearts, that everything is already lost. Humanity thinks in herds, and it shall go mad in herds. However, the modern world has done nothing more than close your eyes to the unseen wonder of chaos."

There was a furious thrashing in the pool beneath Barlow.

"Your future is anxiety, despair, and insanity, and there is but one way that you can go. You cannot run or hide, and you cannot reason with your own flawed nature."

Damn, but his words were starting to make sense. Winfield tried to distract himself. He gazed again at the faces around him, which had all grown sober. There were some among them that he recognized.

118

"You cannot force your own evolution, but it will come to you in the arms of anarchy. In order there is only fear of what you can lose, but chaos is to lose all of that fear. Stability brings only habit and repression, but chaos . . . breeds life."

There was a bartender from one of the River Street pubs. There was an old woman whom he had seen in the lobby of St. Mary's Hospital, and the newlywed couple he had watched holding hands in the Peabody Street Park. There was the minister of Christchurch, witnessing a sermon of an entirely different kind.

"You can choose to become the chaos, or you can wait and be devoured by it."

The surrounding crowd pressed in toward Barlow, carrying Winfield with them, their jackets and gowns becoming prison bars. The sky above bore down upon them all.

Barlow's voice had grown more silent, more intimate as his audience closed in. He was nearly whispering now, imparting some great and terrible secret. "There are sleeping gods," he said. "Ancient ones who are dreaming of you right now. The shadow of them is sweeping in on cosmic winds that can extinguish a flame or raise it higher than any fire you have created."

He knelt down upon the edge of the basin.

"Sharing stories is as old as fire," he said. "Through stories, dreams, visions, and ancient rites, societies have discovered who they are, where they came from, and where they are going. Let me share the story of your race's fate."

Barlow reached into the pool with both hands, lifting them above the throng to reveal a pair of

119

tentacled, squirming nightmares. A hushed gasp passed through the nicely dressed folks of Arkham. The creatures were not large, but seemed to take up more space than they should with their bulbous heads and their eight flailing limbs. The beady black eyes that stuck out of their heads appeared to consider the crowd that had gathered for them. Possibly sensing what was about to happen, they began to writhe frantically in Barlow's hands.

Winfield had seen an octopus before, and it was obvious that these were babies. He was nonetheless wracked by a wave of revulsion as he looked upon them. Images from other places and times began to seep into his brain, which he fought against as stubbornly as the little monsters fought against Barlow's grasp.

The man and woman who had been in Barlow's arms pushed through the crowd, dressed now in shabby earth-colored robes, approaching him from both sides of the pool. They knelt before him, raising their hands up as if in supplication. He reached down with his offering. The man opened his mouth wide, extending the long pink meat of his tongue. On the other side, the crimson-haired woman did the same, her eyes delicately closed to receive her slippery host.

Barlow pressed the creatures into their mouths.

The crowd watched, silently, as they closed their lips around the squirming octopi. Each of them began to whine as if in the throes of ecstasy. The man was obviously aroused, clenching at his groin with both hands. Something wet had splashed across the woman's heaving breasts. She grasped at them in a delicious frenzy, tearing them free of the

120

flimsy robe. The gathered masses began to murmur, shifting and rustling edgily.

The sensual moans felt strangely at home in the near darkness. Even as the man and woman would occasionally gasp for a breath, struggling with the throbbing sea-creatures in their mouths, their grunting sounds formed a fitting music to the night. Then, finally, the woman released a long sigh, stretching her mouth wide to show that the octopus was gone. She had swallowed it whole.

The man struggled for a moment more, a few desperate tentacles slipping from between his lips. But then there was a faint crunch and he swallowed hard. He turned to the crowd with an open and empty mouth.

Barlow rose above them both, lifting another wriggling octopus into the air.

The Christchurch minister was the first to come forward. Winfield thought that the man might try to speak out, to rail against whatever abomination was taking place, invoking the words of his own religion. But he dropped to his knees between the man and the woman, raising his hands toward a new god. Strangely, he crossed himself before opening his mouth wide. Barlow's face twisted around in an unearthly grin and stuffed the octopus in the minister's mouth.

Then they all began to come forward, crowding around the circumference of the pool. Barlow towered above everyone, reaching into the water below, offering his cephalopodic communion. Winfield bowed his head, eyes closed. Trying not to see. The darkness behind his eyelids only offered worse images, accompanied by the sounds of slurping, gagging, and gasping for air. The vile symphony went on and on for what felt like an eternity. Breathing deeply, trying to shut it all out, he could feel them all moving around him. Receiving the creatures into their mouths and then staggering away from the pool.

Some were retching, unable to get the animals down. Others had begun to choke and tumble to the ground with paling faces. The old woman from St. Mary's reached down to retrieve her octopus from where it had fallen into a puddle.

The newlywed couple fed each other like they were eating wedding cake. Their eyes reflected both horror and amazement. Then they began to make love, right there on the asphalt, with the moon and countless eyes watching them.

Winfield began to move slowly forward.

The basin was engraved with symbols he had never seen before. He tried to focus on them, rather than the writhing multitude within. One glimpse revealed chaos itself, countless tentacles slipping over and under each other, flailing, reaching out, as if there were salvation to be found anywhere.

Barlow was across the pool. His mouth did not move, but his voice was in Winfield's head. *There is no other way, detective.*

Winfield reached into the throbbing pool of alien life. The tiny creatures squirmed around his fingers. Clenching tightly, he found purchase, and lifted one into the air. The thing wasn't much bigger than his hand. Tentacles snaked into the air, wrapping around his fingers, trailing down his wrist. It looked like something from a science fiction invasion movie.

He raised it to his mouth. *Do it quick, like that first shot of gin.*

Barlow was beside him now. "The octopus' reaction to pain is the same as any vertebrate," he said, barely a whisper. "They *do* feel pain, August. They remember it, like the child of someone who has known slavery can feel it in their soul. You will feel this animal's pain within yourself."

He closed his eyes, but the monster was still there.

That dry, rasping voice said, "The octopus decorates its lair, and is known to play with its brothers and sisters. It's been said that they can change into other creatures."

He felt tentacles against his lips, cold and yet still very alive.

"Do you feel that predatory instinct burn within you? The desire that all of you have to destroy anything that is weaker than you? The primitive urge you feel to take life away from another living creature?"

He opened his mouth.

"The lust to become powerful and to know everything."

He thrust it toward the back of his throat.

"Now you shall begin to know, and soon you will begin to see."

In his mouth, the octopus fought bravely to escape. Slimy tentacles grasped and held to his teeth, tongue, struggling against the back of his throat. He felt the air closing off, blocked; panic rising. It was like he was trying to consume some flailing, renegade portion of himself. Then he bit down with desperate ferocity. Something snapped

123

and flowed.

And he engulfed it.

The wriggling slowed, but did not cease. It was still moving as he forced it down his throat. Slowing, slowing, and then stopping, somewhere deep inside of him.

The world swam away from him, tumbling down to the slime-splashed pavement. The Miskatonic roared somewhere beyond. Even as the light began to fade, he had already begun to know things that he had not known before.

And they terrified him.

And still we watched and still we waited.

He was drowning in darkness, and the darkness smelled of wisteria. Strange unearthly things were there with him. Many-limbed things that howled with ungodly voices, entangling themselves around his arms and legs, seeking furtive entry into his every orifice. Things devoid of limbs or faces, but possessing immense yawning maws lined with hell. Things that were as familiar as his own mirror image, but then turned to reveal more and more faces and limbs and mouths that croaked ancient words he could not understand.

Yet beneath it all came distant, delicate sounds that he had not known since he was a child. The soothing song of the birds that he listened to for hours outside the old house on Boundary Street. The whispering flow of the Miskatonic before it curved into Arkham, where he once went fishing with his father. The plaintive timbre of everyday voices he had not heard in years, but could never forget.

124

The hellish and the heavenly wrapped themselves together, weaving images, sounds, and tastes within each other, inextricably, as if both realities existed at the same time.

Rising up from the center of everything came an insistent voice that called *detective, detective, detective*.

With eyes finally open, he found Theda Lang wrapped in his arms.

He bolted awake. Pulling away, he tried to push himself up, slamming into the wall behind his desk. Light slipped through the blinds, making strange polyhedrons on the carpet between them. She rolled away from where they had lain together on his office floor. Rather than get up, as he would have expected, she propped herself up against the wall across from him.

"Thought you were taking a dirt nap in the car last night," she said. "I managed to get you inside, though I must say, detective, you could stand to lay off the pastries."

His mouth tasted of milk and rot, and a great yawning abyss drew him steadily near. He reached out to touch the floor, the books on the wall behind him, his desk, anything solid and familiar. Everything was reeling, strangely cast in yellow and blue. He wanted to vomit, to get that damn thing out of his stomach. He wanted a drink, but couldn't remember where he kept the gin. He wanted to scream, or to rip himself apart.

Theda considered him silently. She looked younger than she had in the dark. She also looked tired, as if she had been watching him all night.

"You talk in your sleep," she finally said.

125

"Hope I didn't offend you."

"Maybe if you would've made any sense."

Though the chilly edge in her voice had not diminished, she looked softer than she had before. He figured that probably happened when you spent the night with someone. The scent of her clung to him, mashed into his skin and clothing, fighting for supremacy against everything else he had encountered the night before.

He looked at her with an unvoiced question.

"Your virtue is still intact," she said, "in case you were wondering. Unless you lost it before you crash landed outside the office last night."

Images were flooding in, things he did not understand. Thoughts he did not recognize circled through his head, memories that did not seem to be his own. He tried to force something familiar into his mind: his address, the numbers on his license plate. But they would not come, swimming somewhere just beyond his reach.

His mother was in his head, and his father too. There were horrific things with them. He saw how death would come to almost everyone in Arkham. Except for Theda, or himself.

And there was more.

Much more.

"I've got to see Jupiter," he muttered. He knew how Biddy had died now, and it wasn't those white boys and it wasn't dogs. It was much worse. It was beyond what he could even comprehend. Then he said, just as much to himself, "No, no, I can't tell them about that."

He looked at Theda.

Theda looked back. "Look, ace, I made a bad

call hiring you. I've been thinking about it, and..."

"You can't have your money back," he said, and then offered up a lie. "It's all been spent. You know, expenses."

She chuckled softly, hopelessly. "You must've put a lot of gas in your tank, detective, or stashed a lot of gin under your desk. In any case, I don't care about the money."

"I know where she is," he said.

"Who?"

"Your *mother*, you fool. At least I think that's what they're telling me."

Her face showed nothing, but there were a hundred untold stories in her eyes. Winfield was glad that he still didn't know even one of them. He reached out toward her, waited, and then she reached back. They almost looked like lovers.

"Get whatever you need together. We've got a lot of driving to do."

We were there with them, and we watched and we waited.

Winfield almost believed the spell would be broken when they passed the Arkham city limits. He went to the drug store for more ammo, though he figured it would be useless. The trunk was full of flashlights, guns, axes, and numerous sources of fire; anything that might be used as a weapon. He sent a letter to Meursault, trying to put everything he knew into words that made sense. He stopped by the clapboard shack that Jupiter Lucius called home and made a donation – specifically, the cash that Theda had given him. "The only condition," he

127

said, "is that you take this money and get the hell out of Arkham. I hear Chicago is nice." He didn't tell them what he knew about Biddy.

Theda was beside him as the Plymouth approached the outskirts of town. If everything that was in his head suddenly vanished, they might have other options. They could just keep driving, refilling the gas tank until the money ran out, then make some kind of home together wherever they finally stopped. Pipe dreams, he knew, but he had begun to like the thought. He looked over at her, staring vacantly from her window, as the sign approached in the late afternoon sun. It announced that they were now leaving Arkham. Someone had scrawled beneath those words, *God rest your soul*.

But Winfield's soul was not at rest.

The foreign thoughts were still in his head. Without knowing how they were there, he was contemplating Riemannian equations and fourth-dimensional passageways. Languages he did not understand stalked through his brain, leaving undecipherable messages in words like *hokan*, *Shugoran*, *Lu-kthu*, *Y'golonac*, *Yog-Sothoth*, and *Azathoth*. There were terrifying visions of strange, faraway places that left him feeling colder than any winter he had ever known.

And something inside was pulling him onward to some yet unknown destination.

The radio crackled and hissed, grasping for signals. Winfield moved the dial, finding Bessie Smith's voice reaching out from the past. *The Devil's gonna get you, oh the Devil's gonna get you, man the Devil's gonna get you, sure as you're born to die*. The trees on either side began to get

128

taller, moving in like an army closing ranks.

Every song became another warning. *Can't tell my future and I can't tell my past, Lord it seems like every minute sure gonna be my last.* And, *This time another year, I may be gone, to some lonesome graveyard, oh Lord, how long?*

He decided that sometimes silence is better, clicking off the radio.

The car hurtled toward Aylesbury, and then past it, somewhere in the direction of Freetown and Fall River. They were over two hundred miles southwest of Arkham. The Miskatonic began somewhere in these hills, running through town like a serpent until it reached the sea. The town itself had begun as a trading post in the seventeenth century, built with supplies from the surrounding forests. If there was some strange malignant force responsible for everything in Arkham, as many hushed whispers claimed, then they were headed directly into its wooded heart.

Winfield considered saying these things aloud, but then thought better of it.

He contemplated the books he had read about the Freetown area, books that rested peacefully on the shelves in his office right now. The forest here had a history rife with conflict between settlers and the native people. During the war of King Phillip, the Pocasset had fought on the side of the English in hopes of removing all of the tainted invaders from their land. Later, greedy Indian chiefs sold much of that land to even greedier white people, who would ultimately give the original inhabitants a two hundred acre reservation. Winfield always felt like

129

the constant trading of the land wasn't for the love of acquisition, but because anyone who lived here soon realized the place was just no damn good.

His insides writhed around in fear and anticipation.

The trees had begun to block out the dying evening sun. All around them the forest felt very much alive, but sleeping. It was like something was waiting patiently for their arrival. Winfield figured that was exactly how it was going down, but he still had no idea what to expect. Nor did he have any idea what to do about it.

From a distance, through his open window, there came the wavering, lonely tremolo of a loon. Then, nothing. Just a darkening gloom, mile after mile.

His own voice broke the stillness. "This is what it must be like in the womb," he said.

They could not see each other in the darkness. Only the occasional breath parted the silence. It was as if each of them were alone in the barren depths of the woods.

Without a word, she reached over for his hand. He did not draw back.

After a few miles, she pulled it closer.

He felt the smoothness of her leg beneath his fingers. Still he did not draw back.

Her hand slowly led his across the softness of her thigh. His breath was so shallow that he barely breathed at all. But he did not draw back.

She led him higher, past layers of silk, toward where he knew it would be even softer. She drew him up and up, through a flimsy blockade of cloth, until she pressed his hand firmly into the center of her. The hot and verdant center of her.

What he felt there horrified him.

"My mother carved me up pretty bad," she said.

He wanted to pull his hand away, but she held fast.

"Don't cry, detective, I don't remember any of it. I was still a baby."

Her grip tightened. His fingers were pressed into jagged folds and hollows that had all begun to fill up with moisture. Some of what he felt, he knew, was exactly as it should be. Some of it was not.

"When I was older and understood what she had done, she told me that she was saving me from them."

The inside of her had begun to feel like a strange cave with numerous tunnels and alcoves. With Theda's hand still on his, he started to gently investigate her, moving his fingers around like little explorers. Her own breath had gotten ragged now.

"She said that at least one of her children wouldn't have to endure the monstrosities that she had endured. That's what she called them...*monstrosities*. I was such a fool that I never even knew she'd had other children."

She pressed his hand into her so hard that he wondered if he could reach into her very guts. His wrist ached with her grip. He struggled to keep his eyes on the road ahead. Things he was glad not to see moved and swelled against his wriggling fingers. It felt as though velvet waves had begun to wash over his hand.

"But by then, since I was old enough to ask, I was old enough for her to dust."

She was nearly panting now, and so was he.

131

"Detective, if you stop the car, we can finish this."

He stopped.

But even as she began to reach for him, he turned to cradle the steering wheel. His head was down and his eyes closed. He could smell her on his hand, and even this held the scent of wisteria. She was warm and eager, urgent against him. Something inside of him squirmed in rising panic.

And now he drew back.

"Maybe later," he said. "After all of this is done."

"It will be too late then."

He pictured a house, any house, somewhere further up the road. They were together in the house, and none of whatever was going to happen had ever happened. They weren't the same people they were going to be.

The world wasn't the same as it was now.

"My mother's people went all the way back to the colonial period," he said. "Massachusetts Bay Colony, 1631."

"Well, congratulations, ace."

"When she was a little girl, her family moved down south. That's where she met my father. She never told me much about their life down there, but we all know how they feel about black and white mixing." Theda settled back into her seat without expression. "I always figured that was how they ended up back here. She wanted to find her roots, and he preferred to not get lynched."

The engine hummed beneath them, unmoving.

"But that wasn't what he was trying to get away from."

The headlights stared into the darkness of the road ahead.

"The only problem was he jumped from the frying pan into the fire. I mean, for them to end up in *Arkham*..."

He was opening doors now.

...moving down the hallway, ever so quiet. It only seemed to stretch further, to get darker, with each heavy step he took. The terrible scream was still echoing in his head, his body soaked in fear. His heart was a rabbit trapped in his chest.

And those sounds, those terrible wet sounds.

Reaching up toward the doorknob of his parent's room, his hand so small.

The door, opening like a veil, and the sound is so much worse now, so much worse, and he sees the thing on top of his mother. He doesn't know what it is, only knows that it has long arms like snakes and they are moving, the whole thing is moving, fast, so fast on his mother, and she has no clothes and her legs are open and she's crying and she's looking at him and this thing this monster is between her legs she's crying looking at him and his father where is his father he has to stop the monster but his father his father is there too, he's in the corner and his back is turned and even with his back turned he looks sad, but he's not doing anything to stop the monster monster inside his mother his mother his

He chuckled, but the sound wasn't right.

"I know things," he said. "I don't know how, and I don't even understand most of them. What I'm getting is strictly from nightmares. One of the things I know is that they want me pure, at least as pure as someone like me can be."

133

"I didn't take you for a Bible-thumper."

He shook his head, mournfully. "I'm not. This couldn't be further from the Bible. But somehow it makes everything easier."

"It makes what easier?"

"I don't know."

With a heavy sigh, her hand slipped inside one of those deep pockets for the gun that he knew was there. For just a moment he hoped she was going to use it on him. Theda placed her derringer on the dashboard of the Plymouth. She slowly lit two Virginia Slims, exhaled, and held one out toward him. He took it from her, already regretting that he hadn't taken more.

"Well, let's get this over with," she said.

And we were watching and we were waiting.

When the trees no longer moved, and there were no more animals, Winfield knew they had almost found the place. The road had become craggy and the woods leaned in close. Silence hung in the car like the smoke from Theda's cigarettes, neither of them willing to comment on the strange shapes just beyond the reach of the old Plymouth's headlights. Winfield had begun to know too well what might have been lurking just beyond his sight. He understood why human beings had not become a nocturnal race, preferring to spend most of their waking hours in the light. It was a defense mechanism based in denial and the childhood maxim, *If I can't see something, then it can't see me*. Because things really were different in the dark.

The car slowly rumbled to a stop. He switched it

off, then climbed out to gaze into the deepening forest. The wind moaned like lost souls overhead, through the stiff, silent ranks of trees too old and stubborn to be moved by it. He turned to look at Theda Lang through the frost-encrusted windshield.

"We have to walk from here," he said.

They gathered together the flashlights, matches, and ammo. Winfield checked the Colt in its holster and grabbed the axe, slamming the trunk with a thud that sounded too final. Something didn't feel right at all. He walked slowly to the forest's edge, turning to face her with his hand extended. The flashlight made her features devilish.

She took his hand. "I hope you really are a bloodhound."

Winfield hoped that he wasn't.

They waded into the murky depths of the forest, pressing through the unforgiving New England foliage. The earth crunched and snapped beneath their feet. They breathed in the ancient woody scent of the trees, the earth, and something else. The beams of their lights bounced off the ever-widening trunks of maple, oak, and hemlock trees, casting misshapen figures all around them.

Sometimes they stopped, having heard something rustling nearby. Theda reached out for Winfield's arm – the one that held the axe. Neither of them breathed. But whatever was there mimicked their silence. They pushed on, with nothing but Winfield's newfound instinct to guide them, until the next sound made them stop, then the next.

Winfield knew they were in a two hundred square-mile area near the edge of Freetown and Rehoboth that was drenched in the unexplainable. If half the stories were true, here there had been floating orbs of light, large apelike creatures, ritual sacrifices, and strange crafts that coasted amongst the trees. There was documentation of cattle being strewn in bloody pieces just beyond the edge of the road. Lesser known were the endless reports of people who had merely disappeared somewhere in these woods. The assumption of local law enforcement was that most of them had gotten lost, or come here to commit suicide.

But Winfield knew there were other reasons too.

Some unseen river was making sibilant whispers to the moon, hidden high above in the trees. The hemlocks seemed to have pulled closer together. *They're listening to our thoughts.* He wanted to laugh at this, but was afraid that laughter, here in this desolate black place, led the way toward madness. The barriers between the known world and whatever lay beyond, he knew, were much thinner and more frail than he had ever believed.

They had to stop several times for him to cut away at some entangled brush. He reached out for Theda, silent behind him, and indicated the axe. Both of them had decided that their voices sounded unnatural here, relying instead on touch and hand signals. Even these, within the flashlights' pale moons, threw nightmare shapes against the surrounding trees. So they stopped and he started swinging. The thudding axe was like slow, primitive drumming that bounced corrupted and alien sounds back from all directions.

Somewhere beyond them came the faint accompaniment of a flute.

He held the axe in mid-swing, listening intently,

but the music did not come again.

They passed a yawning gulf darker than the surrounding blackness. It was *felt* more than seen, a sudden urgent and unshakable sense of foreboding. Her hand reached for his at that very moment. He turned the bright circle of his light through a copse of trees; it seemed to reach into the chasm of space itself. He had read about this place, an ancient ledge above a nearly eighty-foot drop into the rock quarry below. If the flashlight could have reached the bottom, they would have seen a crater full of abandoned cars and suicides.

And fools who had taken a wrong step in the dark.

He almost broke the silence to tell her this.

Eventually a kind of crude path presented itself, then widened out, as if the trees had begun to relax in the certainty that they would end up where they should. Winfield, too, knew it was the way they were supposed to go.

...There is but one way that you can go. You cannot run or hide, and you cannot reason with your own flawed nature.

He also knew that avoiding this place would only have altered the sequence of events, not stopped them.

Something very large moved quickly through the shadows.

Theda pressed up against him. He felt her breath, warm against his lips, but he could not see her face in the darkness. There seemed to be a gaping emptiness where her head should have been. The flashlight beams crossed and made a strange pattern against the forest floor. It looked like a gateway to the underworld.

They stood together, almost swaying, long after the sound had passed. Finally, he nudged her flashlight with his own, guiding it just a little further up the path. There was a mass of fallen timber and tangled brush, carpeted with old dry moss. It shone like bones in the beam of their entwined light.

"Deadfall," he whispered.

Though only about twelve feet in height, he knew they had to be careful climbing it. He would hate to get this far only to die from falling on some kind of crude spear.

But climb it they did, branch by cracking branch. Each time a limb snapped under his feet it felt like breaking someone's arm. With the flashlight in his pocket, he climbed blindly, but was aware that Theda was already above him. After a few minutes, she reached down for the axe, then helped him to the top of the pile. He retrieved the blade, then turned to see what her eyes had fixed upon on the other side.

The moonlight fell into a clearing, splashing it with more light than they had seen in hours. There was a grove of warped and twisted trees at the furthest edge of the field that was occupied by monstrous, unearthly shapes. He already knew many of their names. A large abandoned church stood crookedly in the middle of everything, ghostly and gray in the luminescent night. He knew that it had not been used for holy purposes in a very long time.

Standing in front of the church were two figures, looking back at them. They were Lord Barlow and Winfield's mother.

138

Theda grabbed the front of Winfield's jacket and pulled him toward her. Their eyes locked; he began to understand. She dragged his face toward her own and kissed him. Her mouth burned like a fever, but was as soft as heaven. The kiss was more gentle than he would have imagined she was capable of.

Then she was climbing down the other side of the deadfall, going to meet her fate.

And we were watching.

And we were waiting.

Winfield made it to the bottom of the deadfall. He didn't need the flashlight anymore, for the moon showed more than he had ever wanted to see. The vast leaping shadows of even larger terrors loomed beyond the misshapen grove of hemlock trees. His insides churned, the world around him twisting, turning.

Theda had already crossed the field toward the old church, like she had nothing left to fear. She now stood only a few feet away from Lord Barlow, draped in flowing black that made him look like part of the night, and from Winfield's mother. The sound of their voices carried on swirling gusts of wind, stripping away only the words. He didn't want to hear the words anyway, because then everything would be real. He wanted to run, but knew that he would be devoured by unearthly teeth before he could even clear the deadfall.

There would be no more running.

Barlow turned his back to the women and proceeded toward the shimmering mouth of the church. As he vanished into its abyss, Theda and

Winfield's mother turned to follow. So, with the useless axe in his hand and a pointlessly loaded firearm strapped to his chest, Winfield lifted his chin and began a measured, purposeful walk toward whatever waited for him.

The wind bayed sadly through the nightmare-haunted field.

"I hope you weren't going to start without me," he said as he entered the church, but he already figured that he was the guest of honor.

The dilapidated building flickered and hummed with candles and torches, making it seem even more ancient than it was. What had originally been built for the Christian god had been used as a place to worship the Devil for much longer. But now, somehow, even that blasphemy had been outdone. Crosses that had once been inverted by devil worshippers were now tilted at even more senseless angles. The skulls of various animals, known and unknown, hung from the edges of the crosses and adorned the walls. Like Barlow and his congregation, it was something entirely different.

Barlow stood before the broken shards of stained glass where the altar once had been, the women coming to stand beside him.

All the things from Winfield's nightmares were real, and they were here. Swollen inhuman bodies and scaled membranous ogres that could not have been from this planet lurked at the furthest edges of the church. Chimeras, glistening beasts with palpitating gills, and chittering insectoid creatures filled the seats like the vilest Sunday service. The randomness of their conception, and that such a variety of monsters should appear together in one

140

place, threatened to tear away his mind. Among them were things that had been meant to pass as human but had failed miserably. They filled the pews, making a mockery of humanity.

He knew that this was Barlow's idea of fun, almost expecting him to address them all as "dearly beloved." Winfield approached the altar slowly, like a bridegroom.

Barlow grinned his terrible, unnatural grin.

Winfield's mother almost managed a smile as well, but something had died in her long ago. She looked even older than she should have, black hair going white, but her eyes were still as dark as the void. Winfield figured that happened when you'd spent years staring into the face of hell. Even more so when you'd become a breeder cow for all of its demons. With the wind moaning through the broken windows of the church, carrying the croaking, baying voices of a hundred different abominations, he knew that none of these demons were of the earthly type. He also knew that most of them had been here for a very long time.

His mother was looking at him intently, he would almost have said proudly.

"Most of my children didn't make it," she said. "But I always knew that you were special. I knew that one of you would not be a monster."

He could see them like she did then. The slithering progeny, babies born with pink crustaceous bodies and bulging eyes that never closed. Things that would never have passed for human. He could see her now, concealing pregnancies and smashing tiny skulls. He could see the faces of all the men she had been with, and even worse than that.

"You're ready to join us now," she said.

But there was something else in her fire-flickered eyes.

He understood that she had wanted to get out of all of this. That was why she had gone to Meursault, hoping to reset the clock. But there would be no such option.

"No, I'm going to die instead," he said.

Barlow chuckled, a rattling hellish sound, but still said nothing. He didn't have to. Winfield knew that he had been the architect of this meeting all along. He also knew that death was not necessarily what this thing wanted to accomplish, for he could have done that at any time.

His mother was shaking her head. "No, son. It's already begun. You're not going to die. Everything I've done has been to make you safe. That was the deal that I made with them, from the beginning. There would be one who was protected, one who would have the good life your father and I always wanted. It made him so happy to know it was the one that looked like him."

"I doubt it," Winfield said.

He was holding his stomach like he might be sick.

Them things come in after you, that's how they do it. And he was there in the room while they did it, while these things were crawling over her, inside of her. His back was turned, his head down, but he was there. Because he had to be. Because the monstrous seed wouldn't work on its own. It had to be mixed with that of a human being.

As it was when Winfield's mother conceived

142

him.

There was a subtle click, the sound of a bullet being loaded into a chamber.

"So what about the one that looked like *you*, mother?"

It was Theda. There were tears in her eyes, her mouth twisted in a mask of anguish, and her arm was stretched out to hold the derringer in the other woman's face. The hand that held the gun was trembling. Winfield gaped at her, trying to understand.

But, really, he already knew.

She looked back at him, eyes glistening. She wiped the free sleeve of the fur coat across her face. "I'm sorry, ace," she said. "I tried to save you from this, I really did. If you would've just taken me up on my offer."

Barlow was nearly cackling now.

Winfield's mother, and Theda's, was enraged. "You *gave* yourself to him? When it could have ruined *everything*? I tried to *save* you, by making sure that you could never have a child, so they would consider you *useless*. I made sure you were taken care of. *And this is how you thank me?*"

It all happened very fast, but Winfield saw it in slow motion.

There was the look on Theda's face, mournful sadness sparking into rage. He knew that she was going to pull the trigger. There was no discussion to be had; this was why she was here. Remington, forty-one caliber, two-shot. Not a very fast gun, but still lethal at close range. The barrel was inches from his mother's face. His mother, her mother, his, hers -

Theda cried, "*Thank you, bitch.*"

The gun barked.

He shouted her name and swung the axe.

It wasn't meant to be a kill shot. But the blade sank into Theda's skull like a rotting vegetable. Parting bone as easily as hair. The dull thud that echoed across the field could have been the sound of someone chopping wood. Her body shuddered, then slumped. Blood and brains spurted across her face, trailing into her eyes.

The eyes that, in one moment, still had life, then in the next, did not.

She gave a few grotesque shivers and began to drop.

The bullet tore into his mother's left eye. Her cheekbone and brow were scorched with gunfire. There was a bright red hole where her iris had been, and fluids were pouring forth. She turned to look at her son, red and gray spilling onto her chest. Her mouth opened to speak, but something in her brain had been disconnected.

She stumbled, like she was looking for a chair to sit in. But there was no chair.

She, too, began to drop.

Both women hit the ground at the same time.

Through it all, Barlow had never stopped laughing.

Winfield dropped to the floor between his mother and his sister. On his hands and knees, his head spun from one to the other, mother, sister, mother, sister. His breath was coming hard, his insides burning. He closed his eyes, then opened them again to contemplate the ground beneath him.

144

Leaves and mud covered layers of rotted wood and cold, wet soil. Their blood and brains would already be meeting the earth, seeping into the dirt.

He reached out toward the slumped form of Theda Lang, fingertips barely touching the exposed white softness of her thigh. He pulled his hand back. The unholy congregation made not a sound. The night, spinning around him, was silent and still except for the moaning wind and the cruel laughter, rising in pitch and speed behind him.

He spun from the ground. Pulling the Colt from its holster, he fired several rounds in the direction of that foul voice. Barlow took each one of the bullets. Hand, arm, chest, and face. Took them and barely wavered, though something dark was oozing from every hole. Something that was not red.

But he had stopped laughing.

He slapped his hands together. "Well, that was fun," he said, though his voice didn't sound so human anymore. "I just love family reunions. However, now that we've gotten all of that out of the way, it's time that we got down to business."

Then Barlow began to change.

At the great Miskatonic library, Winfield had read ancient lore in which men lost all reason merely by looking upon some beast that should not have existed. He never believed in any of it. The things they claimed to have seen were the result of derangement, drink, or some bizarre mutation. Regardless of how these men came to see such horrors, no matter how repulsive, how foreign to the human conception of a living creature, he knew there was nothing he could see that would drive him mad.

But the thing that oozed and morphed and slithered before his eyes made him question everything that he ever knew.

It was both anthropoid and insectile, and then it was vaguely canine. Without even blinking he watched it become bipedal and forward-slumping. There were brutal red gills from which a mass of feelers sprouted, thickening, then flowing out into throbbing tentacles. Embryonic wings erupted from its back and then caved in upon themselves, forming gruesome gelatinous mouths. Barbed and scaly tongues thrust from the open maws, which snapped shut and disappeared, while the tongues stretched into fleshy cables that wrapped tightly around the erupting flesh of the thing's body.

Even on the ground, Winfield was reeling.

The unearthly display continued, one terrible organism giving way to the next, until he squeezed his eyes shut. Trying not to lose consciousness. Not here, where this thing could do whatever it wanted to him.

But the sodden sounds of transformation were no better, pulsing and splashing in the darkness of his mind. There were voices inside him now, with rasping drenched accents, making sounds that were almost familiar. There were words he had never heard, but knew the meaning of, invoking images of desolate temples in places far away. There were movements inside of him that squirmed and gnawed with dark unholy recollection.

The ground beneath him rumbled with the approach of every bloated, bulging thing in the god-forsaken forest. They were all coming, from the trees and the lakes and the deepest holes that led into the center of the earth. These hellish things that were his new family. The shapes and shadows of them surrounded the church, filling up the broken windows and the doorways.

He thought about sending the last bullet in the Colt straight into his brain. It would only take a few seconds to die. But then he considered what they might do to him in that one eternal moment before he was gone.

Barlow, or whatever his real name was, spoke to him again. But what he had become had no proper vocal cords to make human sound. The words nonetheless entered Winfield's mind without permission or resistance. *We can really be ourselves out here, August. Your brothers and sisters, me . . . and you.*

Winfield felt movement around him, heard slithery rustling against the earthly grave of fallen leaves that covered the church floor. Then the stench of the earth, rotting wood, and the sky. The damned thing was right in front of him. *Open your eyes and look at me, my son.*

"Oh, you son-of-a-bitch."

The thing now had the form of a massive, partially humanoid creature. From beneath it coiled numerous thick tentacles, black and glistening with mucous. The rudimentary skull was marked by eyes like pustules and a gaping mouth full of jagged bones. And it bore the arms and chest of a man, from which the twisted face of Winfield's father peered out.

When the voice entered Winfield's brain again, the misshapen mouth of his father opened and closed in a cruel mockery of speech. *You might have guessed that I'm not from around here.* It crackled with laughter, which the father-face crudely pantomimed. *Some of your societies have given me more earthbound names. They have called me pharaoh, prophet, and trickster – they have even called me the Devil. But I have never found him or any of your other gods.*

Something was moving inside of Winfield.

I have come from the empty spaces between the dying stars.

He could see an overwhelming vastness inhabited by nothing, and then the slumbering something that existed beyond. It festered with the dark, curdled emptiness of eternity. There were shadows, beyond our understanding, lurking in the ruins of burnt-out civilizations; hooded inhuman forms peering beyond the ash of the many dimming suns.

I have come seeking a new home for my countless races.

He could see the rotting dreams of chaos in the mind of a blind idiot god.

The nightmare gallery of monsters had settled into a malformed circle around them. He couldn't look at them for very long, but he'd seen enough to know they made an impossible barrier of teeth, wings, and scales. What passed for their eyes were wide and fixed upon him. Their mouths hung open in hungry grins.

He looked down at the still form of Theda Lang, an axe buried in the pulpy mass of her skull. He followed the blood-spattered sleeve of her fur coat to where it turned into a gun. The derringer continued to point at their mother, even in death.

148

Their mother's eyes were still open, and he wondered if she could see how everything had ended.

"You're going to destroy all of us."

The laughter in his head was writhing with worms. *You still don't understand.*

Another voice was thrust into Winfield's mind. *Where you going so late, boy? Take your hat off when a white man talks to you.*

"Why are you doing this? If you're going to kill me, why don't you just get it over with?" He wasn't sure if he was talking to the monster or to the monstrous people in his memory.

He was answered by a wave of sounds, twisting and weaving in and out of each other like another transformation. Whips slashed across bare flesh. Animals cried out. The stomachs of children groaned in forced starvation. Tank engines rumbled while explosions rained from the sky. Flames roared, engulfing a wave of screams. Crumbling buildings of fire lifted a city's cry into the heavens. Air raid sirens shrieked like the end of the world.

He yanked the gun up to the father-face, then to the yawning maw above it.

"Just another evil bastard, that's all you are, then."

You don't understand, August. Sometimes a thing does not destroy because it is evil, as a fire burning down a house has no real desire to destroy, nor interest in the house. It burns because it is fire. But your people -

"Tell me about us, pal."

Your people destroy because you are afraid. Your fear infects you with the cancers of

149

superstition and hatred.

Something was definitely going haywire in his guts.

Your brothers and sisters are anxious to see your new form. It's not often that one of us can walk undetected in your world. We have already reached your mind, limited as it is, but in just a moment now we shall have it all.

Winfield lowered the gun, tossed it aside. It landed in his mother's lap.

"Look, you can do whatever you want to me," he said. "I didn't figure on getting out of here alive anyway. But whatever kind of hokum you've got going isn't going to wash with everyone out there. Humanity...we've got a survival instinct."

No, you have an instinct for destruction.

Winfield looked at his hands, then at the bodies of his mother and Theda.

All of your precious humanity is nothing more than an abandoned experiment. None of you was meant to be anything more than slaves to us, but you believed that you were something else. Some of you even enslaved each other, if you can imagine the irony of that.

The monster inside of Winfield had begun to climb higher now, seeking to escape. Surely it couldn't have survived. Nor could it have grown so large as to reach into his every limb and organ, wriggling deep into his arteries, his heart, his brain.

We can take an entire world, and it's not even tiring. But it's more fun to watch as you destroy yourselves.

"I don't believe you."

Tentacles curled around Winfield like an

150

obscene caress. The Barlow-thing oozed closer, reaching up with arms that looked human. It placed its hands, as cold as the bottom of the sea, on either side of his skull. He looked into the pustulant alien eyes. Then it pressed him down, pushing him toward the father-face in its belly.

And it showed him the world that was to come.

It showed him everything.

When he had seen it all, Winfield bowed his head. Tears were falling from his eyes. The cruel alien faces of Nyarlathotep pulled away, twisted in malicious, grinning glee. The tentacled arms slowly drew back and Winfield dropped to his knees.

He said nothing else, nor did he look again upon the bodies of his mother and sister. He did not think about the city of Arkham, or the great university called Miskatonic. He did not think about his friends Meursault and Jupiter Lucius. He did not ask if the people of earth would ever stop killing each other. He did not wonder anymore about missing girls, or if monsters actually existed. He did not think about his father, or wonder if he was ever really loved. He did not even think about himself.

He just cried silently.

He did not make a sound, even when the first tentacle squirmed out from between his lips. Another quickly followed, then another. He didn't need to open his mouth for the octopus, for it frantically pushed itself out of the warm human nest. He could feel pieces of himself tearing away inside. The head of the creature, which had grown considerably in a very short time, pushed itself out of his mouth in an obscene mockery of birth. It hung precariously from his face and looked out upon a new world. For just a moment, it looked like Winfield had an octopus for a head.

Then the thing tore itself free, dragging a glistening mass of organs and serpentine intestines with it. It dropped to the floor with a sickening splat. The congregation of monsters watched as it wriggled a few feet away. Watched as it slowly throbbed into stillness. And watched as it died.

Then the detective known as August Winfield fell in a dead heap to the cold earth.

We gathered around, pressing up close to the empty corpse of what had been human. It was nothing more than a vessel now. Those of us who had attempted to pass for human, but had failed miserably, looked on with the most interest of all. Many of us dropped to our knees, barely expelling a breath. But there was no envy in these wriggling almost-human hearts. There was only anticipation. The way we knelt beside the still-warm shell on the church floor would have looked like prayer to most of you. In many ways, we *were* praying.

It was not long before those prayers were answered.

The eyes of the detective opened again, but what looked out through them was not the same. The human face smiled a perfect smile, but what was lurking behind it was no longer human. It was much better. It was many, it was ancient, and it was one in purpose. It smiled, and we smiled, because we knew that it could be done now.

The thing that had once been August Winfield, and looked like him still, rose and greeted its brothers and sisters. It did not bother to look at the bodies that lay on the church floor, for there would be many more bodies to come. There would be many civilizations to fall.

The future we have dreamt will be ours.

We will infiltrate and we will be patient. We will not have to kill many of you. We will only have to work in subtle ways, for the seeds of your destruction are already within you. They have been with you from the beginning.

It is nothing more than a matter of time now.

We are here.

And we are watching.

And we are waiting.

Dan Shadduk's Bad Luck Day

by

R. Mike Burr

Something told me not to answer the door buzzer, but it was nearing the end of a long day smack in the middle of the coldest, darkest age of the minor hell-mouth in which I found myself, through various misfortunes, residing. I was due for some good luck.

Instead, *she* steps gingerly into the doorway.

"May I enter?"

"Can I stop you?"

"I think we both know the answer to that."

Nice that she remembers some of my more disreputable skills, but also knows the hierarchy of things. I'm powerless to stop her.

I gesture to the only other chair in my office. She takes mine, unconsciously rubbing the weathered bone of the armrest.

"Nice place."

"Finding a new appreciation for the lived-in aesthetic?"

I temper the acid in my response, despite myself. She had me the moment she walked in the door. No black magic. No talisman. That's bad. Worse is that she knows it. She dispenses with the cursory work of buttering me up. Better to get down to business. I haven't even made peace with what a schmuck I am when she lets it drop.

"I need your help, Dan."

"You don't say."

She slides her single slender arm into a drawer, tips the bottle.

"It's bad this time."

"Must be."

A lizard scurries, disturbed by the opened drawer. Cyn plucks it up and seductively drops the wriggling thing into her mouth.

"I just can't take it anymore. It's madness. He's gone too far this time."

"So you left. Keep leaving."

"It's not that easy and you know it."

"I don't know. It's always been your strong suit."

She regards me with familiar contempt. I know she could manufacture a pity tear, but it's beneath her.

"I made some bad decisions. I know that."

"Us?"

"Oh, Danny."

She stands, attains her full height: majestic, terrible, and beautiful. I see a thousand of her. She's around the desk, tendrils reaching for the eye that isn't there. The eye they took. I shy back. The sweetness is there, but cut with a new corruption, like a novitiate freshly spoiled. Positively intoxicating. He did a number on her. I can only imagine the things she has seen.

She explores the cheek, tentatively inches toward the socket, where I don't see anymore. I let her.

"I felt so bad."

"Not me. Face like this, scumbags know you're an operator. You and your paramour did me a big favor."

"You've really landed on your feet."

"I was flat on my back for a time, so this is an improvement."

"I don't have time to rehash the past. Will you help me?"

She's nice to act like I have a choice in the matter. I can't say no to her.

"What do you need, Cyn?"

"I need to get away from him. He wants me back."

I point to the eye.

"I don't have the greatest record."

"I know. If there was anyone else, do you think I'd be here?"

"Thanks for the vote of confidence."

"If you couldn't do it, I wouldn't have come at all."

She walks around the table, takes another pull from the bottle and pushes it toward me. My paw is shaking something fierce, but I need my wits about me.

"Were you followed here?"

"I don't think so."

They were probably already here, no doubt waiting to see if there was any fun to be had before dragging her back and pitching my sorrowful monocular carcass into the nearest pit of despair.

"If we're going, we need to go."

I open the other drawer. Get a piece of good luck. Contemplate ending it now. Remember that there's no such thing as rock bottom.

"Thank you."

"Save it until I've done something."

I take a second, wonder who is going to be

responsible for taking out the trash before the next loser sets up a failing venture here. I'm pretty sure I won't be back.

The pus-colored hallway is undulating and moist with residual heat. It would be oppressive, but I know what I'm doing. I'm chilled to the bone.

"Where are we going?"

"Best you don't know. Let me worry about it."

The hallway exists in the fourth dimension, seems endless, tapering down to nothing. It will take forever to get anywhere, but we're going nowhere. The space folds around me. Every step is a chore. I imagine what it's like for her, the dread of fate, and the small spike of guilt that she's dragging me along with her. Maybe she cares a little; maybe misery really does just love company.

I check the stairs and motion Cyn to follow me. She shouldn't be graceful in descent, but my focus shifts to her momentarily, how all the funhouse mirror parts of her move in liquid lock step. I still want her. I want to be doing this for her, even though I know better.

I can't dwell. The storefront window buckles and shatters with a thunderclap. I step in front of Cyn. It seems like the thing to do.

There are three of them: faceless, wordless bulks that won the lottery by eating their siblings and immediately putting those skills to use in the thriving atrocity industry.

They are all wearing the eye, meaning they belong to Byatis. The old toad's a player in the game; the question is whether he's working a contract or freelancing. These gibbering abominations might not even have the brains to tell me, should they for some reason decide to do so instead of playing hide and seek with my internal organs.

The three unfold themselves with a papery crackle. Chains hit the floor. Knuckles pop. The middle one breathes a fetid exhalation onto his eye medallion. Maybe Byatis has remote viewing capabilities. Maybe Byatis likes to watch.

"Dan! Do something!"

"Any suggestions?"

Middle burps out a rasp that might be a form of communication or a simple demonstration of what hopelessness sounds like. I recognize it immediately, try not to let my legs buckle. Right and Left step forward, show us some teeth. They're taking their sweet time with it. A one-eyed old housefly like me is lacking in the intimidation department.

Cyn isn't having any of it. She tries to push past me to the door. Doesn't seem like the most considered plan. I pull her back behind me.

"Things are going to get a little wet. My advice is not to look."

Middle is standing there. Then he isn't. Left and Right stop their advance and try to assimilate the new information. Before they can, a sheet of viscera sprays through the window. Chaos reigns.

Cyn screams. Left and Right turn toward the window, where they are met with my insurance policy.

Vibur. Six feet and change of soul-stealing violence. Bound to me, thankfully, by a few tenuous black magics. He'll squash me like a bug if he ever gets out from under them, but the upside of his carnage is worth it.

Vibur tries to find purchase in Right's fleshy underbelly. The goon starts slithering away, maybe allowing for a split second of hope. Vibur finds a chin and yanks up. There is a crunching that could be the separation of bone from sinew. A high keening escapes from a newly created orifice. What passes for a smile forms a rictus on Vibur's face. Fangs follow fangs. Right is not spared this last indignity. Vibur makes a gentleman's lunch of the goon's face.

Left takes an instant to plot his course of action. In this instant, Vibur gently places his furry mitt on Left's head and turns it around. Left's arms and legs go limp. Vibur drags a rough tongue across his cheeks, and then Left's, whose arms and legs spasm stupidly. The possibility exists that Left died of fright or went insane before Vibur went to work on the eyeballs. Depends on how lucky he was.

Cyn wraps her arm around me and tries to find some measure of protection behind me. She is optimistic…or desperate.

Vibur tosses Left to the side and makes a small attempt at cleaning parts of three different beings from his already rumpled suit. He quickly realizes the futility of the enterprise. His scream opens three dimensions and shuts down four more.

"Sorry, Boss. I know what you said about thinking ahead. I did bad, huh?"

I flick away some bone fragments and attempt to blot a heroic blob of vitreous humor.

"You did fine, guy. Cyn, meet my driver."

Vibur thrusts out a sticky paw, then quickly withdraws it. He has second thoughts. His whip-like

160

tongue finds the paw, smearing the vitreous humor further. He shrugs.

"I'm not exactly street legal anymore. Vibur here is a good man in a pinch. He's hell on upholstery, though."

"Where are we going, Boss?"

I gingerly pick up a medallion from what used to be Left.

"Let's return this to sender."

Cyn moves from behind me, considers the medallion.

"Dan! You can't be serious. You might as well take me straight back to him."

She goes to leave, but I enwrap her arm and spin her toward me.

"Damn it, Cyn. You were the one who came through my door. Now I'm in it up to my neck, and we're going to play it my way. It's pretty damn clear that every two-bit bad man from the hell-mouth to the great drain knows you're on the lam, sugar. What we need to figure out is if the big man is writing contracts, or the toad is working on his own. What I don't need, one minute after saving your skin, is anything but gratitude. You got it?"

I gauge her reaction to see if she's buying the idea or if I'll have to do some more convincing. Cyn looks at me and then at Vibur. She shakes her head.

"Whatever you say."

She heaves a sigh of resignation, and we shuffle out into the cold, wet night.

Vibur hunches down over the wheel and maintains a death grip on the shifter. He keeps a running dialogue with someone while he drives. I try not to interfere, and vigil for any more of Byatis' boys. I find myself distracted by Cyn slipping ever so gently into the back seat.

The car creeps into a slightly better neighborhood. A majority of windows are intact, and a few streetlights, while doing nothing to guarantee safety, at least dissipate some of the sheeting, rainy darkness. The streets are relatively empty. There isn't a twenty-four hour bazaar here. The homeless are shuffled down a side street or swept down to sleep on my stoop.

The corruption remains, but under a veneer of legitimacy. The nondescript building where Vibur now eases the car to a stop has seen enough in the way of abomination to make the pope renounce her vows. It might just be the contrast, but dirty deeds always seem just a little worse in the nice part of town.

Vibur and I exit the car and are not immediately assaulted. This could be viewed as an improvement to my evening, or another indication that I'm playing right into the old toad's hand. I motion to Cyn, and she reluctantly exits the car.

Two goons appear when we approach the door. They are not immediately hostile, but lethal intent is apparent.

"I'm here to see the wizard."

I hold up the medallion for effect and Vibur gets huge. Either this gets some traction, or, more likely, Byatis knew we were coming. The goons step aside, and the three of us enter a hallway lit by the requisite light bulbs hanging from chains. I take the lead and leave Vibur to watch the rear.

His door is at the end of the hallway. A greenish

light glows behind it. I consider knocking. It swings before I hit it. I guess he knows we're coming.

"Enter and be amazed at the glory of the all-seeing Byatis! Exist in awe and horror at his corruptive obesity. Kneel before Byatis!"

"It works a little better when you have someone else say that kind of stuff."

The toad sits shadowed on a table near the back of the room. The half-light leaves his grey skin glistening and highlights the streak of malevolence in his one centrally located eye. I knew there was something that I liked about him.

"Good help is hard to find these days."

"I regret to inform you that you have three new openings."

Byatis forms his oral anus into some version of a smile. Slime drips from the upturned corner of his mouth and oozes through rows of little sharpened teeth.

"Are you here for a job interview, Dan Shadduk? I could definitely find a position for you… and your delightful friend, too."

Vibur steps forward. I put out my arm to hold him back.

"As much as I would probably benefit from your expertise, infrastructure, and superior sense of grooming, I think I'll remain an independent enterprise."

"Very well. Then why have you and your associate and your lovely lady friend decided to pay me a visit?"

I hold up the medallion.

"The guys who broke my window were wearing this. Why did they pay me a visit?"

The toad maintains his anal smile. Definitely thinks he's in charge, which might mean that my game's over.

"Dan Shadduk. Don't ask questions you know the answer to. Your companion has made certain assignations that my employer considers to be more permanent."

The toad stops short of saying the name, invoking the presence.

"Things don't last forever, Byatis."

"We both know better than that, Dan Shadduk."

His exhalation is the sound of a thousand corrupted souls. Vibur's paws fly up to the side of his head. Cyn steadies herself on my shoulder. I try to remain standing and muster something resembling authority in my voice.

"Can the show! Why were they there?"

"Leave now, Dan Shadduk, and your suffering will be much less. Leave her to her blessed consequences."

I see every one of his teeth.

"I think you're freelancing. I think you're out of your depth. We'll walk out of here. You never saw us. That's the best outcome for you."

"There is only one outcome!"

The toad tries to diaphragm up another round of soul keening. I throw a hex to stop him.

"Think for one second. This does not end well for anyone in this room unless she disappears."

"You bargain like you are the viceroy of a thousand soul farms. What can you offer me? I feast on corruption and debasement. I will bear witness. I am the all-seeing eye. I am Byatis!"

The toad lets loose a string of syllables from the

164

old language before I can block him again. Vibur goes limp and lashes an arm toward me. I throw Cyn out of the way and barely duck. I'm not as lucky the second time. I land flat on my back and slide for what seems like forever. My one saving grace is that he's not that fast, but he's still on top of me before I can get to my feet. Byatis is masturbatorily delighted. Two of his goons burst into the room. The toad waves them off, enjoying what is sure to be the separation of meat from my bones.

"Capitulate now. The corpse desecration will be minimal."

I try to frame my response. Vibur spins me around and shakes me like a rag doll. I dribble some words from my rattled brain, and he drops me. I throw up a little and Byatis seizes the opportunity. Vibur's eyes glaze over, and he takes another wide swing at me. I throw a hex, but it doesn't take. He's sluggish, but still manages to shred a sleeve of my coat. I smell the rancid odor of my blood and then I hear her shriek.

Cyn wraps her arm around Vibur's neck. She pulls her bulk onto him, and Vibur sinks to his knees for an instant. The hold is strong, however. Even as her rows of pincer teeth are digging in to his shoulder, Vibur is shaking Cyn off and coming after me again. I don't have the mojo to break Byatis' hold on him.

The instant plays out in ultra-slow motion. I see Vibur for the first time, the most voracious of larva devouring the carcass of some poor unfortunate; his pupal stages and how surprised each of his hosts were when he erupted from a cavity; the first hex that bound his service to me. Vibur, hissing with anticipation, raises his paws to bury them in my abdomen. I've gone soft. I don't think I can pull the trigger. I've played right into Byatis' excessively articulated finger appendages. This is the end of Dan Shadduk, scourge to no one, many-faced horror of abject failure. I close my eye folds and try to make the best of the situation. I know that Vibur is a quick eater. And nothing happens.

I hear Vibur choke and hazard a look. Cyn has produced a tendril that's wrapped around his throat. He's struggling, but losing inches. My inner conflict falls away and I feel the familiar sheen of indifference. It's good to be back.

Wriggling away from the immediate area of Vibur's eventual consumption, I draw a bead on Byatis' amulet.

"Dan Shadduk! I command thee–"

My finger is faster than his words. The slug slams into the amulet, and it shatters into a thousand mirrored shards. Byatis wails. So does Vibur. For a short time before Cyn takes a fatal amount of flesh, he knows what it is to have a life and lose it. The abject misery is delicious, if a bit baroque. I turn my attention to Byatis, trying to effect a quick exit. I step on his leg and twist my foot until I hear something solid give way.

"Let me alone! I will damn each of your organs to a separate hell!"

"Hard to do without your little trinket."

Byatis grunts and tries to pull his ruined leg from under my foot. He knows I'm right.

"Are you working for the unspoken?"

"May a thousand flies take residence in your

eye!"

I step on the other leg, work my foot a little right and left.

"Why did you come for her?"

"I am the unholy and unloved Byatis!"

I grind my foot before he can finish. I have the feeling I don't have time to listen to a long-winded explanation.

"I'll make it quick. Just tell me. How did you know?"

Byatis tries one last heave and collapses face first onto the floor.

"Everybody knows she had a thing for you. When I heard she bolted, I came looking."

"Why?"

"Don't you want to know the mystery, to feel the rain of corruption wash over you? Don't you understand what he can offer?"

"Dan, don't listen to him."

Cyn, covered in Vibur, has edged up behind me.

"There's darkness and pain, and there are other forces that are not to be tampered with at any cost. Don't let him tempt you."

"Do you think that he can tempt me with his little stories? Is that why you came to my door, Cyn?" I spit the words out. They taste like ash.

"It's not a story! You know it's the truth. Let me live. I will gladly lick your boots and live in your filth for an iota of your knowledge. Please!"

He actually flops over to attempt to lick my boot, which elicits a sickening sound from his ruined leg. Cyn looks terrified, so I kick him free and bury three slugs in his head. It's a mercy really; he's nothing without the jewel. Maybe some part of me *is* going soft.

"You did that for me?" It's hard to gauge her expression, but Cyn sounds incredulous and appreciative.

"I did something."

I try to look away, which is enough of a tell in itself. Her bulk shudders and deflates. It's hard to realize you've been played for a fool. It was harder for her, since she had played so many before.

"From the beginning?"

"Pretty damn close. The frog was an unexpected complication."

"I don't need to ask why."

She telescopes her arm to its full length. The delicate, horny protrusions beckon me closer.

"Is there anything I can do?"

"It's nice that you ask."

The wall shifts. Cyn screams. I feel microscopic maggots being born and feasting on every atom of my flesh. The degradation is exquisite. A tentacle seizes Cyn and she offers a parting curse.

A cloud of flies explodes from me. His emissaries had promised riches and power. I hoped for death. It felt like I was winning on that count, but I was still stubbornly aware of what was happening to me. I see Cyn struggling through the portal and being dragged back in, screaming the entire time.

"Why?   Why? Whhhhhhhhhhhhhhhhhhhhyyyyyyyyyyyyyyyyyy."

On the edge consciousness, where I might be spending the rest of eternity, I raise what's left of my head on a rickety neck.

"It's Nyarlathotep's world, baby. We're just

living in it."

In the Shadow of Reality

by

Dan Johnson

A cold October rain fell as Detective Geoff Wilheimer climbed the stone steps of the posh Providence Estates home that was now a crime scene. Uniformed officers searched the slick, muddy grounds surrounding the property as neighbors peeked out their windows, trying to find out what was going on.

Wilheimer nodded at Michaels, one of the patrolmen who stood watch at the front entrance, and the two proceeded down a hallway on the first floor.

"When did you hear about this one?" Wilheimer asked as he and the officer approached the living room at the end of the hallway.

"Call came in around 6:45," Michaels said, holding up the police tape across the door. "My partner and I got report of a disturbance and came straight over. Neighbors had heard shouting coming from the victim's house; we were en route when shots were fired."

They walked into the living room, which showed signs of a recent struggle. There was a huge dent in the wall, apparently where someone had been thrown against it. The detective reasoned it must have been the murderer, as the victim had no signs of the displaced plaster on him. The victim did have two bullet holes in him, one in the chest and one in the shoulder. He was dressed in a bathrobe

171

and boxers. On his coffee table was a TV dinner that was half eaten.

Wilheimer noted the distance from the dent in the wall to where the victim fell. "You said the shots were fired en route?"

"Yes, sir. We got the follow-up call three minutes after the initial one came in."

"Looks like the victim was settling in for the evening."

"Could he have caught someone breaking in?" asked Michaels, stepping aside so a member of the CSI team could get to the body. "We haven't seen any signs of forced entry."

The detective examined the door for himself. "He was arguing with whoever shot him...That tells me he knew his attacker well enough to let things heat up for a few minutes before someone complained and the gun was finally drawn."

Wilheimer turned to Michaels and motioned to the dead man. "Have you ID'd the victim yet?"

Michaels nodded as he took out a notepad. "Yes, sir. The victim was Professor Darwyn Clement. He worked at Arkham College in their anthropology department."

Wilheimer turned as he heard commotion out in the hallway. He stepped out and saw Michaels' partner, Delanie, trying to keep a visibly distressed woman from entering the house, and not having much luck.

"I must see him," the woman said through muffled sobs. "I have... have to see Darwyn, *please!*"

Wilheimer tapped Delanie on the shoulder and the policeman stepped aside. The detective stood in front of the woman to keep her from going further down the hallway and seeing the body.

"Miss," he began, "I'm Detective Wilheimer. I'm afraid…"

"He's dead, isn't he?" The woman asked as she looked in Wilheimer's eyes. "Darwyn is… gone…"

Wilheimer didn't say anything. The woman broke down, no longer able to stifle her sobbing as she fell into the detective's arms. He patted her back stiffly in an effort to be consoling.

After a few awkward moments, Wilheimer led the crying woman to a chair in Clement's kitchen. She eventually calmed down enough for him to learn that her name was Dr. Patricia Wilmoth, she was a colleague of the deceased, and she was his girlfriend. He also learned who Clement's attacker might have been.

"Dar and I…well, we began seeing one another shortly after he came to work at the college," Patricia said as she struggled to compose herself. "You could say it was love at first sight as far as I was concerned. He was such a brilliant man, so kind…so…"

"And the head of your department, Dr. Combs, he didn't take kindly to this fraternization?" Wilheimer asked, as he underlined the name 'Dr. Stuart Combs' on his note pad.

"Stuart was furious," Patricia said. "I have known him since I was his student – almost twenty years. I always knew he was infatuated with me, but this resentment he had towards Dar and I dating was so irrational. It was just uncalled for."

173

Wilheimer flipped through his notes, circling a date Patricia had given him. "Dr. Clement joined your school's anthropology department over a year ago. Was there tension the whole time?"

"Tension? No," Patricia said as she rubbed her hands together. "Dar was hired so Stuart could supervise an archeological dig in Africa. He was away for almost nine months and just learned of Dar and I being together two weeks ago."

"You said you and Dr. Combs had words this afternoon? That was why you came here tonight?"

"Yes," Patricia said, nodding her head. "Stuart told me that if he couldn't be with me, no one would. He's an old man, almost at the college's retirement age, and normally so gentle. But he was so angry today, it scared me. I just knew he would do something to hurt Darwyn."

Michaels came into the kitchen. "Detective," he began. "The CSI boys are done. The morgue is here to take the body...Dr. Clement, that is, down to county."

Wilheimer and Patricia rose from the table together.

Patricia smiled sadly at both policemen. "I thank you both for your kindness," she said. "I still can't believe Dar is gone."

"Do you need a ride home, Dr. Wilmoth?" Wilheimer asked. "Given everything you have been through, perhaps you shouldn't drive."

"I would appreciate that, detective."

"My partner and I can take the lady home, if you like," said Michaels.

"I'll take care of it. In the meantime, I'd like you two to run down a possible suspect for me."

174

Wilheimer handed him a piece of paper, torn from his pad, with Dr. Combs' name and address on it. He escorted Dr. Wilmoth out the door and down the front steps to his car. By now the rain had stopped, the neighboring windows were all shut, and the nightscape glistened under a bright moon.

Patricia Wilmoth lived a short distance from Clement's residence. It wasn't an inconvenience to Wilheimer, but it was unusual for him to bother doing something like this. The detective knew that. Most times he would have let Michaels and Delanie handle such a routine thing as running a witness home.

"So," Patricia said suddenly after sitting in silence for several minutes. "How long have you been a policeman, Lt. Wilheimer?"

"Twenty-two years this coming July," Wilheimer said as he kept a lookout for an upcoming turn. "I joined the force right out of college. And please, call me Geoff."

"It must be fascinating," said Patricia. "And so dangerous, too."

"It's had its moments," Wilheimer admitted. "But I knew the risks when I signed up."

"I do hope you'll be careful when you go after Stuart." Patricia sighed. "I…I just don't want to see you get hurt too."

Wilheimer stole a glance at Dr. Wilmoth as she stared out the window. She was middle-aged and not unattractive. But there was *something* about her that the detective couldn't quite put his finger on. He had dealt with other witnesses before, and he knew better than to get involved with them. It was

Day One stuff. But Patricia Wilmoth wasn't coming across as anyone that was just ordinary.

The two rode in silence the rest of the way to Patricia's home until Wilheimer pulled up to her driveway.

"Once again, you have been most kind, detective," Patricia said, fixing his gaze with a coy smile as she turned slowly toward him...

He was still studying her smile when Patricia lunged forward and kissed him hard on the lips. At first he resisted the advance, but soon enough Geoff found himself giving in to the kiss.

When Patricia finally let him go, she smiled and told him good night. As he watched her walk into the house, Wilheimer again sensed that something most unusual was happening.

"Victor Nine," came a voice over Wilheimer's radio. "Do you copy?"

"This is Victor Nine," said Wilheimer. "I copy. Over."

"Victor Nine," said the dispatcher. "You are requested to proceed to 412 Baker Lane. Unit 9 is already on the scene."

Wilheimer threw his car into gear and prepared to head to his destination – the address he had given Michaels earlier.

"Victor Nine, acknowledging," said Wilheimer. "Inform Unit 9 that I am en route."

Twenty minutes later, Wilheimer pulled up to a small house on the grounds Arkham College, right behind the patrol car that belonged to Michaels and Delanie. As he got out of the car, he noticed all the lights were off in Dr. Combs' home. By now the wind had picked up to a howl, making stray leaves dance across the lawn.

Wilheimer got out of his car and walked over to the uniformed officers outside the residence. "What's the situation?" he asked briskly.

"We arrived a short while ago and found the residence empty," said Michaels. "We knocked on the front door, and it swung wide open. No one answered when we called out, but the place looks like a tornado hit it. When we saw no sign of Dr. Combs, we called it in, requested a search warrant, and figured we should wait for you, detective."

"We just got the word the warrant has been issued," said Delanie, as another patrol car pulled up. "That should be it now."

As two more uniformed officers joined the group, Wilheimer took possession of the search warrant and command of the situation.

"Delanie, keep an eye peeled out here." Wilheimer motioned to the new arrivals with his left hand. "You two, check around back. Question anyone who approaches the house. Michaels, come with me."

The detective and the officer walked up to the house and onto the porch. The door was still wide open. Wilheimer took a deep breath and stepped inside. Combs' house did indeed look like it had been ransacked. Furniture was overturned, drawers were open and papers lay scattered all around the living room.

Wilheimer holstered his piece and began looking around the room. He noticed a small pile of clothes tossed onto Combs' couch. When he examined a jacket on the bottom of the pile, plaster residue fell from the shoulders. It was a match for the plaster that had been dislodged from Clement's wall. As he examined the sleeves he found the right one had a trace of residue from a recently fired weapon. No doubt about it, this jacket made Combs the leading suspect for the murder of Dr. Darwyn Clement.

"Michaels," Wilheimer said as he laid the jacket down carefully, "go call this in. Have dispatch put out an APB on Dr. Stuart Combs immediately. Tell them he's wanted for questioning and possible murder."

Michaels acknowledged the request and went outside to call in this new development.

Wilheimer walked over to a ransacked desk, picked up a piece of paper from the floor and examined it. On one side was writing that looked like scribbling, until Wilheimer realized it was a foreign language. From what he could tell, several key words were repeated over and over again. He flipped the page over and saw the image there of some unearthly monster. It looked it had been drawn by a child, or a madman. Its mouth was open, with tentacles coming out of its maul, surrounded by rows and rows of teeth. It had eyes that seemed to bore into Wilheimer's soul, even though it was just a drawing. Wilheimer dropped the paper, taken aback by how hideous the creature was and the chill it sent down his spine. Reluctantly, he picked up it up again, folded it and put it in his pocket. He couldn't explain why, but it just seemed important to hold on to.

Wilheimer and the officers searched the rest of

178

the house and found the upstairs in as much disarray as the downstairs. They also found a wall safe and a lockbox; both had been emptied. As soon as the search was complete, Wilheimer ordered Michaels to have a copy of the report ready by morning and to have the evidence tagged and logged in at the station sooner than that. Meanwhile, the detective drove straight home. Within thirty minutes of stretching out on his couch, Wilheimer was asleep and had begun to dream.

In his dream, Wilheimer sensed a shadowy figure that he only saw out of the corner of his eye. He thought he heard the figure speaking to him. It said, "Your dreams...my dreams..." over and over again. He then felt as though he was spinning around in circles, twirling and twirling until he caught sight of someone. Each time he spun past this person, they came into focus a little more, until finally he recognized Patricia Wilmoth. Patricia was smiling at him as he finally came to a stop. As she walked towards him, she began to disrobe. By the time she reached him, she was fully nude and reaching out to stroke his face. She said not a word in this dream, but slowly stripped the detective bare. At one point, she grabbed his face and thrust her tongue deep into his mouth, down into his throat. At first the sensation was otherworldly, divinely intoxicating; but then Wilheimer felt something wiggling down his throat. He felt like he was going to vomit. He watched as Wilmoth pulled away from him, and, instead of a tongue, she had a large, pink tentacle that was invading his mouth. She opened wider, and several smaller tentacles wiggled from her mouth and began to engulf his head.

179

With a start and almost gagging, Wilheimer woke up. He spat and coughed until his mouth felt...*safe* again. The detective leaned his head back on the couch to compose himself, staring up at the ceiling for a few moments before sitting back up. Feeling he had only been asleep for a few minutes, he was shocked to see the clock reading 6:06 a.m. He had slept for almost five hours.

The dream had seemed so real, he felt shaken. He thought about the kiss the two of them had shared and only now did he realize how wrong it was. After all, evidence pointed to Combs being the killer of Darwyn Clement, and Wilmoth as a witness who knew about the motive. But this wasn't an open and shut case yet. Wilheimer reminded himself that he should be thinking of Patricia as a suspect as well.

When he checked in at the police station, Wilheimer got the report from Combs' home and began to study it. The APB had gone out on Dr. Stuart Combs just after midnight, along with the year, make and model, and license plate number of his car. Wilheimer had the autopsy report on Clement by 8:00 a.m. and learned that the bullets that killed him were from a .38 revolver. A quick search revealed that Combs was licensed to carry such a weapon. More and more, the evidence against Combs was building up. But something still wasn't sitting right with Wilheimer. As he looked over the file he was quickly amassing regarding Combs, there still seemed to be a missing piece to this puzzle. The detective pulled out the piece of paper he had taken from Combs' home and examined the side with the writing on it. He dared not look at the hideous creature on the back again. He hadn't logged this as evidence, not yet, at least. He folded the paper up and stuck it in his shirt pocket, then leafed through the report on Clement. According to the records from his college, he had a doctorate in anthropology and was regarded as an expert in dead languages.

Wilheimer also took the liberty of having a file on Dr. Wilmoth put together. As he flipped through it, he learned she was a renowned expert on sociocultural anthropology. The report also included a copy of her college ID. Wilheimer looked at the picture and studied it for a long while. She wasn't a beautiful woman, nor was she ugly. She was just plain. He actually had a hard time reconciling this image with the woman he had met last night, or the one he had had such an erotic dream about a few hours earlier. That woman seemed so much more dynamic than the woman in this picture could ever be. Still, he couldn't stop thinking about her.

Wilheimer got up and grabbed his jacket. He was hoping there might be a clue at Combs' office at Arkham College; he was also hoping to run into Patricia again.

"This is a most shocking turn of events, I must say," muttered Dr. Jonah Kyle, the dean of Arkham College, as he led Lt. Wilheimer to Dr. Combs' office. "A beloved member of our faculty murdered, and the lead suspect is one of our most admired professors? Just so shocking."

Dr. Kyle stopped at Room 301 of the Human Studies Building and unlocked the door for the

181

detective.

"I just hope you'll find something that could perhaps clear Stuart rather than damn him further," said Dr. Kyle as he turned on the lights inside the office.

The first thing Wilheimer noticed when he walked into the office was a huge map of Africa with one region blown up, pins and notes all over it. Surrounding the map were photos of an archeological dig somewhere out in the desert. What really drew his attention, though, were several inscriptions posted to the side. Wilheimer took the paper from his shirt pocket and realized these were similar to the ones he had discovered last night.

"I hear Combs just got back from a large expedition outside the country," Wilheimer started. "Africa, right?"

"Indeed," said Kyle. "When Stuart returned two weeks ago, he said he had unearthed something that could lead to a find rivaling any before, perhaps even that of Tutankhamun."

"So, he was back here for what, exactly?" Wilheimer asked, looking over photos of the dig.

"Stuart returned to request an official extension of his leave," began Kyle. "As well, he needed to arrange additional capital and assistants. Mostly though, he wanted to show his find to Dr. Clement and get his aid in translating that language you see there. It stymied even Darwyn, initially."

This bit of information made Wilheimer turn around. "I heard Combs and Clement weren't that chummy."

"I don't know where you could get that idea," said Kyle, shaking his head in disbelief. "It was Dr.

182

Combs who recommended Dr. Clement come and teach at the school in his absence. Darwyn was like a son to Stuart. That's why all of this is so baffling to me – I could never see Stuart hurting Darwyn for anything."

"I spoke with Dr. Wilmoth last night," said Wilheimer. "She came to Darwyn's house after he was murdered and indicated there was bad blood between the two."

"Dr. Wilmoth...yes..." Kyle began, then stopped himself.

"Is there something about her I should know, Dr. Kyle?" Wilheimer crossed his arms.

"Patricia is a fine employee, very capable," the dean said as he tried to figure out the best way to phrase what he had to say. "But Dr. Wilmoth, well, she really bothered Dr. Clement initially. She rather made quite the fool of herself when he first arrived. Practically threw herself at him. He almost quit after the staff Christmas party when she became a bit tipsy and...well, fondled him in front of another professor."

Wilheimer was concerned by this revelation. "Really?"

"Indeed!" Kyle exclaimed. "In fact, it was only Dr. Clement's respect for Dr. Combs that made him stay on; otherwise, he would have resigned on the spot."

Wilheimer turned and looked again at the map and the photos of the dig.

"I was under the impression Dr. Clement and Dr. Wilmoth were close," said Wilheimer.

"I had heard through the grapevine they were keeping company these days," said Kyle, "which just struck me as odd. That seemed to have developed overnight, practically. I can honestly say I never saw that coming."

"Dean," Wilheimer started. "Just what was Dr. Combs looking for? In Africa, I mean?"

"Stuart thought he had discovered the buried ruins of an ancient civilization – a society even more advanced, perhaps, than the Egyptians."

"Is that *so…*"

"Yes," said Kyle. "Truthfully, this civilization had already been described, but was considered to be just a myth. Its center was said to be a great palace known as Gz-eh, close to the Valley of the Kings. The people there worshipped a great force, a member of a race of ancient beings that sought to rule Earth as they ruled the heavens. It was said they could take a man's dreams and make them come true. They could take the shadows of reality and bring them into the daylight."

"That's perfect, since it's almost Halloween," said Wilheimer, trying to lighten the mood.

"You would think," said the dean. "But Stuart thought it was real, and he believed he found something on his dig that indicated there was more fact than fiction yet to be uncovered."

After searching Dr. Combs' office, and finding nothing to suggest where he might have fled, Wilheimer decided to have another talk with Dr. Wilmoth. In light of what had happened between Combs and Clement, Patricia had taken the day off, but her home was nearby. It would be easy enough to drop in and get some facts straight.

Wilheimer pulled up to Wilmoth's home. He

was determined to find out what the real story was with her two suitors. The detective pounded on the door and was ready to unload on the professor. But as soon as she opened the door, something changed. Wilheimer couldn't explain it, but rather than wanting to talk to her, he now found that he *needed* her.

Patricia smiled as she opened the door. "Geoff, I was just thinking of you."

Without a word, Wilheimer stepped in and grabbed her. He kissed her long and hard, and she kissed him back. The two began stripping away their clothes, and the detective took the professor right there in her living room. The sex was raw and animalistic. Wilheimer wasn't thinking, he was doing, and Patricia cried out in pleasure.

The sex that followed was like a marathon, with Geoff and Patricia repeatedly pleasuring one another, back and forth. Finally, after three hours, they fell asleep in Patricia's bed. As Wilheimer slept next to this woman he had met less than twenty-four hours earlier, he dreamed; and the images again troubled him. In his dreams, he again saw a shadowy figure, but this time it was an older man who came into focus quickly. He was in a rundown motel in the heart of the city, and he was frightened. What's more, he seemed to sense Wilheimer's presence, and he cried out in such terror that Geoff sat up with a start.

Wilheimer looked over and saw Patricia still sleeping. He shook his head and cursed himself for what he had done. Sleeping with a witness?! He could lose his badge for this. He scrambled to get his clothes and left without waking her.

Out in the car, he tossed back his head and rubbed his eyes. The image of the old man and that hotel were burned into his mind, but he was more upset about what he had done with Patricia.

"Victor Nine, please respond," came a voice over his radio.

Wilheimer looked at his watch. He had been out of contact for hours. He knew there would be hell to pay. He picked up the radio, trying to think of a rational reason why he would have been out of touch for so long.

"This is Victor Nine," he said, waiting for the questions he had no good answers for.

"Victor Nine," the voice began. "The vehicle registered to the suspect in the Clement investigation has been located in a downtown parking deck. We are beginning a sweep of the area now, and your presence is requested."

Wilheimer sighed in relief and acknowledged the call. And then it hit him. The hotel he saw in his dream...he knew it. It was a rundown flophouse. The perfect place for a man on the run. The perfect place to find Dr. Combs.

Straight away, Wilheimer drove to the hotel from his dream. It was the Standford Inn, a place well known by the police as a hotbed of prostitution and drug dealing. When he described the man from his dream to the desk clerk, the man behind the counter knew just who the detective was looking for. He gave him a room number, 407, and watched as Wilheimer proceeded up the stairs. Once on the fourth floor, Wilheimer approached Combs' hotel

186

room with his revolver drawn. A drunken lug stepped out of a room to the detective's right, cursing under his breath. A flash of Wilheimer's badge drove him back into his room.

Wilheimer stood with his piece cocked and his badge in the other hand. He kicked in the cheap, plywood door and stepped into the musty room. Sitting on the bed with his back to Wilheimer was a man in his sixties, clad in a sweat-soaked t-shirt, his few remaining hairs disheveled. All around him were empty pill bottles and coffee cups.

"Dr. Combs," the detective began. "I don't want any trouble. Stand up and keep your hands where I can see them. You're under arrest on suspicion of murder."

The old man raised his hands in the air and slowly stood. He turned, and it appeared that Combs had been crying. His eyes were red and his face drawn and sad. He had bags under his eyes, and he appeared to be disoriented from a lack of sleep.

"I know you," Combs said as he pointed to Wilheimer. "I saw you in my dreams. You're with her, aren't you?"

Wilheimer was shocked, and he lowered his weapon.

"She's not what she seems, my boy," Combs began. "Don't trust her. You can't trust her, not anymore!"

"You mean Patricia?"

"It's not Patricia!" The old man screamed. "It's something else…something not of this world! It took control of Darwyn! That is why I had to kill him! Her control over him made her powerful! That is why she tried to control me, too! The more

187

people she corrupts, the stronger *it* becomes!"

Combs then looked stunned, and his eyes grew wide. He spoke just two words, "God forgive," and then his neck twisted and his head spun fully around. Dr. Stuart Combs fell to the floor, dead.

Wilheimer spun around and came face to face with Patricia. She smiled and shook her head slightly as she locked eyes with the detective.

"I had my doubts you could be so effective," she said as she approached Wilheimer. "I was sure it would take you much longer to find Combs. But here you go and locate him so, so quickly. You impress me, detective."

Wilheimer raised his weapon and aimed it at Wilmoth. Her smile grew bigger, and as she threw back one hand, the gun went sailing across the room. She threw her other hand forward and Wilheimer went flying back into an armchair that sat in the corner.

"What the he--" he gasped as he caught his breath.

"But just because I am impressed, don't think I will let you live," Patricia said as she walked past him.

Wilmoth walked over to the papers that Combs had been looking through and tossed them aside. Then she looked in the drawers of the nightstand and the dresser.

"Poor Stuart," she said as she searched for something. "He could have shared this all with me. But his male ego couldn't accept that *I* had been chosen. But then, why should I be surprised? He only asked for my help because he and Darwyn struggled to understand what he had unearthed.

Only then did the force behind his discovery make itself known to me. It chose me over the both of them!"

"*What* chose you?" asked Wilheimer, as he struggled against the force that kept him restrained to the chair.

Wilmoth shrugged as she flipped the bed over with one hand. She shook her head when she saw there was nothing there.

"What were you chosen *for*?!" Wilheimer demanded.

"I was chosen to be the instrument of his return!" Wilmoth said as her very gaze pressed down on the detective, threatening to push all the air from his lungs. "Great and powerful Amon-Gorloth. His is the power to shape and alter reality from dreams. When I unleash his magnificence on the world, it will be reshaped to match his whims and desires. In the meantime, his glory gives me the power to make men like you and Dar desire me, whereas before you would have never given me a second look. And it gave me the power to find Combs, who had stolen what I needed to cement my pact with my master!"

"And here it is…" Wilmoth reached down near the armchair and brought up a glowing red pyramid, whose light somehow bathed the room with a sticky feeling. Smiling, she held it out in front of Wilheimer.

"Behold, the instrument from which my lord and master shall come forth," she said as her eyes began to glow with the same red energy. "Combs unearthed it, shattered into three pieces by the fools who thought to banish mighty Amon-Gorloth after

189

he invaded their dreams! Their dreams that gave shape to his power and made their nightmares reality!"

Wilmoth stepped closer to the detective, who still struggled against his invisible bonds.

"I was there when Combs and Clements reassembled the portal, when my master reached out and chose *me* to be his anchor on this plain." She smiled and the red energy now shined through her teeth and gums. "And in return, he made my dreams, my desires, come true! For Darwyn, and then you, Geoff."

"Shape... shaped reality..." Wilheimer spat out.

"To what I wanted!" Wilmoth said as she held the device in front of Wilheimer. "The more I use this power he grants me, the stronger the bridge becomes. Soon, he will return to our plain and rule as he did centuries ago. Combs thought he could stop us by taking this back. But the old fool had to sleep sometime, and when he did, I had him. You just happened to sense him, too, because of our bond, which is a pity. We could have had so much more fun together."

"Never... get away..." Wilheimer said, struggling to the very end.

"Brave fool," said Wilmoth, as the pyramid grew dark in its center. "We already have."

Within the void, a shape came forward. It was the monster Combs had scribbled on the paper, the face of Amon-Gorloth. The creature's hand sprang forward, and Wilheimer was dragged into the void, screaming as he disappeared between its dark folds.

Patricia Wilmoth placed the pyramid in her handbag and walked out of the Standford Inn. Once on the street, she hailed a taxi. One pulled up immediately and stopped for her. The cabbie snarled, "Where to, lady?

As Patricia settled in, her eyes shined briefly with the red energy of the triangle. Suddenly, the cabbie's tone and attitude changed.

"That is...where you headed, ma'am?"

Patricia smiled and then licked her lips with a pink tentacle. "As far as my dreams can take me, little man."

Into the Valley of San Fernando

by
Rick Shingler

I was just about to pack it in for the day when she oozed her way into the office on legs that went all the way up to her chin. And that's not a metaphor. What I mean is her legs went all the way to just below her mouth. And there were a lot of them. Legs, that is. As far as I could see from where I was sitting, she only had the one mouth.

"You're Phil, right? Phil Howard?" she warbled. "I need your help."

Christ. Help one evil cloud-like entity find a couple of her missing goat-spawn, and all of a sudden you're on speed-dial for the Elder Ones. I don't have time for this shit.

"That's the name on the door. Listen, not to be rude, but I've got a pretty full caseload at the moment, ma'am. Maybe try Al Edgar down in Bellflower."

I had just gotten up to show her the door when she threw a couple dozen of those tentacles around my shoulders.

"Please! You have to help me find my little girls!"

Sonuvabitch. I don't know if she was purposely tapping my weak spot, but it sure as hell worked. I can't turn away a missing child case. I untangled myself from her embrace and closed the door.

193

Turning back to her, I gestured to the bench under the office's only window. The bench had begun its existence in this world as the back seat of an old Buick Skylark, before I salvaged it and bolted to my office floor, but it was wide and spacious enough for her to sit on.

"Coffee?" I offered, as she noisily settled onto the faded green Naugahyde.

"I would, please," she replied primly.

I poured two cups, handed one to my client, and pulled a chair over to face her.

"Let's start with your name," I said.

"Kassie," she replied. "Kassogtha, actually. I am mated with the great Cthulhu. We have two girls together, twins named Nctosa and Nctolhu. We call them Nicci and Nikky. They've been tethered to this plane for months, but now they've disappeared altogether. I need your help to locate them and help them slip their bondage to this miserable plane."

I took a sip of my coffee and realized with a start that this wasn't today's coffee. This being Monday, it wasn't yesterday's either. A quick review of my morning reminded me that I had taken my morning joe at a diner near a client's office. And that meant the cup in my hand was full of a murky, tar-like substance that had been fermenting in a dirty pot on the crappy burner of a cheap coffee maker since last Friday. Three and a half days ago. Setting the coffee aside, I settled back into my seat and crossed my legs. Ms. Kassogtha took a second gulp to drain her cup and continued talking. I got up to offer her a refill, which she gratefully accepted.

"You've probably seen them before," she said. "For a little while about a year ago, their faces were

194

everywhere."

I couldn't begin to guess where she pulled it from, but she unrolled a scroll to show me a picture of Nicci and Nikky. She was right. I knew exactly who they were. The junk folder in my mind immediately salvaged the jingle from the gum commercial they did together, but I was sure their fame went beyond that. I thought I remembered hearing something about their appearance on one of those stupid teenaged monster hunter shows, but I couldn't think of the details. They must have had an excellent agent, because even without watching those teen shows I recognized them. I know they appeared off and on with other shows and had some movie cameos. Heck, they even did a music video. I think it was Drake making out with Nikky, but I couldn't be sure.

They had been living the dream. But then Nikky botched her line as a presenter at the Academy Awards, and things started to go south. She was supposed to say, "The Oscar for best adapted screenplay goes to..." but it came out sounding more like, "My father's return will mark the end of this ludicrous humanity, save those who bow to his name." And, as if that wasn't embarrassing enough, Nicci had that wardrobe malfunction while dancing behind Snoop Dogg during the Super Bowl half time show a couple of weeks later. Once that happened, their downward spiral was a foregone conclusion. Come to think of it, I hadn't heard anything about either one of them since the dust of the Super Bowl brouhaha settled. I think I heard that Nikky had been passed over for a role in a period drama. And there was some ballyhoo about Nicci stalking off the set of a sitcom because she felt she had been typecast as the token *creature with tentacles*. But that was months ago.

As I was shuffling these memory cards, Kassie continued talking, trying to cajole me into taking her case. She needn't have bothered. I surprised myself with a mildly detached (yet genuine) curiosity about where these two stars could have fallen. Not that I'd ever admit that curiosity to the client.

"Hundred and fifty a day, plus expenses," I interrupted her. "And I'm talking about dollars, not Shoggoth slaves." Hey, I'd been burned before. And trust me when I say: there isn't a scrubber and/or disinfectant in this world (or any other, for that matter) that can completely remove Shoggoth stains from Naugahyde.

The next morning I paid a visit to an old acquaintance at one of the studios. Getting into these places is a whole lot easier than they would like the tourists to think. At least it is if you have a "friend" like Vincent at the front gate. I slipped him a couple of twenties while pretending to ask directions, and he let me in while pretending not to know me.

Now that I think about it, my love life isn't all that different.

Anyway, once you're inside the gates, the key is to look like you know exactly where you're going. It wasn't long before I was walking through a sound stage door with a sign informing me that *Human Pyramid IV: Once More, From the Top* was being shot here. It was lunchtime, so I didn't expect to find any teamsters around, but the guy I was looking for doesn't exactly pay dues. Nor does he have much of a taste for what they're offering at the commissary. I eventually found him in a wardrobe trailer near the closed garage door at the far end of the building.

"How's it been, Phart?" I asked.

I had carefully approached him while his back was turned to me, just so I could enjoy the way he jumped when I spoke.

"Fuck's sake, Phil," he said, turning around. "You wanna warn a guy before you sneak up on him. And it's *Tony*. How many times I gotta tell ya to call me Tony?"

"You're breaking my heart. If it'll make you feel any better, think of Phart as a term of endearment."

I was on a case a couple of years ago when I stumbled upon Phartyaltone's big secret. I had caught him accidentally slipping into his true form in a poorly lit corner of a dingy dive bar near the studio. Comically enough, he had a bad case of hiccups from washing down a handful of pretzels with a mug of badly pulled ale. He's never told me, but I've always assumed he was some sort of Shoggoth prodigy to be able to assume such a convincing disguise. I knew *he knew* I saw him slip, and when I approached him he bought me a round to convince me to keep it under my hat.

His shockingly masterful approximation of the human form, combined with sheer desperation on the part of the fledgling WC network, had been enough to land this sniveling demon his first gig as a production assistant. He liked his job and knew these sorts of hires weren't exactly out in the open, even for a tiny network like The WC. I agreed to keep his secret as long as he agreed to keep his ear to the ground for cases that could prove fiscally advantageous to a man in my profession. Not to get all political, but I knew when I made it that this arrangement had a short shelf-life. It's always been just a matter of time, really.

The way this crazy town operates, it wouldn't surprise me if the various demi-gods and demonic entities working at the studios decided to organize and form a splinter union. God knows, there're enough of them. IATSE Local 666, or some such. I'm halfway surprised no one's organized a benefit on their behalf yet. Maybe Coldplay or U2 or some other socially-conscious bands will record a song about an Outer One trying to make its way in human form, and a new *cause célèbre* will be born. In the meantime, working stiffs like my friend Phart were content to fly under the radar. It's sort of funny how well suited a Shoggoth can be to low-level production work. I guess spending most of your existence toadying to the demands of Elder Things makes one distinctly suitable for work as a PA.

That first PA gig had been on the early seasons of a show called *Lacroix Lacrosse*. As unlikely as it sounds, the show took place in and around the fictitious Lacroix High School in New Orleans, specifically following the demon-hunting members of the ladies' lacrosse team. It was almost as dumb as it sounds. Somehow, it ran for seven seasons. I never watched it, personally. Well, not while sober, at least.

Besides keeping his demonic secret, Phart owed me an actual professional favor. Not long after I first met him and discovered his secret, he fell armpit-deep into a case involving the disappearance of a Craft Services bakery truck. He was still considered the new guy – not to mention he was still mastering how to hold his human-like shape, and people on set *do* like to talk – so everyone was quick to look at the allegedly other-dimensional monster posing as a human when an entire truck full of doughnuts and bagels disappeared. It didn't make much sense to me, considering most Shoggoth are actually gluten intolerant, but I suppose that's not really commonly known. I guess not everyone has my experience with Shoggoths eating pizza then uncontrollably evacuating themselves on the Naugahyde.

Well, in the end it turned out that a member of the show's supporting cast had been on Atkins for a week or two too long, and lost his self-control when he saw the truck double-parked outside the stage door with the keys still in it. He had driven it to a parking garage at LAX and settled into the back to nosh. A buddy of mine who works security at LAX clued me in. I collected a finder's fee from the studio, and I left it for the authorities to determine why the carb-starved actor thought it necessary to be naked, except for a cream horn, while binging on bear claws and pumpernickel bagels. Some mysteries are better left unsolved, if you ask me. Who can figure actors, am I right? It's doubtful if I'll ever feel comfortable eating a cream horn again, I'll tell you that much.

Long story short, Phartyaltone owed me one or

two.

"Whose underwear drawer are you sniffing through this week, Phil?" he asked, turning back to continue sorting call sheets.

"I need find out what you remember about the time those two demon girls first appeared on *Lacroix*."

He stiffened for a second before turning around to face me again.

"Who's got you looking for the twins?" He tried to make it sound casual, conversational.

"Why do you suddenly seem so interested?" I asked, much less conversationally.

His eyes shifted back and forth, studying each of mine in turn. Just when I thought he was about to tell me to go fuck myself, he let his shoulders drop, and his voice broke with a chuckle.

"Knowing you, you'll find out about it anyway," he said. "Nikki and I had sort of a thing. Pretty hot and heavy, I don't mind telling you…"

"I'd really prefer it if you didn't tell me, actually," I interrupted. "How long did that last?"

"Until the night she caught me in a wardrobe trailer with her sister."

Now it was my turn to snort a laugh.

"Dumbass. What were you thinking?"

"I swear, I thought it was her. It was dark, I'd had a few…"

"OK, OK. No need to break out the Cheater's Litany. My line of work, I've heard all of it more times than I could remember. Look, their mom's worried about 'em. You got any info?"

"Well, I was there the night they crossed over, if that's what you're asking about."

"Crossed over?" I asked, tapping a cigarette out of its pack.

"You don't know that story?" he asked incredulously. He pointed at my unlit smoke. "I hope you know you can't light that in here around these costumes, right?"

I respectfully put it back into the pack. I knew all along he was going to say that, and figured my cooperation with his request was likely to keep his gears greased and running smoothly.

"Thanks. Anyway, this ancient text had found its way onto the set when they were shooting that episode. One of the characters was supposed to use it as a prop for a scene. The boy. The asexual one that hung around and lent moral support to the demon-hunting chicks. The problem was that he had been out on a bender the night before and didn't know his lines. So instead of the bullshit hokum in his day pages, the idiot actually read out of the text. When he got to the bottom of the page, the whole set started shaking. Well, even I thought it was just another earthquake, but then the twins appeared immediately behind the actors, in perfect line with the rolling camera.

"An exec from the network happened to be on set that day, negotiating a contract dispute with a couple of the show's stars, and he literally jumped at the chance to sign them as day players. The episode was rewritten to include the newcomers, starting with the fortuitously perfect shot of their arrival. They played out the rest of the season as recurring characters before being killed off along with all of the other fake demons in the season finale. They bummed around the studio for a while, taking bit parts here and there. Their agent landed them the gum commercial, which was pretty huge for their career. The director of that ad was also set as AD for a feature, and the girls began to see themselves on the big studio lot up the road. I know they were involved in a bunch of projects for the rest of that year, but I sort of stopped paying attention. I heard about the Super Bowl fiasco, but that was the last thing I heard until you walked in. By that point I had been cordially invited to stay the fuck out of their lives."

"Think back to that night they first appeared. What can you tell me about the book? What are the chances I could get a look at it?"

"Look, what can I tell ya? Dumb luck. All of it bad. I heard some overzealous prop girl found it in a thrift store while searching for trendy retro t-shirts. Someone told me she found an old 'Three's Company' shirt. It had Chrissy on it and everything."

"So, where's the book now, Phart?"

He exhaled deeply at my continued use of his pet name before answering.

"The book's gone. It burned up in an on-set fire. The way I heard it, that same prop girl tried to hide a lit hash pipe inside of a wooden crate full of shredded paper. The book got caught in the blaze."

"All right, Phart. You got a name for this girl, or do I have to troll the hipster bars looking for a t-shirt with John Ritter on it?"

He thought for a minute.

"I think her name was Charity or Chastity or some kinda stripper name like that. I'm pretty sure I saw her on the lot the other day. Someone mentioned she was working over at Soundstage 13 on that show called *META-Physical*. You know it?"

Sure, I knew it. Two underwear models driving around the country in a muscle car, fighting demons. It was nearly as plausible as *Lacroix Lacrosse*, but with butch guys in denim and leather instead of girls in plaid skirts. I'll admit, I watched the first few seasons when it had a story to tell, but was frankly surprised to hear it was still on the air.

I took leave of my helpful Shoggoth friend and went in search of this mysterious prop girl. I thought if I could get my hands on the book that brought the girls here, it might help me to locate them on this plane. Or something. In all honesty, I wish these extra-dimensional entities would just lose my number. I really don't know from portals and demons. And this making-it-up-as-I-go crap is a pain in the ass.

I crossed the lot to the building with the big 13 on it. The light was on above the door, indicating a hot set, but the door wasn't closed all the way, so I slipped inside. In the minute it took for my eyes to adjust to the darkness inside the soundstage, it would have been easy to believe I had just stepped into a large empty room. Or, as my vivid imagination ran away with me, a large room full of dead, bloody bodies. Shaking that image off, I began to move toward a cluster of lights at one end. As I approached, I began to hear the actors talking on the set. Even in person, the two leads of this show appeared to be genetic anomalies. Some kinda master race bullshit. One sported a perfectly square jaw and pronounced chin dimple, the combination of which exuded a sort of charming boyish manliness (or manly boyish charm, maybe; I'm no casting director). The other was a sort of missing link, towering well over six and a half feet, with a sloped forehead and hair thicker than the pile carpeting my uncle had in the back of his Sun Cruiser van in the seventies. While they worked through their dialogue, the crew moved about the set silently. They were filming a scene that appeared to be happening inside a squalid interstate motel room. The dimpled one was yelling at the giant one for getting sick in the back seat of their car. Except it wasn't puke, the other one defended himself, it was ectoplasm. Dimples went on to yell some more about the car, and Gigantor made light of Dimples' relationship with the car. It went on like that for a few minutes before anyone noticed me standing there.

"Can I help you?" The voice whispered into my right ear from behind. I spun around to face a bespectacled woman holding a clipboard.

Matching her whisper, I went into my best Tinseltown charmer mode.

"Are you one of the producers?" I asked.

She shook her head, but I detected the tiniest whiff of a smile turning at one corner of her mouth.

"*I wish*. No, I'm a production assistant," she intoned. "You, I don't know."

"The union sent me. I need to verify the names of your prop people."

She seemed taken aback, which was exactly what I wanted.

"Oh! Uh…I don't really have that list. If you want to talk to Gypsy, I'll go see if I can get it for you." As she whispered, she led me away from the set toward a table strewn with crucifixes, crystal vials, and medieval-looking weaponry.

Behind this table sat a girl in her twenties. She was wearing a black hoodie, black jeans, and a black trucker cap. Her black boots rested on the corner of the table. But it all looked like washed-out gray compared to her hair. The box of hair color must have been labeled, "Complete and Utter Absence of Light #9." As we approached, she looked up from a dog-eared paperback. She let the pages close over her index finger, and I caught a glimpse of the unmistakably lurid cover of a convenience store romance novel.

"Miss Lee?" my escort whispered. "This gentleman is from the union. He needs to talk to you."

Miss Lee slowly put her feet on the floor and sat forward in the chair.

"Gypsy," she said. "What can I do for you?"

Miss Lee. Gypsy Lee. The "stripper name" Phart couldn't remember.

"Your middle name Rose?" I asked.

She looked a dagger at me and started to return to her book. "Hilarious," she said flatly. "I never get that one."

I quickly disabused her of my ruse, so that I could explain the true reason for my visit. She couldn't even bring herself to try to appear interested. Once I started to talk about the spell book, however, the crack of her chewing gum slowed and her eyes met mine again. I took this for an encouraging sign. When I relayed to her Phart's gossip about the destruction of said book being facilitated by her careless placement of a hash pipe, her nostrils flared, and she leaped to her feet.

"That motherfucker said WHAT!?!" Her outburst brought forth a stunned silence throughout the set, broken only by the director's annoyed command to "CUT!"

"I can't believe that guy," she continued, once we had stepped outside of the soundstage. "I mean, there was a fire on set. I didn't have anything to do with it, though. And the fire was put out quick. A couple props were messed up, but that stupid book wasn't there the next day."

"So there wasn't a hash pipe?" I asked.

"Well, yeah," she snorted, "but I left it in Brock's trailer after lunch."

"Brock…?"

"Brock Nichols." She sounded a little disappointed in me for not knowing who Brock Nichols was. "You know… *Harry*? The lacrosse team manager on the show? He was only, like, the heart and soul of the demon killers, even without any superpowers. The hapless eunuch Jiminy Cricket to the other girls on the show. Did you never watch *Lacroix' Lacrosse*?"

"Was Jiminy Cricket a eunuch? Nevermind. Is it possible that the book could have been stolen?" I asked, hoping to catch a break and get back on track.

"I suppose. For all I know, it was burned beyond recognition and tossed during the post-blaze cleanup."

I realized that someone was lying to me, and it was pissing me off. Not only that, but I still wasn't any closer to finding the two girls than I was before their mom slithered into my office that morning. It was time to call a strategy meeting with Big Rich.

I could always talk to Big Rich. It was probably the best relationship I'd ever had. He pours the drinks, never cuts me off, and listens to everything I say. Occasionally he'll grunt an acknowledgement or laugh, but mostly he just tends the bar while I talk my way through the sticky cases. His place was the living embodiment of a dive bar. It's true. Some Hollywood location scout or another pops in here a couple of times a month, looking to shoot the latest Tarantino, or whatever, in here. And a couple of times a month, a Hollywood location scout spends the evening at home researching how to remove poop stains from his pants and reevaluating his career choices. I can't begin to understand Big Rich's reasons for routing these guys with the gusto he employs, but it's a hell of a lot of fun to watch.

Rich loves to tell the tale of how he was once a semi-famous luchador by the name of "El Ricardo Grande." I looked him up online, and it turned out he was totally telling the truth. During one of his bouts, he took a nasty tumble out of the ring and into a metal table by way of a guy selling cerveza. The melted ice in the vendor's cooler and several shattered bottles' worth of Modelo hit a power outlet under the table at the same instant Rich's body crashed on top of it. Any man less than 6'7" and 280 pounds probably would never have walked away from the arena that night. Even at his size, that level of electrical jolt came with a price.

Big Rich just wasn't altogether there. If you ask me, something in the wiring of his brain short-circuited that night. A conversation with Rich could range anywhere from his wrestling days, to the motorcycle he'd been fixing up for the past decade, to the time he wandered across the border into New Mexico and was picked up as a hitchhiker by a van full of extra-dimensional tentacle-demons who handed him over to aliens. These aliens, in turn, took him aboard their UFO for experimentation. In the latter case, he's more than willing to describe the process by which the aliens installed a device in his rectum, and how no matter how much he strains when he shits, he just can't seem to push the damned thing out. Someday, he's sure, someone is going to come for him. He doesn't know if it will be the aliens or the demons or the government, but he knows it's only a matter of time. He keeps a bag under the bar with a change of underwear and a new toothbrush, just in case.

Don't get me wrong here; most of the time, Big Rich stares off blankly and lets me talk my way through a problem until I spring him into action by asking for another round. Occasionally, Rich will experiment with some new exotic cocktail. For reasons I cannot fully comprehend, he seems to relish using me as his guinea pig for his mixological forays into the unknown.

Like I said, it's the ideal relationship.

But that night, he wasn't feeling particularly loquacious and neither was I. I felt like I was chasing my tail with this case. My leads on the spell book had become dead ends. And I never really had a plan for what to do once I had it, anyway. Not only that, but after a full day I couldn't even report a whiff of a lead on the location of the girls. It seemed I was probably going to be cutting the client loose in the morning. And I hate cutting clients loose. It stinks of failure.

I took my first sip of Rich's newest creation, which he was calling "Shaolin Throat Punch." As near as I could tell, it was composed of rice wine, sour cherry liqueur, and lime. While waiting for the tendons in my throat to relax from the drink's unique assault, I began to settle comfortably into a vigorous session of wallowing self-deprecation. I was interrupted by Rich's wondering voice drifting across the bar.

"What in the twelve fucks?"

This was Rich's favorite expression of disbelief. I had playfully asked him one night whether he could tell me what it meant and explain the twelve fucks. I had made a crack about it being like the twelve days of Christmas. With a gleam in his eye and a wide smile, he had merely said, "You've never been a famous luchador, my friend." I'm still not sure even *he* knows what he meant by that, but I'll be damned if I'm ever going to ask about it again.

I glanced up to see what had elicited his outburst this time. He was standing at his post behind the nearly empty bar, watching a television mounted to the wall behind me. I casually spun on my barstool just enough to see the screen. Call me a cynic, but I couldn't tell you of another time when something genuinely made my jaw drop in awe. There, in a box in the top left corner of the screen, floating over the shoulder of some blonde sitting behind a news desk, were Nikky and Nicci.

"Yo, Rich!" I called out without removing my

eyes from the TV. "Where's the sound?"

I heard a small rustle behind me, then the volume bars appeared on the screen, ascending from left to right as the sound faded up.

"...are they now? Well, there's no longer a need to ask that question. The twins have landed in Vegas. Nicci and Nikky will be headlining at the Seven Rings Casino starting next week. Just what will their act be like? We spoke with Empty Lot operator Conway J. Zarh, Jr., who had this to say: 'I tell ya, these girls aren't really what I'd normally put on my stage. I doubt I'll be doing any surprise dressing room inspections, if you know what I mean. But there's no denying that they'll draw a crowd.' The new show is scheduled to begin early next month..."

I tossed money on the bar as I gathered myself to get up from the stool. My barely-touched drink stared up at me.

"You missed the good part, man," Rich laughed. "Before the news anchor started talking, it showed those two tentacled chicks dancing. It looked like a rehearsal or something. They were covered in those, whattaya call 'em...*sequins,* and had feathers at the ends of all their tentacles. I tell ya, the last time I saw tentacles like that, they were on their way into..."

I was out the door before I could hear any more of Rich's newest abduction story. I needed a fresh change of clothes and a cup of coffee. It was already late in the day to start the four-hour drive to Vegas.

Several hours later, as my hatchback crept along

210

the Strip, I began to recall how much I hated Vegas. There are those who see it as an oasis in the desert, as some kind of a Bacchanalian playground where the rules of the outside world no longer apply. Like Disneyland for adult sensibilities. I look at it and all I see is a roiling pit of people who have come on a pilgrimage to get whatever it is they feel they don't have. The whole town reeks of desperation sweat and cheap body spray. It's like Times Square exploded into an entire town. The lights are too bright and the sounds are too loud. Every doorway of every building tries too hard to get your attention. It's seedy and debauched, but not in the good way. Not like a Tom Waits song. There's nothing musical or truthful about the Vegas version of seediness and debauchery. It's a compliment from a lap dancer; as soon as your money stops flowing, you know the show's going to be over.

I paused outside of the front entrance of the Nine Rings after handing my key over to the valet. As noisy and assaulting as the Strip was, I knew it would be worse in the enclosed space of the casino beyond the doors. Especially this particular one. The Nine Rings was named thus because of its distinction as the only structure in all of Vegas built as eight progressive subbasements, each one a ring and each deeper underground than the one above it. It reminded me of an inverted Guggenheim Museum. It was started about a decade ago by a couple of slimy real estate developer brothers named Gareth and Allen Durante. It's believed the structure was built as the foundation and parking garage for a high-rise hotel/casino; when the funding fell through for that development, the

211

Durantes swept in and purchased it for a song.

Rather than build on top of it, they repurposed it, put a single ground-level story on top, and opened the doors. The front doors from the valet loop open into a revolving lobby, which constitutes the first of the nine rings. The inner wall of this eternal waiting area is lined with elevators, each of which lowers guests down into the literal depths of depravity. Word is that the lowest levels are reserved for the elite and are strictly "invitation only." There is an urban legend about some sort of death matches taking place nightly down in subbasement seven, and a longstanding unconfirmed rumor that anyone caught cheating or stealing from the casino on the fourth sublevel is taken down to the eighth, never to be seen or heard from again.

The majority of patrons of the Nine Rings don't descend any deeper than sublevel four, which is the casino floor. Sublevel three is the kitchen level, where various eateries, bakeries, and lounges surround a full food court. I wouldn't need to go any deeper into the joint than the second level, if my study of the building's directory was accurate. Even if I weren't slightly claustrophobic, I couldn't imagine anyone voluntarily descending into the ground under this desert. Still, I had to grudgingly admit that installing a casino eight stories into the desert floor was a pretty cool idea. Taking a deep breath, I stepped into an open elevator.

I stopped short inside the compartment, faced with a grotesque portrait of casino co-founder Allen Durante. It was painted directly onto an American flag in what must have been some sort of ersatz political statement, sealed into a gold frame, and hung on the back wall of the elevator. I don't really follow politics, but this particular paragon of avarice is currently sitting in the Senate Chamber, representing the barren wasteland of Nevada. The continued success of this family is a mystery to vex even the savviest analyst. The Durantes had appeared on the scene in the mid-eighties, their sleazy gilt opulence quickly discovered by syndicated newspaper cartoonists and late-night talk show monologue writers alike to be an easy source of comedy gold. So to speak. Somehow, the constant lampooning and satire embedded them in the collective consciousness of the nation. A bestselling book, a few hundred radio and television interviews, a reality show or two, and Al found himself positioned to become the self-appointed anointed savior of modern conservative politics. His brother Gareth ("Gaz") has been running the casino while he "moonlights" at his other gig in Washington.

All I know is *I* wouldn't have voted for the guy.

I stepped out of the elevator onto the second sublevel. According to the sign above the stairs, the Nine Rings' theatre concourse, with all the stage acts and nearly-nude dancing girls, was on this floor. Lacking a better plan, I chose to throw myself on the mercy of Lady Luck and hope that the girls were here and rehearsing. Discovering a sign announcing the impending premiere of Nicci and Nikki's stage show on the wall outside of a set of dark-paneled, closed doors, I decided to play a hunch. I only had to wait outside the theatre doors for four minutes before someone exited. I quietly

213

grabbed the door as it swung shut, and I waltzed through. Glancing over my shoulder, I looked back through the closing door and saw the stage technician who had unwittingly given me access crossing the hallway toward the men's room. I started to think that luck might be on my side, for once. This, of course, gave me pause to wonder whether I should bag this plan and head down to the tables instead.

"No, no, no!"

A male voice echoed from somewhere in the direction of the stage. Light rigs littered the area, and a couple of technicians were quietly running cables and making adjustments to the instruments mounted on the rigging. Another hand pushed a mop and bucket around the apron of the stage. The voice I had heard hadn't come from either of them. Scanning across the stage and the tables directly adjacent to it, I spotted an upright piano in the aisle. It had been placed along the far end of the row.

"You come in on the fourth beat, not the third!"

The voice had come from a man sitting at the piano. He had spun around on the bench to face one of the tables. And at that table sat the two tentacled entities I had been hired to find. Occasionally, this job is as simple as figuring out where to look. As far as I could tell, they both looked like they were ready to devour the piano guy. Or at least drop his piano on him. It seemed he was able to sense their impending mutiny as well.

"Look, let's take fifteen," he said. "I need a Quaalude."

Their tension dispelled, the girls allowed themselves to slump back into their seats. Watching

214

the piano player disappear through a side exit, I sidled down the aisle toward the stage. I generally don't like to sneak up on people, so I followed a slightly-longer-than-necessary track in order to cross in front of the first row of seats, in full view of Nikky and Nicci. They watched me approach them through red-rimmed eyestalks. The shared begrudging daze with which they regarded me spoke of many hours of rehearsal and very little sleep.

"Who are you, now?" one of them asked. It might have been Nikky.

"Girls, you mom's worried about you," I stated plainly. "She hired me to track you down."

It looked to me as if Nicci was relieved by my presence, but Nikky immediately began to huff and puff.

"Oh, is that right?" Nikky asked. "Well, dear old mum can go and—"

"Dear old mum can buy a ticket just like everyone else," said a voice from the stage behind me. I spun around to find myself looking into the eyes of Gaz Durante his own damn self. "Now, who the hell are you, and what do you think you're doing with my newest stars?"

He stalked out of the stage right wings, flanked by three casino security guards. It's hardly a secret that I'm not in the best of shape. One guard probably would have been enough. I couldn't help but feel slightly flattered by the gesture, if I'm being honest.

"I'm afraid I'm here to take the girls back to their mother," I said, hoping that my voice didn't betray how taken aback I was at being confronted by such a famously pugnacious son of an infamous son of a bitch. His chuckle forced me to think that my attempts at calm bravado had failed.

"Well, that's going to pose a problem," he sneered. "They've already signed a contract. Now, if we have nothing further to discuss, I'll ask these three gentlemen to escort you to the elevators."

Now, it's a four-hour drive from Los Angeles to Las Vegas. Radio reception is lousy, and there's not much to see along the way. All of which meant that I had spent the past several hours deciding on a course of action in case of this exact scenario. I pulled out my cell phone and found a number in my contacts.

As the girls looked on and the three security guards lumbered down from the front of the stage, I listened to the phone ring on the other end. I looked up at Junior, offering him a reassuring nod as I held up my right index finger to indicate that I would appreciate one minute of his patient forbearance. The three security team members looked back at their boss apprehensively. Truthfully, my heart was slowly crawling up through my throat a little more with every unanswered ring. It occurred to me that I should probably have coordinated this part of the plan with my client before setting foot into the belly of the beast.

Standing, looking from one of the three galoots surrounding me to another and then the other, I tried my damnedest not to show any visible relief when I heard the click and the raspy voice at the other end.

"Ms. Kassogtha?" I asked the phone. "I want to put you on speaker. Is that OK?"

She growled her consent into my ear and I held

216

the phone out in front of me.

"Can you hear me?" I asked the phone in my hand.

The speaker crackled slightly before she assented.

"I'm here with Mr. Durante," I said, "and I have a question I'm hoping you can clarify."

"It must be Gaz! How have you been?" Kassie crackled through the speaker. "How's M'Elle?"

The man in front of me squirmed as he realized who was speaking to him. As for me, I had no idea who this M'Elle was or even how she might have known the man in front of me.

"He's..." Gaz stammered. "He's OK, I guess. Our arrangement is a bit confusing. I have to act like his servant, but I'm also his guardian, right? He still begs me to let him out. I won't, though," he added hastily.

"My husband told you M'Elle was a craven negotiator," she said. "But I know you're standing firm against his entreaties, considering all that Cthulhu has done for you and that brother of yours. Amassing wealth is child's play, but political manipulation isn't nearly as easy as it once was. It wasn't really that long ago that Warren Harding had that 'indigestion problem,' which offered such benefits for dear Mr. Coolidge. I'm certain you can appreciate the debt you owe my husband and, by association, me."

I still wasn't sure I understood this conversation.

"Well, yeah, sure," Gaz said. I could tell by the way his shoulders stiffened that he was beginning to regain his footing with my client. "Of course I do. He's still sealed exactly where he was confined centuries ago underneath this very stage." Watching him talk, I remembered the reasons why I have often fantasized about testes-punching this man whom I've never met before. "And as such," he continued, "I fail to see any reason that I should extend any further favors to you."

See? Right there. The shit just went sideways. Now THAT'S familiar territory for me.

"Meaning what, exactly?" I asked.

His eyes moved up from the phone in my hand to my face.

"Meaning that these girls of hers signed a legally-binding contract with our company, and I expect them to follow through with it."

"Ms. Kassogtha, quick question," I said to the phone. "How old are your girls?"

"It has been nearly twelve millennia since they sprung into the cosmos, clawing their way from the cavernous maw of my womb," she answered.

"And, as unnecessarily robust as that answer was," I said slowly, "I'm wondering something. After twelve millennia, the twins must have racked up quite a slew of ex-boyfriends, right? Pretty things like them, and all…"

I turned my attention to the twins. One of them seemed to have released some form of excrement, but neither seemed willing to acknowledge it.

"Certainly not," Kassogtha said with derision. "Cthulhu and I have enough to worry about without entertaining the possibility that our sweet girls could be establishing themselves as mating partners to lesser entities. We have been really working on our relationship lately, and it's been seriously all-consuming."

218

"Ok, so how old would the girls need to be before you would give them your blessing?"

"That's a well-established house rule: no dating a day before their eighteenth millennia," she said flatly, before resuming her explanation of her marital woes. "Cthulhu is just so consumed with his work. It's always 'conquer this' and 'destroy that' with him. We just don't talk anymore. I remember a time when he would take me along on his sieges. Not anymore, though. And it just makes me so sad. I can't even appreciate the acrid smell of burning flesh like I used to…"

"Thanks…talk soon," I replied, flipping the phone shut.

I knew that hang-up meant that I would have to explain myself later, but hoped she would exhibit some benevolence with regard to my process. I just really hate it when clients get too comfortable and start oversharing.

In the meantime, I had a slightly disoriented son of a casino owner in front of me.

"So, Gareth. Gary? *Gaz*," I began, embracing my inner cheekiness. "I'm not sure it would look that great for your senator brother if word got out that the casino he half-owns was employing two under-aged girls in a stage show without the consent of their parents. Am I right?"

His cheeks flushed a shocking shade of purplish crimson. I wish I could say that I am not the type of person who takes pleasure in moments like this, but I'd be lying. Behind me, the girls were whispering to each other. I could feel them moving around to stand behind me, as if they were seeking shelter.

"This changes nothing!" Gaz spluttered. "I have

signed contracts! I'll tie this up in the courts for the rest of the decade! I'll… I'll…"

"Give it a rest, kid," came a gravelly voice from backstage. "For shit's sake, have a little dignity."

Around the corner slithered a worm-like sack of a creature. Much to the chagrin of the stagehand with the mop, this newcomer left a visible trail of slime across the stage. The techie quietly shook his head as he wrung out the mop and went back to work.

"I swear, I don't know what goes on inside that tiny head of yours, child," the worm said to Junior. "Hey, how's it goin'?" he cast casually toward me before turning his attention back to Durante's reddened face. "You really think it's a good idea to piss off Cthulhu? Let the dick in the cheap suit take the girls back to their mama."

I could tell that the next words to come out of Gareth Durante's mouth were quite possibly the most difficult he'd ever had to utter.

"Yes, Lord Shudde M'ell," he squeezed through clenched teeth. "I live to serve you."

"Damn straight," Shudde M'ell said. "If you're angry, you have my permission to go down to one of the kitchens on sublevel three and beat on a sand dweller or two. Just make sure not to disrupt dinner service. It's Taco Tuesday."

We both watched Gaz sulk his way out of the room before M'ell spoke again. On a side note, I had to give the younger Brother Durante credit; for a man in his late forties, he could sulk as well as any teenager I've ever seen. After he was gone, M'ell turned back to me with a sharp intake of breath.

"Listen…" he hesitated, "uhh…?"

"Phil," I cued him. "Phil Howard."

"Mr. Howard, I hope you'll extend my best to your client. I've been stuck in this burrow of a casino for so long, I didn't even recognize the girls. The last time I saw them, they were still suckling at Kassie's elongated teats. How well I remember that day, watching the salty saliva glistening…"

I needed to stop this demonic worm entity from embarrassing himself (and/or sickening me) any further.

"Look," I said, holding a hand up toward him, "as far as I can tell, no harm was done. The girls seem OK, right?"

He looked over my shoulder at Nikky and Nicci, who had been watching the proceedings with detached interest.

"Yeah," M'ell said. "Yeah, sure." He leaned in toward me, close enough that my eyes watered at the fungal odor of his breath. "I'd appreciate it – as a personal favor – if you'd put in a good word for me with their mom, you know? Maybe her old man could do something about this *under-dweller* situation I can't seem to escape?"

"I'll be sure to tell them how cooperative you were about all this," I assured him. I was ready to go. Turning, I cocked an eyebrow at the girls. "Ladies?"

Topside, we held up the valet loop outside for nearly a half hour trying to find a way to fit my passengers into a two-door coupe hatchback. In the end, we laid down the back seat and pushed both front seats as far forward as they would go. Even

221

then, both girls had to clamber in through the back hatch. It was likely they hadn't been that close to each other since the womb. I had to tie their luggage on the roof. Luckily, Shudde M'ell was forthcoming with strong bungee straps. I didn't ask.

Not only was my driver's seat pushed far enough forward that the steering wheel was causing the kind of chafing they don't make ointment for, but the seat back had to be completely upright. And this was a four-hour drive. Between that and the weird swampy smell (which one of the girls was trying to cover up with inordinate amounts of patchouli), my patience for this job had worn as thin as my car's balding tires.

The ride had started with the typical tropes of a sibling road trip.

"Stop touching me!"

"Hey, that was my chewing gum!"

"Watch where you put that tentacle!"

It went on for about a half hour. Then it settled into a half hour of sullen silence, during which one of the girls farted sporadically, filling the vehicle with the kind of rotting pumpkin aroma you just can't ever get rid of. I tried the radio, but the front speakers were fried – and the girls were pressed against the rear speakers, effectively blocking them – so I turned it off. By the time we reached the second hour of our journey, I had found some sort of Zen self-preservation space, deep inside myself, where my knees didn't ache and my lower back wasn't screaming and I wasn't awash in pumpkin-fart-laden air. I became aware of them whispering to each other just moments before one of them (Nikky, I think) leaned forward.

"What is our mother's plan for us?" she asked.

I looked back into the rear view mirror.

"How should I know?" I snapped. "Do they practice corporal punishment where you come from?"

I felt her body shrink away from the back of my seat. Glancing in the mirror again, I saw her expression fall just as her sister's eyes went livid.

"Oh, you think we deserve a spanking? We should be punished for being ripped from our home dimension and trapped here on your miserable, stinking plane? Where we can't slither five feet without getting dog shit or chewing gum or a cigarette butt on our tentacles? Because it's been nothing but a party for us, I'll tell you!"

"Hey, look, I'm sorry," I relented. "I'm just... I'm sorry. I shouldn't have answered like that. I don't know if I understand what your sister was asking. Is she worried that you'll be in trouble with your mom?"

The first one found her voice again.

"No, nothing like that. We've been in the shit with Mother before. What I'm wondering is if she has a plan for releasing us from this plane."

I didn't answer immediately, because I hadn't given it any thought. Sure, I was hired to find them and bring them back to their mom, and that's what I was doing. But did the job stop there? At what point does my responsibility end? Their mother never gave any explicit indication that she expected me to assist in the cleanup of this situation – but did she ever imply it? I ran through the mental tapes of every interaction I'd had with Kassogtha in the past couple of days, searching for some missed signal.

Meanwhile, her girls gazed at me with impatience from the back of the car. I was certain that the wrong response to this query would very likely result in my continued involvement with this damned family. My aching hips and borderline claustrophobia were triggering a primal need to wash my hands of this case as quickly as possible. I just wanted to drop the girls off with their mom, collect my check, and go drink a six-pack or two under a pier somewhere.

"She didn't really say, that I recall," I confided. "How would that sort of thing happen, do you think?"

"It should be simple enough, really," one of them said. I didn't bother looking back to figure out which one was talking. "All we need is the book with the incantation that summoned us and the person who performed it."

"The person who…" I trailed off, considering this requirement. "You mean that actor who read the incantation?"

The sister who had become nettled a few moments ago demonstrated her continued disagreeableness.

"Yes, that's who she means. God, you're thick!"

Silence fell in the car, save for the whine of tires on the desert highway and an occasional quiffle from shifting, enclosed tentacles. After several uncomfortable moments of searching frantically through my brain for a new topic of conversation, seeking something (anything!) to keep the question from coming, Nicci asked quietly: "Do you think you could help us find him? And maybe even track down the book?"

Dammit.

After a bit of strategical discussion, one of the girls was able to extract her apparently-water-resistant smart phone from I'd-rather-not-know-where and find Brock Nichol's agent's number on the actor's movie database page. Nikky surprised me a little with her vocal performance as the actor's syphilitic jilted lover. She played it sympathetic, but with a resolve that made it impossible to argue with her. Having seen some of her prior work, I didn't expect her to have the depth, frankly. It became clear that the agent found her performance equally revelatory. After some minor persuasion, she was able to extract from the agent the address where he expected his client to be working into the evening. I exited I-15, readjusting my route to take us to Burbank and from there into the Valley.

This rerouting proved to be a deep miscalculation on my part. From a strictly geographic standpoint, it was the quickest way to reach our new destination, but I failed to take into account the effect of curving mountainous terrain on the constitution of a several-thousand-year-old preteen cramped into the back of a compact car with her twin sister. In a grasp for the slimmest of silver linings, I noted that the transformation of my vehicle from modest hatchback to rolling vomitorium seemed to be confined to the passenger side. I pulled the car over at a wide spot in the highway, joining a broken-down tour bus. A dense group of giggling sugar-saturated Harajuku girls, returning from a day trip to Angeles National Forest, was milling around the graveled area while their driver radioed for assistance and swore profanely at the smoking front end of the bus.

My car's approach garnered much curiosity and more than a few flashbulbs, but when I opened the hatch to let Nicci and Nikky clamber out, the entire squadron of chittering rainbow-haired tourists exploded into a frenzied paroxysm of instamatic camera flashes and squeals. I stepped in to try to protect the girls, particularly Nicci, whom I would have expected to need plenty of fresh air and open space to prevent further hurling. But they seemed happy to interact with the swooning fans.

After an hour of autograph signing, selfies, and gummy bear consumption, the tour bus choked back to life, and we were finally able to get back on the road. This impromptu fan junket gave me the time I needed to clean and air out the right half of the car. I eventually pulled my passenger-rich car around the still-loading bus and back onto the highway. Thanks to my deft negotiation skills with the sole English-speaking member of the group, Nicci and Nikky waved to the gathering with tentacles bearing thirty-seven anti-nausea wristbands. I honestly didn't know if the acupressure points for my charges would be compatible with those of humans, but they seemed to do the trick. I'll admit to experiencing a twang of guilt when I thought of the likelihood that thirty-seven candy-laden stomachs were now eighty-five percent more likely to void themselves inside that poor driver's bus. The other result of my negotiation was a strawberry-scented plush snail with big cartoon eyes dangling from the rear-view mirror, which masked the worst of the smell from Nicci's earlier regurgitation.

We made it the rest of the way to the address in Chatsworth without further incident. Kassogtha was already there, waiting for us next to an enormous SUV. She and her girls shared a joyous reunion involving what seemed to largely consist of waggling their extended tongues in each other's directions and slapping their tentacles on the ground. While this ritual was observed, I took a moment to regard the house to which we had been directed. The agent Nikky had sweet-talked had said that Mr. Nichols would be shooting here into the evening, but I could see no indication of a film crew. There was no Craft Services truck, no equipment van, and not even a single production trailer. With my client and her daughters still reconnecting, I crept up the driveway to investigate.

I approached the front window, where I was relieved to see the glow of the scoop lights commonly used for indoor filming. That sense of relief puddled around my ankles when I peeked through the window to the scene inside. I stood transfixed, and only the muffled chime of a doorbell broke my trance.

Unbeknownst to me, Kassie and her girls had crept up the driveway behind me and were standing at the front door. Even as I moved to stop them, the door swung open and a sallow man in a ball cap blinked at them.

"Can I… help you?" the man asked hesitantly.

"We seek the one called Brock Nichols," Kassogtha stated simply.

"Listen, this is a…" Yankees Cap stammered, "I mean, we're in the middle of a…"

I stepped up behind them just in time to see

227

Brock Nichols step around the corner wearing nothing but a smile.

"Nikki! Niccy! Or is it Nikky and Nicci? I never was able to keep that straight!" the naked actor beamed. As he bounded up to the girls, his half-mast member bounced jauntily like a dog's uncertain tail wag. "What the hell are you doing here? Where have you been? God, I haven't heard anything about you since that Oscar thing. I know how much they hate it when you go off-book at those things. How the hell are you?"

As we all entered the living room, he gestured toward his four equally-naked co-stars. The room reeked of cheap lube and latex. "Ladies, can we take fifteen?" The brunette needed some help from the other three in getting down from her perch on the back of the sofa, because of her high heels.

A placard on a nearby chair identified the cinematic masterpiece in the making as *Miss Congeniality 5: Warts and All*. I waited until someone brought Brock a robe, and he sat down with Nikky and Nicci before I approached the three of them. He hadn't stopped talking since the front door, and there was rabid wildness in the back of his eyes. This kid probably should have joined half of his co-stars and gone directly from the show's wrap party into rehab. But instead, it would seem, he chose a career in porn. I can't say I blame him. At least this way he's more likely to get laid.

Kassie was in a corner, talking on her cell phone, while the young(ish) star and his former cast-mates played catchup. The guy with the ball cap who had answered the door, as it turned out, was the director of this libidinous cinematic treatise.

He paced the floor in the adjoining room, muttering to himself. I could tell he was annoyed with the filming delay, but he seemed far more interested in listening in on my client's phone conversation. I turned my attention back to the young actor and the twins on the sofa.

"…and remember the time they were filming the restaurant scene and the characters had to share a cheese plate and all the cheese turned out to have been replaced with slivers cut from bars of soap and everyone blamed Kirk Cameron because he was a guest star that episode but kept complaining about the characters using God's name in vain and so he got fired? That was totally me. Oh! And remember…"

"Excuse me. I hate to break up your…whatever you're doing, but..."

Brock and both of the girls looked up at me from where they sat on the sofa.

"Hey," he said with a sudden flash of smile. "Have we met?"

I nodded toward Kassogtha across the room.

"Their mom hired me to track down her girls for her."

"Well, all right! 'Cause here they are. You must be pretty good at your job."

He smiled expansively at me.

"Uh, yeah," I replied. I looked questioningly around the room. "Listen, do you mind if I ask…?"

He leaned forward with his elbows on his knees, suddenly *all business*. Well, except for the fact that this move shifted his robe to reveal the tool of his new trade. He didn't seem to notice. I determinedly kept my eyes locked on his face as he began nodding his head.

"Uh-huh. Uh-huh. The thing is, I spent seven seasons as the sexless mascot of a show with seven incredibly hot girls." He looked fondly at Nicci and Nikky. "Well, nine for a while there." Both of the girls' typically mottled, grey coloring turned momentarily brownish, and I realized they were blushing. "When it ended, I took a break. Did some drugs. Did a little traveling. Checked into rehab for a few days. You know, the typical Young Hollywood package. One of those nights at the clinic, I had a moment of clarity. Or I got horny. Whichever it was, I checked myself out the next morning and launched my porn career. It turns out they love it when the mainstream actors cross over like that. Sasha Grey had it all wrong."

None of this had anything to do with what I wanted to ask him. While he prattled, I had time to consider just how bad a porn set smells.

"Yeah. Fine," I growled, still trying not to look at the alarming length of his exposed dangly bits. "The girls here need to be released from the spell you used to trap them here on Earth. Any chance you remember the incantation that brought them over?"

His glassy eyes stared up at me for a significant percentage of a full minute before he shook his head.

"Dude, I had a hard time remembering my lines for today's scene, and they mostly consist of grunts and moans. Actually, it's a pretty great acting exercise, if you don't mind me getting all 'it's about the craft.' The key to really selling those noises is the timing. The timing is extremely crucial. An ill-placed grunt when it should have been a moan can turn a hot scene into a comedy. I did an intense study of Peter Boyle in *Young Frankenstein* to prepare for this shoot tonight. Usually, I dig into my Stanislavsky techniques for the really challenging scenes. For example, when I walk on set for a gangbang scene, I reach down deep into my emotional memories and acquire my core feelings of intensely needing to have sex with multiple women. I was thinking of doing a workshop, actually…"

"Great. That sounds great," I interrupted. "Hey, sorry to jump off-topic here, but if I can find the book with the incantation, and a way to reverse it, do you think you'd be able to help free your friends?"

"Well, if it's something that'll help the ladies here," he grinned, "I'm the hero you're looking for."

"Great." I turned toward the door. "I'm going to leave them here for a while. Back soon."

Kassogtha put a tentacle over her phone and turned toward me with some alarm.

"Where are you going?" she demanded.

"I had some time in the car to piece all this together," I told her. "I know who has the spell book."

The situation had changed a bit by the time I returned to the house two-and-a-half hours later. It took longer than I had imagined it would. I had to track down Phart, then threaten and beat him until he gave up the location of the book. Then I needed to find a way to restrain Phart so I could retrieve the book, then navigate from Burbank back to Chatsworth with my less-than-favorite movie industry insider.

The first and most unsettling difference in the scene was the attendance of Cthulhu himself. Or, I supposed later, an aspect of him. The entire house felt colder and damper for his presence. He and Kassogtha were talking with the adult film director in the front room, where the cameras and scoop lights had been turned off after our disruption of their shooting schedule. Kassie had just turned toward her husband/spawning partner/eternal consort. I couldn't see her face, but a shiver of hopeful entreaty quivered the base of several of her rear tentacles. The director tried to appear detached, but his hawkish stare and the way he rocked slightly on his heels, clutching the bill of the Yankees cap now held in front of him, betrayed his anxiety. They seemed to be discussing some sort of business deal.

"What do you think, beloved?" she said. "We've been looking for ways to reinvigorate our partnership…"

Cthulhu looked from Kassie to the director and back.

"I just don't know, Kass. A sex tape?" Cthulhu's bass rumble shook the room.

"A CELEBRITY sex tape," the director corrected vehemently. "THE celebrity sex tape to end all celebrity sex tapes. It would be bigger than Pam and Tommy! And think about it: we could cross-market internationally as the first-ever live-action hentai tentacle porn flick!"

Cthulhu drew a breath and exhaled audibly, seeming to take offense.

"Any project involving the great and mighty Cthulhu should never be addressed with an appellate as reductive as 'flick'!" he stated, raising himself up to an even more imposing stature. The director shrank away from him, raising his hands to plead mercy for his poor word choice.

At that instant, Cthulhu noticed me standing in the doorway with Phart, the ancient text tucked under my left arm.

"What is the meaning of this?" he demanded.

Kassogtha turned to see the focus of his newest outburst. Her eyes narrowed when they reached my captive.

"Not sure how much the old ball-and-chain filled you in, but I have the book and the guy responsible for hiding it." I explained. "I thought you might have some words for him."

The ancient one slid past me to invade the personal space of my bound informant, who, I suddenly realized, was pale and quaking with fear.

"*You.*"

The simplicity of Cthulhu's accusation was shadowed by the ferocity of its subtext. I suddenly felt like I had come in at the end of a movie. Phart, to my surprise, exhaled a chuckle.

"I can't believe you didn't know this was my doing," he laughed. "I did my best to put my fingerprints all over it."

"You will suffer a millennium of scabrous wounds for this," Cthulhu stated simply.

"Do your worst," the man I knew as Phartyaltone sneered. "It was worth the laugh."

I sidled over to Kassogtha while the two continued to barb each other.

"What's going on here?" I asked.

"How do you know this being you have brought before us?" she asked, her eyes never leaving the verbal duel.

"He's just some stage hand I know," I replied. "I use him as an informant for cases that lead me to the studios."

"You will need to find a new font of information, I am afraid. It seems Nyarlathotep will be accompanying us back to our home dimension."

I nodded, turned back to watch the debate, looked down to the floor, nettled by eyebrows, finally processed her statement, then turned back to her, only to find my vocabulary had gone missing. I looked down at the floor again. After a moment, I smiled slightly with the confidence of a rediscovered grasp of spoken communication, which I utilized to its fullest extent when I looked at Kassie and said: "Nyarlant-whuh?"

"Nyarlathotep and my companion have a long history of strife. I see now that he was the one who supplied the ancient text which locked my girls on this miserable plane of walking meat."

I realized she was right. I had seen it, too. I just hadn't realized the full extent of the deception. I knew Phart had lied to me about the destruction of the book, which meant he must have been hiding it. I suspected he had some involvement in the sequence of events that summoned and trapped the girls here; but without a clear motive, his subterfuge had been little more than a footnote to the case. Later, I would sit at my desk with pen and paper and unscramble the letters of Phartyaltone's name and slap myself on the forehead. At least I had

234

arrived with the culprit already bound and ready for transport. Maybe I could claim a bonus for the extra service.

Cthulhu, satisfied with having upbraided Nyarlathotep for his mischief, looked around the room.

"What happened to Nctosa and Nctolhu?" he rumbled. "Where in the Hells have those girls gotten off to now?"

A creak on the stairs betrayed their descent. They slithered along the curve of the staircase, sheepishly avoiding their father's narrowed gaze. Behind them, Brock followed. He was cinching his robe tight again, but looked drawn and rather exhausted. His cocksure smile faded as he entered the room.

"Er… Hey, everybody. Looking for us?" Brock asked.

With a savage movement, Cthulhu turned to me and ripped the book out from under my arm. He wordlessly riffled through it, stopping on a particular page. I could see over his shoulder that the words on the pages pulsed and moved as he scanned them. Turning one more page, he spun the book around and shoved it into the young actor's face.

"Read," was all Cthulhu said.

"Oh! Uh…" Brock stammered, trying to focus on the pages held in front of his face. Then, haltingly: "Ne lasu la pordon pusxigxas via azeno sur la vojo ekstere!"

A hollow whistling slowly filled the room. A sweeping wind swept through the house, moving curtains, mussing hair, and lifting Brock's robe. In front of the sectional sofa, a glowing portal began to grow. Cthulhu, holding the closed book, shoved Nyarlathotep through the portal first. He gestured to Nctosa and Nctolhu to enter next. When they attempted a last look back at Brock, their father grudgingly pushed them through as well. As Kassogtha moved toward it, I stepped forward.

"How can I contact you with my bill?" I asked her.

"Er… I'll call you," she said and dove into the light.

Yeah, I've heard that line before.

As Cthulhu stepped through the slowly shrinking portal, the director stepped over to Brock. He smacked his star over the head with his ball cap.

"What is wrong with you?" he asked Brock. "You know I need you to finish this scene tonight! And you were upstairs frolicking with the calamari twins?!?"

Brock pulled his phone out of the pocket of his robe.

"I know, I know, but check out this POV I shot. I'll put you as producer if you'll give me the director credit."

As the director craned his neck to look at the screen, a single bolt of eldritch energy erupted from the remnants of the portal. It snaked across the room, crackling until it reached Brock's phone. The phone immediately erupted in a burst of smoke.

"Dammit!" Brock shouted, dropping his now-worthless piece of technology.

I left the house, a smile on my face. I wasn't sure when I could expect to be paid, but at least this whole mess was over with. I really hate these Elder

Ones cases.

As I headed back out to my car, I wondered out loud if it was too late to get another one of those Throat Punch things from Big Rich.

The Shadow Over Braxton County

by

Paul Brian McCoy

In my dream, Dad was still alive. Younger than when I'd left home. Vibrant. Like he hadn't been since I was a little girl idolizing him and pretending nothing bad was ever going to happen again. The old house was laid out the same: same furniture, same decorations, same lingering sense of unease. Mom was already dead, I guess. She wasn't there, and we avoided mentioning her like we always did. He led me to my room and told me that I was safe. Nothing would happen to me while he was there to protect me.

Then the bus pulled into the station and I was jarred awake.

Morrison, West Virginia still smelt the same after eight years, even nearing midnight: the hint of garbage, the touch of exhaust, and the slight fishy smell of the Elk River slinking its way through the middle of town. The two or three other people disembarking the bus had rides waiting – families hugging and crying, welcoming them home. As soon as I left the relative safety of the bus station, a meth head, all bad teeth and scabby skin, asked if I had any money to spare. I glared, said nothing, and kept walking.

"Fucking bitch. Can't even smile for me? Cunt!" His voice reverberated through the station

239

and out into the street, but nobody else was near. Nobody else heard. I turned and walked backwards, glaring at him, and he slunk back to the doorway in which he'd been lurking, muttering about fire and damnation. Coward.

I shouldered my backpack and slipped away into the shadows, making my way across town toward the Emerson Motel, where I had a room reserved. Reflexively, I tried to keep out of the pale blue of the streetlights. Years of avoiding cops had burnt those instincts into me, and being back home brought them out even stronger. Not that it was going to matter.

I knew the police car was there before I saw it pulling up alongside me. Ignoring it, I kept walking. There was no other traffic out this late, so it was creeping up the wrong side of the street. When the window rolled down, I glanced over from the corner of my eye, not looking up from the sidewalk, and saw why it was shadowing me.

It was my Uncle Jack. I should have known he'd be here, waiting to pounce.

I jumped as he whooped the siren and laughed.

"Hey Sammy! That's you, ain't it? All grown up?"

"Hey, Jack."

"*Uncle* Jack."

I kept walking, not moving an inch his way. He kept creeping along.

"Where you heading?"

"My motel."

"You don't have to do that. Come on home."

"No thanks, Jack."

"*Uncle* Jack."

240

"No thanks, Uncle Jack. Money's already spent."

He laughed and I cringed.

"I can get you a refund, Sammy."

I shifted the backpack on my shoulder and kept walking, wishing this would all just be over. That tomorrow was over. That the funeral was over. That I was back on a bus leaving this shit stain of a town and I would never have to come back again.

"Does your parole officer know you're here?" he laughed. I stopped walking and held my breath. I knew he'd go there, but I didn't think it would be his go-to intimidation technique. I bit my lip and tried not to shout at him. "Don't worry, girly. Nobody else knows about your little indiscretions. Nobody else even knows you're here.

"You're lucky you've got family looking out for your best interests." He laughed again and I imagined stabbing him in the throat.

"I'm clean, *Jack*," I said softly, trying to keep my voice even. "Have been for nearly three years. I'm taking care of myself."

He smiled that same smile from the days just before I left town. The smile that said he knew something I didn't. The smile that I knew meant he couldn't wait to destroy my illusions. "We both know that's not entirely true, Sammy."

I started walking again, faster this time. The patrol car moved forward at the same pace. Jack was about to say something else when his radio crackled to life, demanding his attention. *We got another one, Jack. Out at the Lucas place. Says the dogs are going nuts and they think somebody's outside the house. Says it's the monster again.*

"Goddammit." He picked up the microphone and took a deep breath. "This is Jack. I'm on it." The radio buzzed into silence as he replaced the mic into its cradle. "Fucking crazy people," he muttered. "I'll see you at Billy's service tomorrow."

Without another word, Jack pulled back over to the correct side of the street and drove off towards the outskirts of town. I still remembered the Lucas place. Alcoholic redneck with an alcoholic wife and three dipshit kids. The dogs were smarter. They lived on the edge of the woods, up a dirt road with "Keep Out" signs posted every thirty or forty feet. They had a reputation for causing a ruckus whenever possible, so it was a bit odd hearing them call the police for help. Old Man Lucas must be up around sixty now. Maybe dementia's setting in. Or maybe he's just drunk.

Fuck 'em. I just needed this night to be over. So I kept on walking.

I've never been religious. Not counting just after Mom died, I couldn't remember the last time I'd been to church or considered praying to something. I never thought Dad was religious either, but the service was being held at the Baptist church just a few blocks away from my motel, so I waited until the very last minute before heading over. It was a small red brick building. All sharp angles and limited parking without a single car in the lot. Opening the door, I was greeted with a rush of warm air and not much else. The casket sat up front in its place of honor, but the minister was nowhere to be seen.

I slipped into a pew toward the back of the room

and tried to be invisible. The casket looked cheap from here. And it was closed. There'd been no viewing the night before, and with this kind of turnout, I guess that was understandable. I remembered Dad having lots of friends when I was younger. Friends who would have sent him off in style – drinks, singing, crying, more drinks. But meth friends don't really stick around when things go bad. And they rarely, if ever, go to funerals for their other meth friends.

"Figured we'd skip the memorial and just get this over with," Jack said from behind me. I jumped and heard him chuckle. No idea how he was able to get into the pew behind me without me knowing. I guess I was distracted.

Even though I knew parts of the story, I had to ask. I turned around in the pew to face him.

"What really happened? Nobody had any details for me."

"A fire. Horrible one." A pause. "Billy was cooking again." He shifted and the pew creaked loudly, the sound reverberating through the empty church. "That's why the closed casket." He kept rubbing his hands together, nervously. He wouldn't meet my eyes. Nobody should see that. Not their own father. Not their brother.

"I told him to be careful. To not take any unnecessary chances. No shortcuts. But then we got the call that a trailer was on fire up in the woods on the other end of town, and by the time we got there, it was over."

"So you knew he was cooking?"

He shrugged. "Yeah. I knew."

"He was living with you, wasn't he?"

Jack's face went blank. Cold.

"Yeah. Mostly. He'd been spending more time at the trailer than home lately."

The words hung in the air for a full minute before I looked away. He refused to look me in the eye, so I went ahead and turned back around, giving him the back of my head to stare at. I threw my next words out softly, bait on a hook.

"So if he was cooking again, I guess that means there's no inheritance?"

That got another laugh out of him. A real one this time. No condescension or hostility. He really thought that was a hilarious question. He leaned forward, gripping the pew on each side of me, framing me up and putting his face near the back of my head.

"You need money, girly?"

I could smell bourbon. He'd already been drinking, and I was beginning to think he had the right idea.

"I don't *need* money. But it would have been nice." I sounded disappointed without really meaning to. Money *would* have helped. Money always helps.

His breath was hot on the back of my neck. For the first time in forever I wished I'd grown my hair out to my shoulders.

"I might be able to get you some money." A long pause. "Depends on what you're willing to do."

"I'm not a whore, *Uncle* Jack." I stressed the 'Uncle' there, hoping he'd move away from me. It didn't work.

"I'm not a pimp, girly. But I've seen your rap

244

sheet."

There it was. He knew. And now he was going to actually do it. He was going to tell me the truth.

"You know how to cook meth. Turns out I know a guy who just lost his cook." Another long pause. I concentrated on my breathing. Keeping it steady, even though my heart was pounding.

"That's how you knew Dad was cooking."

He huffed another blast of hot air onto my neck.

"Shit, Sammy. It's a little more complicated than that."

"So explain it."

He sat back, freeing me to turn around and face him again. He still wouldn't look at me.

"Do you know how long I've been a cop?"

I shrugged.

"Too damn long. Too damn long to still be a deputy. Deputy Sargent. I'm a fucking joke around here. I get sent on the shit calls. I get no raises. I can't advance. I'm turning fifty this year and the only reason I own my home is because I inherited it.

"I inherited your dad, too. Little brother Billy with all the promise. The artistic one. The one with the big ideas and brains. But he was sick. Maybe crazy. Always had been. Always prone to getting drunk or high, too."

He shifted and creaked again.

"You know that. You might not want to admit it, but you know. You're a lot like him, from what I can tell."

Now it was my turn to shift and send creaks though the church. But I refused to respond beyond that.

"Yeah, you knew. So when he fell off the

245

wagon this last time, I was ready. I've spent the past two years preparing for this. I worked long shifts, I busted the fuckers who stumble around our streets, I got names and addresses of dealers. I put them all on notice and decided to start building a future for myself. I'd drive out the suppliers, and your dad would cook for me. I'd make sure it was distributed."

He paused again, weighing his words carefully.

"I need a new cook."

"*You* do?"

He smiled. "Well, to be honest, I'm not the one at the top of the food chain here. But the guy I work with, he's big time. And he needs a new cook."

"I'm clean. I told you that."

"Even better. You'll be safer than your dad ever was."

"I can't do it. I can't go back to jail."

"You'll never see the inside of a cell. I can promise you that. We're safe. Protected." He leaned forward again. "The Egyptian has everything covered. I think he'd even prefer it if we kept this all in the family."

I stared at Jack and, for the first time today, he looked me in the eye without hesitation.

"It's good that you're home, Sammy."

"I have to think about it."

"Of course you do. We'll get your dad taken care of and then you go back to your motel and get some rest. Think it over and I'll run the idea past The Egyptian to see if he bites."

"He doesn't have a real name?"

"You don't want to know that. That's a question you don't ask again."

246

The service was practically non-existent, and the burial was over before I could even wrap my brain around the fact that we were lowering my father into the ground. Jack said nothing more about his offer, just gave me a ride to the cemetery and back to my motel. There was nothing more to say, really. Everything else was silence. I felt like my skin was peeling away from the muscle, and my bones were vibrating some deep, dank signal that could only be heard through the dirt.

Jack said he'd see me in the morning and pulled away. The Emerson wasn't a big motel; two floors, doors opening onto the parking lot. There was a pool, but it looked like the pump was busted and no one was ever going to get around to fixing it. Garbage floated in the green water. I pushed the long sleeves of my t-shirt up and rubbed my wrists, first the right, then the left, feeling the old scars, the first scars, and fought down the urge to relax with a little bloodletting.

I hadn't cut myself in three years, since right around the time I got clean, but every day I remembered the gentle calm of the razor, the endorphin release, the peace. If this day got any more fucked, I wasn't sure I could keep from falling off the wagon.

With a sigh, I swiped the lock on the door to my room and swung it open to darkness. Stepping inside, I closed the door behind me and exhaled loudly. Where was the light switch? I haphazardly flipped it, and the light by the bed flickered and buzzed, sending the darkness retreating into shadows, revealing the battered furniture, the

247

stained wallpaper, and...

"Oh shit!"

The Fed was sitting in the back corner of the room, watching and waiting for me. He fit right in with the motel décor. His suit was shabby and probably used to be black; his shoes weren't shined. He was so pale I was surprised I didn't see him glowing in the dark when I came in. It looked like he cut his own hair. His entire appearance seemed to be an afterthought.

"Did he bite?"

No "hello." No "how are you feeling?" No "was it difficult burying your father today?" *Did he bite?* I ignored the question and dropped onto the bed. The squeaking of the springs in the ancient mattress was so loud I knew people in the next rooms could hear them. If there had been people in the next rooms. The Fed had taken care of that. We were isolated.

"I watched my father's casket get lowered into a deep hole today."

"And did Jack bite?"

"Of course he bit. How could he not? You made sure I was irresistible. He's convinced I'm an ex-meth cook with a past that I'm trying to escape."

"Well, you *are* an ex-meth *head* with a past you're trying to escape. And we taught you to cook just for this occasion." He crossed his legs. "You're sure he took the bait?"

"Fuck." I sat up and looked the Fed in the eye. His look didn't waver. "Yes. I told him I'd think about it. He's contacting The Egyptian tonight."

The Fed's mouth twitched into the brief semblance of a smile.

"He actually told you about The Egyptian already? That's a good sign. He must be desperate. His dealers are already running low on supply and if he doesn't get the operation back up and running quickly, The Egyptian might move on to another town. This is very good news. He's got his fingers in any number of drug pies in this crumbling state."

"I don't think I can do this."

"Of course you can."

"I don't want to be around drugs all the time. I'm an addict."

"You should have thought about that before you agreed to this."

Did I ever actually agree to this? I tried to remember just when I had actually said this would all be okay, and got nothing. One day the Fed was harassing me about my past and my family, then the next I was going along for the ride. My criminal record was never all that flashy. Some possession, public intox, a couple of domestic violence calls. I've never been slow to anger and it's gotten me in more trouble than it should have. Smoking meth was something that I also barely remember beginning. Like it had always been there, lurking in the background.

Maybe it had. Maybe I'd been around it when I was little and it just seemed natural to slide into this particular addiction, like my father, like my mother. When she OD'd, Dad finally got his shit together and got clean for me. But he was always odd, never the "normal" dad. His strangeness had wormed its way into me, and by the time I was seventeen I was on the road. And I guess, when left to his own devices, Dad just went back to his old habits.

Jack had actually been okay when I was a kid. He looked out for me when Dad was crazy. It was hard on him, watching his little brother fall apart, pick himself back up, then fall apart all over again. Sometimes it felt like whatever madness was inside of Dad had skipped over Jack. I'd thought he was a good person for most of my life. But he had nothing but shit for me when I decided to leave. I was abandoning my father. I was a coward. I wasn't using yet, but he thought I was. He said he could see it under my skin, the disease just waiting to come out. Had I abandoned him, too? Probably.

I had abandoned this whole place. This shit town, all churches and yard sales, petty squabbles and barely restrained white supremacy. There had to be something better out there. So that's what I tried to find; something better. Someplace better. That craving to find someplace worth staying.

But people are the same wherever you go. Shitty.

"It's The Egyptian we're after. Your uncle is just a means to an end. Don't worry too much about him. And with any luck, this will be over before you even start your first cook."

"You think that's likely?"

He chuckled. "No. But it's possible. Depends on how desperate The Egyptian is." He reached into his jacket pocket and pulled out a small black flip-top cell phone and tossed it onto the bed. "My number's preprogrammed. If you need anything or get any new information, call me. I'll be in the area, but it will be best if you don't know where."

"It'll be best. Sure."

He was gone before I even realized it. I guess

I'd zoned out. It was a cheap-ass phone, probably bought in bulk just for losers like me. Bait. Dangling on the line. Without even thinking, I got undressed and went to the flimsy dresser, shifting aside the two or three tops and the handful of panties to find my knife. It fit perfectly in my hand, like it was a part of me. Like it had never left.

It was my security blanket. I took it with me wherever I went, but rarely did I ever even touch it after stashing it away. It was comforting sometimes just to know it was there. But this was all getting to be a little too much. I could feel it calling to me. The knife blade was going to help me take control. I wouldn't be afraid. I wouldn't be alone. I wouldn't fail.

I sat back on the bed and slowly pressed the blade into the flesh of my thigh. Not deep. Barely even enough to break the skin, and even then it was just the hint of a cut. A trace of blood dotted the line the blade left behind, fresh among dozens of other faint scars, and the pain was so slight it barely registered as pain. It registered as comfort. Relief.

I could do this.

In my dream, Dad is still alive. I am lying in bed, deep in sleep, when I hear a shuffling sound from the corner. I open my eyes. The clock says 12:34 but it feels as though I've been sleeping for more than just two hours. It feels like years. He is older than when I'd left home. Tired. His face sags on his skull like a mask that doesn't fit quite right. He looks like he did at his worst, when he was crazed and scared.

The motel room is laid out the same as when I'd

fallen asleep; same furniture, same decorations, but with a new lingering sense of unease. Something isn't the same. The walls seem to be sinking in at odd angles, and my eyes can't focus on where they meet the ceiling. They don't line up properly and I feel nauseated at the sight.

Dad is standing in a corner that doesn't connect, like an image in a broken mirror. He is hooded, wearing a long robe. I've never seen him dressed like that and it increases my nausea. He is trying to speak to me, but the air between us is thick; viscous and dense. The words reverberate, their echoes reaching me before the actual sounds. He doesn't sound like my father. The mannerisms are exaggerated but his hands are less animated than when he was alive.

He tells me I'm not safe. Something bad is going to happen. He can't protect me.

I climb out of bed, struggling to push myself up and toward him, fighting with gravity like I'm slogging through mud. He tries to wave me back, yells at me to stop. I reach out to him, trying to touch his hand, and his face shifts in terror as he falls backwards through a sliver in space. There is a deafening roar, a waterfall, a freight train, a tornado. The floor shifts and I tumble forward, following him into nothingness.

I'm on a balcony, high above an ancient cityscape. It smells of mold and dust. Towers bend and shift, flowing and changing with every glance. Clusters of iridescent, spheroidal bubbles gather and swim through the air below me. They change colors rapidly, cycling through hues I know and some I can't identify. There's a pain behind my eyes and a

252

pressure in my ears. Is this what a stroke feels like? Rising up between the towers, on the edge of the horizon, is a rapidly changing polyhedral figure. It acknowledges me watching and the air rushes from my lungs. It's alive. The bubbles are alive. Everything here is teeming with unnatural life-like things from a familiar nightmare. Intimately otherworldly.

I scream, and my voice is distant. Small and tinny, as if broadcast through a busted speaker. A wave of vertigo sends me to my knees. Tumbling backward, I know I'm dying. There is no way out of this. I'm abandoned and lost. I close my eyes and feel the new cuts on my thighs split open, my blood pouring out in waves.

I opened my eyes and it was dawn. My cuts had bled through their bandages, staining the sheets. The bed screeched in agony as I sat up and tried to make sense of my dream. Fragments of it were already fading from memory, and for some reason I was thankful. By the time I'd gathered up the sheets and taken a shower, I could barely remember anything from the dream other than seeing my father.

I guess that's why I called Jack. I wanted to see where Dad had died. What was left of it. I was starving, too, so I suggested we meet for breakfast. That I had something to discuss with him. He sounded like he hadn't had much sleep either, but he immediately perked up when he thought I was going to agree to cook for him.

"Not over the phone," he whispered, and agreed to pick me up in just a few minutes.

One of the only good things about a town as small as Morrison is that you can get from one end to the other in no time at all. Especially if you're driving a police cruiser. Within fifteen minutes I was in the front seat of the car, and we were on our way to have biscuits and gravy - one of the only things I really missed about living here.

Once we were seated in a window booth and our orders had been taken by a waitress who clearly knew Jack but pretended she didn't - her nametag said Brenda - he started in.

"So you've decided?"

"Not yet."

"Not yet. What do you mean *not yet*?"

"I mean *not yet*." I smiled politely as Brenda returned with our coffee, expertly pouring two cups while giving us both the stink eye, and then disappearing without a word. "I have questions."

"You have questions. Shit." He took a sip of coffee, watching carefully as I popped open three creamers and turned my coffee from dark black to pale brown. Watching the creamer swirl up and around the cup made me feel uneasy. Like something from my nightmare coming back, but just below the surface.

"You don't have to have questions. You can just trust me on this. The money will be good, you'll be protected, and we'll both live happily ever after."

"Like Dad?"

He sat his coffee down.

"Your dad was never stable. You know that. He couldn't be trusted to be in the lab and not tweak the recipes. No pun intended. He wasn't safe. I see that now."

"You see it now? Nice. How do you know I'm safe? How do you know I won't fall off the wagon? Because I sure don't know."

He scowled and leaned forward. He smelled like soap and bourbon. Before he could say another word, Brenda was suddenly at the booth, taking our orders before slipping away yet again. He huffed.

"You'll be fine. You're stronger than your dad ever was." It was my turn to huff. "You don't think I remember, Sammy, but I do. You were a big part of keeping him clean for as long as he was. There was just never going to be a future where he wasn't a junkie."

He paused and looked out the window at the parking lot.

"You never knew your grandparents. He got a lot of his crazy from them. Somehow it missed me. It's like they were normal people until after I was born, then sometime around when I turned ten, everything started going to shit. Weird shit."

I'd never heard much of anything about my grandparents before, other than I was named after Grandma. When I was little, nobody mentioned them. They were just gone. Long dead. We never even visited their graves on Memorial Day. It was like they never really existed. In my mind, I'd pictured my dad and Jack always just being there, living in Morrison their whole lives, never going anywhere or doing anything.

"What kind of weird shit? Sex stuff?"

"No!" He glanced around the restaurant. "Not really." He took a drink of coffee. "Shit, I don't know. Like I said, they were normal until I turned ten. Then things went strange for a long time, until

Mom got pregnant with Billy. She was on a lot of drugs during that. Real drugs. Prescription. She wasn't well. And Dad...well, it *seemed* like he was on drugs." I don't think he was even aware that he was tapping his fingers rapidly on the tabletop. "*Not* prescription." He got very quiet for a minute or two except for the tapping, almost forgetting I was even sitting across from him. That's when our biscuits came, and we ate in silence.

Despite having been anxiously awaiting the taste of homemade biscuits drowning in sausage gravy, I couldn't really taste anything. Eating was a mechanical process that morning. We both seemed to pay no attention to what we were doing; the meal was efficiently finished in a matter of minutes, and then the plates and silverware were just as efficiently taken away by Brenda.

"I want to see where Dad died."

Jack glared at me.

"I need a fucking cigarette. Come on." He threw a handful of cash on the table and stalked out the front door. I followed, noticing a strange look on Brenda's face. A little bit of pity, a little bit of disgust. I couldn't tell if it was for Jack, or for me, or for us both. Regardless, I quickly caught up with Jack in the parking lot, and then we sat in silence for nearly a full minute in the squad car as he lit a cigarette and exhaled smoke out the driver's side window.

"You saw that look she gave me, right?" He was pissed. I suddenly realized it wasn't because of me. "That bitch. Thinks she's too good for me. She grew up here, same as me. She never left, same as me. Bitch." He sat and stewed, dragging on the cigarette, fingers tapping rapidly on the steering wheel. I had no idea what to say or do, so I said and did nothing. I looked out the window at the woods across the street.

Morrison was like that. Not only could you get from one end to the other in minutes, you were always close to woods and not too far from actual forest. I thought I saw a deer move through the trees, but then it was gone.

"Forget about her, Jack. I want to see where Dad died."

"I fucking heard you the first time." He threw the cigarette out the window and started up the car. "I have to go do a follow up at the Lucas place. The trailer you want is about a half-mile up in the woods, five minutes from there. I can drop you, point you in the right direction, and come pick you up when I'm done with that drunken lunatic. Then you need to make a choice. The Egyptian needs an answer."

It wasn't the news I wanted, but it would do. I grew up here, too. The woods weren't scary.

Jack couldn't keep from bitching about Old Man Lucas on the drive over. Seems the Lucas place, a palatial double-wide trailer with a five-dog kennel on adjoining property, was the sight of recent Braxton County Monster sightings, despite this not being Flatwoods. This wasn't the first reported sighting of the monster since the original one back in 1952, but over the past few months they'd picked up. And being the favorite son of the Morrison Sheriff's Office, Deputy Sargent had been assigned the case, which meant that he was getting

257

repeat calls about weird sounds and strange sights, and more than a couple of meth-fueled paranoid rants - usually in the middle of the night.

"There was something about that last batch that your Dad cooked up. It's selling fast, but it's making weirdos weirder. I'm used to paranoia and nonsense - shit, I lived with your dad after all - but these tweakers are seriously fucked in the head. And I can't tell if it was always that way or if there's something different about the crank. A lot of them aren't paranoid about their neighbors, or their families, or even the law anymore. They're getting high and getting freaked out about the end of the world. Lots of fear of fire and shadows. But then they just go right back to smoking and shooting up."

He pulled off by the side of the road. There were no houses in sight in either direction.

"Fucking junkies. God love 'em. Your dad's trailer's just up that path there. About a half-mile, like I said. Nobody goes up into the woods these days, especially not with these stupid-ass monster stories going around. You can't miss it."

I exited the car and crossed in front to the edge of the woods. The trees were especially thick here and the path was barely noticeable. A deer path, maybe.

"I'll be back in an hour or so. If you're not back down here, I'm leaving without you."

As he drove away, I realized I'd forgotten to ask how a trailer got a half-mile up into the woods with hardly a path to get to it. There's probably another way. This was just handy to where he was going. God forbid he cut me a break. So, cursing both under my breath and out loud, I started into the

258

trees, trying not to notice how quickly they blocked out the sun and how chilly the air suddenly became.

It took around fifteen minutes to make the hike. Should have been quicker about it, but a lot of the path was overgrown and uphill. Had to cross a goddamn creek at one point. Fucking Jack. There had to be an easier way to get to the trailer. Not only was it dark and cold, but after about five minutes I realized I hadn't heard any birds. No animals rustling through the underbrush, either. It used to be hard to walk in the woods for more than a minute or two without flushing a squirrel or a rabbit. I hadn't even seen any bugs to speak of. Not that I was looking.

Before I'd realized it, I was stumbling out from a line of trees into a small clearing, just barely large enough to house the single-wide trailer that sat at its center. Or what was left of it, anyway. More light was breaking through the foliage onto the trailer that, before it became a burnt-out husk reeking of chemicals and smoke, might have been nice at some point. I'd forgotten how much space a single-wide actually had inside; as I moved closer I could see that although the framework was still intact, the walls had burnt down almost completely. The insides were a shambles, an ashy, sooty chaos. Police tape hung from the remains as though it had only the vaguest intention of keeping anyone out.

The strangest things, though, were the mushrooms. What was left of the trailer was teeming with pale, fleshy mushrooms. They grew across the clearing in waves, as though exploding out from the trailer, or perhaps they grew the opposite way, like dozens of Yellow Brick Roads leading to Tweaker Oz. I knelt down and ran my hand across a patch and my fingers came away coated lightly with pollen. Did mushrooms spread pollen? Were they spores? There was a faint luminescence to the entire scene, as the mushrooms seemed to faintly glow in the mid-day shadows. I imagined how gorgeous they'd be at night, like a Milky Way in the middle of the forest, making the place where my father burned to death something beautiful instead of just a contaminated ruin.

The mushrooms gave off a strange, musky odor, too, and now it was on my fingers. I wiped my hands on my jeans and took one last look inside, imagining what it must have been like when the chemicals burst into flame, when the fire leapt up his arms, across his chest. His hair sizzling and his flesh charring, splitting. That was when the tears started, I think. I can't really remember. All I remember is Uncle Jack shaking me by the shoulder, asking if I was okay. I was rocking back and forth at the base of a tree, my knees pulled up close and my arms locked tightly around them.

"You shouldn't stay here. Not on the ground like that. This whole place is toxic."

He pulled me to my feet and led me away from the trailer in the opposite direction from which I'd come. The asshole *did* have a shorter way. We were at his car in minutes, and as we drove back to my motel I finally stopped crying. It wasn't even noon yet, but I was exhausted. I had to lie down. We pulled into the parking lot and the cruiser crept to a halt in front of the door to my room. I didn't say anything as I climbed out and took a couple of steps forward, fumbling my key card out of my pocket.

Jack was watching me with something that approximated concern, though I couldn't tell if it was for me or for his meth 'empire.'

As my motel room door unlocked with a buzz and a click, I glanced back, meeting Jack's eye.

"I'm in. I'll do it."

In my dream, Dad is still alive. I am lying in bed, deep in sleep, when I hear a shuffling sound from the corner. I open my eyes. The clock is gone. The room is dark, but illuminated faintly by mushrooms sprouting and sporing as I watch; universes exploding and expanding, living, dying, reproducing. I can barely see him, but he is older than when I'd left home. Tired. His face sags on his skull like a mask that doesn't fit quite right. He looks like he has something important to say.

The motel room is laid out the same as when I'd fallen asleep; same furniture, same decorations, but with a new lingering sense of unease. I can't really see it, but the walls and ceiling don't meet at the right angles. The darkness helps to hide it, but the nausea it induces won't be stopped. I vomit in the floor next to the bed, noting for just an instant that the bedsprings make no noise.

Dad is standing in a corner that doesn't connect, like an image in a broken mirror. He is hooded, wearing a long robe. I've never seen him dressed like that and it increases my nausea. He isn't trying to speak to me, but motions me to come forward. He moves stiffly, as though relearning to move.

The mushroom spores flow about him on currents of air – rising, swirling, diving, expanding in an unearthly glow – and as I watch, I step

261

forward onto mushrooms sprouting from the carpet. I reach out to take Dad's hand, but instead he slips backward through a sliver in space. I follow without hesitation and step out into the clearing where he died.

There is no moon and everything is darkness. The shell of the burnt-out trailer glows with mushroom light. Behind me, in amongst the trees, I see shadows moving. Man-sized. Gliding as though on wings. I want to turn toward them, to try and focus, get a good look, but Dad calls out to me from inside the remains of the trailer. Not knowing what else to do, I move toward his voice, kicking up glowing clouds of mushroom spores that follow me, the air rushing in to fill the space I leave as I move through it.

I pull the police tape aside and slip through the gap where the door had been. Debris crunches beneath my feet, but the sound is softened by the mushrooms cushioning my steps. What furniture there was has been destroyed – charred and broken, in total disarray. The chemical stink has an electric tinge that can't quite cover the smell of scorched meat. I want to vomit again, but I force the urge down. I get light-headed and the trailer seems to shift around me, what's left of the walls breathing and closing in.

The mushroom light suddenly begins to pulse in a wave, as though guiding me to the far end of the trailer. What else can I do but follow? Rubble and wreckage, in what would have been a bedroom before being repurposed for the meth lab, have been shoved aside. A trapdoor is exposed, open and leading down under the trailer. An escape hatch? I

262

want to wake up. I want this to be over. I don't know what's happening. Then I hear them outside, moving through the trees toward the trailer. I feel the floor move as they enter the outer room.

I have no choice. I climb down into the trapdoor, finding a rickety ladder mounted to the side of a hole going down into darkness. I can't see what's below, but I can't stay here. I climb down the ladder. The last thing I see as my head drops below the edge is the first of the figures from the trees. I can't believe it. It can't be real. Then I'm gone.

The ladder leads down to a ledge cut into the wall of a vast cavern. The mushroom glow leads downward along the wall, mixing in with a strange, velvety moss. Looking back the way I came, the trapdoor is no longer visible, as if it has been closed or never existed in the first place. There's nowhere to go but down, so I take a first, trembling step toward the ledge and find a stairway carved out of the stone, spiraling into the abyss below.

Carefully, I take a step. Then another. The cavern is deep but not very broad. Sounds of my footsteps echo across the emptiness. There are chisel marks where the steps were carved, so I know they're not natural. But the angles of the cuts are upward, as though the steps were cut from below. I keep one hand up, fingertips brushing through the moss of the wall, dry lips mouthing voiceless secrets. Tiny glowing motes rise into the air, following my fingertips, and for a second I wonder would happen if I breathed them in? Would they find purchase in my nose and lungs, in my mouth and throat? Would this strange moss grow inside of

263

me, choking me, killing me for simply being here?

But this thought only lasts for an instant. The moss is comforting. Soothing me as I travel down into a pit that may as well be bottomless.

I lose track of time on the stairs. I can no longer tell if I've been walking for minutes, hours, or days. I haven't stopped, and I'm not tired, but I can barely remember when I started this journey. Suddenly the steps are gone and I am falling forward, landing on my stomach just a few feet away from the final step.

Coughing, I push myself up to my feet, and it's as if my eyes have finally adjusted to the dim phosphorescence of the cavern. I'm in a circular chamber that appears to have been carved out of the earth in the same manner as the stairs. Oval entryways lead off in five different directions, into tunnels that each glow with eerie, mechanical lights that flicker to life as I turn to look. Before I have a chance to even move toward one of the passages, they are filled with skittering sounds, and as I begin to freak out, there is movement in each doorway.

The figures I'd seen in the trailer are here. Strange beings fill the entryways, blocking the light. They are large; man-sized. Pinkish and crustacean-like. Where their heads should be are convoluted ellipsoids; pyramided, fleshy rings covered in short antennae. Their armored bodies each have numerous sets of paired appendages, clawed and insect-like. Pairs of membranous wings hang from the backs of each, withered and bat-like, as though afterthoughts of evolution; useless on this world, but maybe not on others.

I forget to scream. My mind locks up as I try to take them in and understand what I'm seeing. I can't move, or at least I don't think I can. I don't really try. I simply stand there, watching, waiting for what comes next. What I assume are their heads begin lighting up, flashing various colors and patterns, communicating with one another. Then I feel it. A wave of hostility and confusion, a psychic battering I'm not prepared for. They move forward into the chamber and I finally find my voice.

I screamed and woke up in my bed. The clock read 12:34.

In the corner of the room sat a man, waiting; watching me sleep. He was bald, with flawless, golden-brown skin and pale eyes. He wore a tailored suit that probably cost more than I could ever hope to earn in a year. His legs were crossed casually, with one hand resting on the arm of the threadbare chair where The Fed had sat earlier, and the other on the golden, star-shaped handle of a shiny black walking stick. I wondered if I was still dreaming.

"You've been wandering," he said in a comforting voice. "Don't be frightened. I'm a childhood friend of your father's. And your uncle's." I should have been frightened, but he was not threatening. Something kept me calm. The bed screeched as I sat and faced him. "I thought we should probably meet face-to-face, since you're going to be working for me."

"They never mentioned you when I was growing up," was the only thing I could think to say.

"Not surprising. I was introduced to them when they were children, but we drifted apart." He put his finger to his lips. "Don't mention that to Jack. He doesn't remember." He leaned forward in the chair, grasping his cane handle in both hands and resting on it.

"You're a bit of a surprise, yourself." He was curious. His eyes glinted in the half-light of the clock. The lights from the parking lot snuck in around the edges of the curtains. "I can't believe I've never met you before."

"I've been away."

"You've been a secret, I think." He smiled, exposing perfect teeth. "But it's good to have you back in the fold, so to speak. Pity about your father. It's hard to believe he's really dead, isn't it?"

He watched my reaction like he was expecting something. Like a cobra eyes its prey, or a serial killer watches his victim's last moments.

"I can't believe it, either," is all I could manage. He tilted his head and leaned back. I turned for an instant to glance at the clock, and when I turned back he was seated on the bed next to me. The springs were silent. I gasped, but he hushed me, running his finger along the scars on my arms. I flinched, and he leaned in close, bringing his face next to mine. He inhaled deeply.

"You've got the scent of entropy upon you." I had no idea what he meant, so I stayed still, desperate not to encourage violence. Which was strange, because there was nothing violent about the way he carried himself. He was gentle, even. But there was something otherworldly about him. Something foreign and frightening.

"I don't like secrets, Samantha. And secrets can't be kept from me." He smiled again. "I have a nose for that sort of thing. I'm glad to have you working with us. Please don't try to hide anything from me; any secrets of your own, or that your uncle might be keeping." His finger kept lingering on my scars and I felt like I wanted to scream.

He leaned in even closer, his face pressed up close to mine. His skin was unnaturally smooth. He had no pores. He reached up with a long finger and pulled one lower eyelid down, saying, "I've got my eye on you."

Beneath the lid were writhing, horrible things, and I dropped down into an icy darkness. I fell backward onto my bed in a shrieking of springs, and he was gone. The cuts on my wrists – my first cuts – had opened up again, and I was bleeding.

I wrapped my wrists quickly, got dressed, pulled up the hood of my hoodie and headed across town to Uncle Jack's. The city always closed up shop early, and at nearly one in the morning there was nobody anywhere. I was surprised the streetlights even stayed on. Despite that, I felt like I was being watched. I kept seeing things moving from the corners of my eyes, but there was nothing when I'd look. After three blocks of fast walking, I started running. I had no reason to think that The Egyptian was following me, but I'd gotten sick of people sneaking up on me when I wasn't paying attention. If someone was going to leap out at me, I wanted to see them coming.

And as if on cue, after cutting through a yard to round a corner, I was face-to-face with two junkies, a man and a woman, both skeletal and practically luminescent in the moonlight, out checking to see if

267

any cars were unlocked. He kept wrenching at the door handle as though if he just tried extra hard it would magically spring open. She turned to face me, creeping forward like a fucking snaggletooth vampire.

"Hey girl. Whatchu doin' out this late?"

"I could ask you the same thing." I fingered the knife in my pocket.

Her rat eyes flicked toward the bandages on my wrists.

"You okay? You need some help?"

"I'm good." I tried to edge toward the street, to get the parked cars between us. You never know what a junkie's gonna do when they're jonesing. If they thought I had any money, I could get my ass kicked. If they thought I had any drugs, I could get killed. "Just going to a friend's house."

"You want some company?" He was paying attention now. His voice was ragged. "You look like you want some company."

"I said I'm good. Keep doing what you're doing. I'll be on my way."

She held a hand out to him, waving him back.

"Bitch don't see it, does she?"

"Don't think she does."

"You're all alone, bitch. It's all coming down on top of us. Fire and brimstone shit." She coughed and spat. "You want to be with your people when the shit goes down."

"That's where I'm going."

"Those ain't your people."

I took a few more steps, almost past them. "You don't know me or my people." I was starting to freak out a little. My palms were sweaty, like I needed a fix.

The woman released a hoarse sound that was supposed to be a laugh. "I know your people. We your people. We gonna ride waves of fire to the end of it all. You gonna be there with us."

"You're high."

"Shit yeah, we high," he answered for her. "Gonna stay high until the end of days, bitch. You should come with us. You can make us some money, looking all clean and shit."

"Fuck you," I spat before I could stop myself.

"Oh ho, that's not nice." He smiled a rotting smile and looked at her. "Were we not being nice?"

"We were fucking nice as fuck."

"I'm going now," I said firmly. If I didn't take control of the situation, things were going to get bad quick. "Just forget you ever saw me, okay?"

He spat on the ground in front of him. "I ain't forgetting you. I'll be dreaming about you for days."

She smacked him in the arm. "You ain't fucking her, asshole."

"I said I'd be thinking about her, not fucking her."

"I know that tone. You think she's good-looking? *That* bitch?"

He smiled and cocked his head. "She look good from here. Meaty. Not like your skinny ass."

She smacked him in the face and he took a swing at her. Before they could even turn back my way, I was across the street, cutting through yards and away. Fucking crazy-ass junkies.

I was pounding on Jack's door for a full minute

269

before he flipped the porch light on and opened it. Before he could say "What the fuck?" I was inside and heading to the kitchen. I was hoping the booze would be out, and Jack didn't disappoint. His half-finished rocks glass was sitting on the counter, and I downed it in one swig, shuddered, coughed, and reached for the bottle of Jim Beam sitting open next to it.

"Goddammit, that was mine," he laughed. "I'll get you your own glass." He was still in his deputy's uniform and hadn't shaved. He took the Jim Beam bottle and poured my drink. "On the rocks? Shot of water?" Without a word, I took the glass from him and took a sip this time. "Okay, then. You all settled?"

I nodded.

"Then what the fuck are you doing pounding on my door in the middle of the night? What the hell's wrong with you? That's how people get shot! I literally just walked in the door from another goddamn idiot monster call and just want a drink and *sleep*."

"Nothing wrong with me." I took another drink. "Your fucking boss was in my room tonight."

"The Egyptian? He was here?" He looked stunned. "I just called him today. Told him you were in." A long pause. "He was in your room?"

"When I woke up from a nightmare about Dad." That was when he noticed my wrists.

"Were you cutting yourself again?"

"No. Not really. I --"

"Dammit, Sammy. You can't be doing that shit." Then he froze. "Did The Egyptian see those?"

"No, he didn't. I didn't cut my wrists." Which

270

was technically true. "I don't know what happened. They just started bleeding. But that's not why I'm here."

"Of course it's not." He took another drink. "Why are you here?"

I wasn't sure where to start with it, so I just said it.

"Could Dad have faked his death?"

The look on Jack's face was something I'd never seen before. A combination of fear, doubt, rage, and unbridled panic. "Did The Egyptian ask you that?"

"He didn't come right out and ask, but he hinted." I took a drink and tried to remain calm. "I *think* he hinted. It was very surreal. I just woke up and he was there. I didn't know what was going on."

Jack picked up the bottle of Jim Beam and walked out of the kitchen without saying a word. I followed him into the living room. He dropped heavily into his favorite recliner, and I slid onto the couch, pulling my legs up underneath me.

"Billy wouldn't do that to me." He added more bourbon to his glass and handed me the bottle. "He knows -- he *knew* how dangerous that would be." Another long pause. "Did he do the whole 'you can't lie to me' bit?" I nodded. "Yeah, he loves that one. Shit. I need to get in touch with him. Assure him that everything's okay."

I didn't think that was a great idea, but I didn't say anything. I had a feeling if I opened my mouth and didn't put bourbon in it, I'd just start pleading with him to leave town with me. Because suddenly I knew I had to get out of there. I couldn't handle it.

It was all getting to be too much. Then there was a knock on the door, and my first thought was, *Oh shit. The tweakers followed me.*

But I'm not that lucky.

"Who the fuck?" Jack muttered as he forced himself to his feet and approached the door. The porchlight wasn't on anymore, but I didn't remember Jack turning it off. He glanced through the window that lined the front door and cursed. "You better be careful, asshole!" he shouted at the door. "I'm a fucking cop!"

He swung the door inward, and The Fed was standing calmly on the porch, looking as nonplussed and disinterested as ever. An obviously fake smile flickered across his face, then vanished. "Deputy Sargent? I'm Special Agent Chambers. I'd like to have a word with you about Samantha." Jack looked confused. "And your illegal meth operation. May I come in?"

His name was Chambers? Had he ever told me that? He had to have identified himself to me at some point, but all I ever remembered calling him was The Fed. What the fuck was wrong with me? Did I even know who he was? Was he really a federal agent?

"Badge," Jack asked, in a remarkable show of restraint.

"Excuse me?"

"Badge. Show me your badge and we can talk." Jack began to finger his pistol, but kept it holstered. I had to do something, so I casually walked over and put myself between the two of them.

"It's okay, Jack." Here we go. "He's with me." Jack's eyes bulged, and I thought for a second he was going to backhand me. "I'm sorry."

"You're gonna be sorry. Goddammit, we're all gonna be sorry." With one arm he knocked me out of the way, back toward the living room, and with the other he tried to draw his gun. It had barely cleared the holster when he froze. Agent Chambers had a badge out, all right, but it was like no badge I'd ever seen - engraved with a weird three-armed symbol, two arms hooked and the third like a scorpion tail, all reaching out from a dot in the center - and as soon as Jack laid eyes on it, he just stopped. He was still conscious, but relaxed like I'd never seen him. Was he hypnotized? What the fuck was happening?

"What the fuck is happening?" I said from the floor.

"I'd rather have done this the old fashioned way," said Chambers, letting himself in. He gently took Jack's arm and re-holstered the pistol, then led him into the living room, seating him in his recliner. He knelt down and looked into Jack's eyes, which were glazed over in a way I'd never seen. The pupils dilated, but there was no other movement. It was like he was dead.

"What's wrong with him?"

"Nothing. He'll be all right soon enough. And then he'll help us clean house around here."

I thought about getting off the floor, but instead leaned against the wall, pulled my knees up and stared hard at Chambers. The elbows of his suit jacket were worn almost through, and the cloth of his pants was thin. There was dirt under his fingernails and he still needed a shave.

"Hand me the bourbon," I said. Chambers

273

paused, looked at me like I was joking, saw I was not, and handed me the bottle. "And my glass, please." He did. I poured myself another drink. After a long pull on the Jim Beam, I took a deep breath and let it warm me up inside. There was a slight urge to throw up, but it passed. "Question time."

Chambers sat on the couch and eyed me curiously. He weighed his next words carefully. "I suppose I owe you some answers."

"Jesus fuck! You think?" I took another drink. "So." Long pause. "Are you really a Fed?"

"I am."

"FBI?"

"No. Not really. Used to be, but I'm part of a different branch now."

"A different branch of the FBI?"

"Sort of. More of a...brotherhood."

I took another drink. I was finally good and drunk. I was ready for this. "Sounds like a cult."

"More of a brotherhood." He relaxed on the couch, perhaps sensing that I was trashed and might not remember any of this in the morning. "You're familiar with the Flatwoods Monster sighting? The first one…1952?"

"I grew up in Braxton County. Of course I've heard of it. There are giant Flatwoods Monster Chairs you can get your picture taken in all over the county. At the fucking Gassaway Dairy Queen. There are souvenirs everywhere. Jack's been driving all over town logging new sightings of the stupid thing. People are crazy for that shit here."

"That first sighting was real. It wasn't an owl, as it was explained away. It also wasn't an alien. Well,

274

it was, but they'd been here for aeons. They call themselves the Mi-go. My brotherhood is dedicated to tracking down their threat and eliminating it."

He paused like he was finished. Like that was all I needed to know.

"Aliens? *The Mi-go.* And your cult hunts monsters."

"We're not a cult. Not really."

"So you're government-sanctioned monster hunters?"

"Well...we don't require government sanction. The King in Yellow gives us our authority."

I sighed. "So you're in a cult." He started to protest again, but I cut him off. "What did you do to Jack?"

"The Yellow Sign can subdue the will of those we need to...persuade."

"And you did that to me, right?"

He frowned and glanced over at Jack, then picked at some fuzz on his jacket sleeve.

"Anyway," he started. "The Appalachians are a known Mi-go territory, but there hadn't been any information about them in the area since that one sighting. No other reports turned out to be credible. Until the death of your father, that is."

That got my attention. "What does my father have to do with alien monsters?"

"That's what we wanted to know. If there was a connection, it seemed it might have something to do with the illegal drug operation your father and Jack were involved with. We did some digging and found references to The Egyptian and the recent rash of monster sightings." He sighed and was clearly agitated. "Sometimes this job is too easy.

275

They get complacent. Think we're just dumb apes they can manipulate."

I'd never seen Chambers get worked up over anything. Usually, he seemed just barely in the game at all. Doing the bare minimum to get by, letting entropy take over...

"He said I smelled of entropy."

"What? Who did?"

"The Egyptian." Chambers sat up straight. "He said I smelled of entropy and he wondered if Dad was really dead."

"You've met The Egyptian already?"

"That's what Jack said. Yes. He was in my room tonight. You didn't see him leave?"

"No."

"I assumed when you showed up here that you were following me."

"I was. You've been under surveillance since you arrived. There was no sign of him entering or leaving."

"It wasn't a dream. I remember my dream from tonight, and that was not part of it."

"What dream?"

I poured another drink, as mine was mysteriously empty.

"I saw my Dad, but he might not have really been my Dad. He led me to an underground chamber, and then these monsters with glowy heads came out and scared me awake. When I woke up, The Egyptian was in my room and he freaked me the fuck out. I don't want to do this anymore. I'm done."

"Man-sized insect-looking creatures with wings?"

276

"Um..."

"Those are the Mi-go." He sat forward. "You dreamt of them? And your father was there?"

Now it was my turn to hedge.

"Not really. I don't think so. It was a dream."

Chambers leapt up and began to pace, muttering to himself. Before I could completely shift into nervous breakdown mode, he stopped and sat back down.

"Dream communication with the Mi-go is not unheard of. I believe you were contacted. Your father may well be alive. He might not be your father anymore, not entirely, but he's clearly sending you a message."

"Whoa whoa whoa…there's nothing *clear* about any of this." I drained my glass again, and things got a little fuzzy around the edges. "My dad is dead. We buried him."

"You buried a box."

"With a body inside!"

"A body burnt beyond recognition."

"They check these things!"

"The real question is why the Mi-go would be hiding your father from The Egyptian. They worship him. In their manner."

"Wait. Worship him? Who the fuck is he?"

"The Egyptian will do for you. The Crawling Chaos is another, more fanciful name. You shouldn't know anything else or he may sense it when you see him next."

"Well, fuck that. I'm not seeing anybody ever again."

"You have to."

"Fuck you."

"Samantha. Don't you want to see your father again? To find out if he's really alive?"

My glass rolled out of my hand and across the floor. I tried wiggling my fingers, and there seemed to be a time lag between the command and the action. I was probably going to be sick. Soon.

"Would a gun make you feel safe?" he asked. He almost sounded really concerned. "It wouldn't help, but I can get you one."

"I'm out. I said it. I'm out."

"I'm afraid not. Turn around, please." I didn't want to, but there was something about his voice. It was that damn badge. I knew it, but that didn't help. I turned around. "Raise your shirt, please." I did as he asked. I didn't know what was coming, but his reflection in the window pulled a long knife from out of nowhere.

"This sign will protect you. He won't be able to read you. I'll make sure you don't remember any of this conversation."

"That's nice," I mumbled, beginning to pass out. Then he began cutting into my back, and I lost consciousness, giving in to a wave of soothing pain and relaxation.

In my dream, Dad is still alive. I'm lying on my stomach on Jack's couch, alone except for Dad, who is trying to speak to me again. I don't want to open my eyes. I don't want to move. Dad stands at the doorway, his face ill-fitting, his hands like gloves. I don't want to question the robes anymore. I think I know what they hide. I think there's light coming from behind his eyes.

He seems to be shouting, but no sound gets

278

through. The more he gesticulates and tries to get my attention, the warmer my back becomes. Not a painful heat, but a soothing calm that spreads through my entire body. My eyes flicker shut, locking out the vision of my father -- not my father. I think I know this for sure now.

I open my eyes one more time just to see if he's gone, and I'm no longer in Jack's living room. I'm in the circular cavern beneath the old lab. The monsters, the Mi-go, are nowhere to be seen. The only sound is the grating and whirring of machinery reverberating through the stone walls.

I stand and feel a powerful urge to follow the noise, despite the fact that I no longer think this is a dream. I can feel the chill in the damp air. The mossy walls provide faint light, illuminating the stairway that leads back up to the surface. I want to run for the stairs, but there's something strange going on here, and I need to know what happened to my father. Is he still alive? Why would he fake his death? It's absurd, but I find myself walking slowly toward the first doorway at the foot of the stairs.

I reach out and touch the stone entryway and the warmth on my back flares up again, calming me in a way I haven't felt in years. Since I stopped cutting myself. Regularly. People don't understand the urge, calling it self-harm, calling it a psychological crutch. A cry for help. Fuck *help*. It's nothing of the sort. If anything, it's a cry to be left alone. To be allowed to get away, to process things, to find my footing. It was different in the beginning. I admit that. I never wanted to die, never wanted to suffer. I wanted attention. That's why the wrists. The obvious.

But that didn't last long. Suicide watch is no way to live.

The cutting brings a rush of endorphins. Yes, there's pain, but it's a small pain. A manageable pain. A pain that I control. The meth fucked that up for me. I don't even know why I started. But I smoked it for some reason. I was never a smoker, not even cigarettes. I guess I saw my parents both smoking when I was little. Too little to understand what they were doing. I was lucky, though; I only lost my mother to it. Sort of. I don't know anymore.

That sense of loss, that pain, flares up inside – a cold that counters the soothing heat. That's when I see it. I don't know what it is I'm seeing. My mind won't quite register. A wall of machinery. Lights. Sounds. There, in the center, a glass compartment. No, that's not right. It's not. I don't know what's happening anymore. I want to be home. I want to be on the couch, sleeping off my bourbon drunk, anticipating the hangover, pretending that everything's going to be all right.

I opened my eyes, and that's exactly where I was. And the bourbon pain behind my eyes was settling in. The sun was setting, a purple-red light slipping through the gap in the curtains that were only haphazardly pulled to. Jack wasn't in his chair. I guess he'd staggered upstairs to his bedroom at some point. I barely remembered falling asleep. How had the whole day disappeared? We were sitting, drinking, talking about The Egyptian...

The Fed.

Waitafuckingminute. The Fed had been here. I jumped up from the couch and cringed. My back was remarkably stiff, and I suddenly knew it wasn't because I'd been sleeping on my stomach on a couch older than I was. I lurched my way to the half-bath nestled back behind the kitchen, pulling my shirt up over my head and off. I flipped the light switch and blinked back rapidly, feeling the sharp hangover pain stabbing into my eyes again. I kind of wanted to puke, but I could still taste the lingering vomit of last night, and I fought it down.

I contorted myself around to see my back in the tiny mirror, and there it was: a variation on the symbol from The Fed's badge. More spiraling than claw-like, with additional markings at the points. Fuck it. Vomiting was back on the agenda, and I fell forward, barely getting the toilet seat up in time.

When there was more bourbon than water in the toilet, I finally gave it a rest, falling backward and knocking my head on the sink. Before I could swear, I heard Jack's cell phone ringing in the living room. Fucking John Mellencamp singing about fighting authority or something. I knew I should ignore it and head straight for the bus station, but an overwhelming sense of existential dread came over me, and I really wanted to throw up some more. Instead, I stumbled back to the living room.

The phone kept singing its stupid song at me while I stared at it, resting on the arm of Jack's chair. I glanced toward the stairs, hoping Jack would appear and take responsibility for answering it before I had to. I took a deep breath and called his name. There was no answer.

Why wouldn't the damn phone go to voicemail? It just kept telling me over and over that authority always wins. It was making me very uneasy. Images of last night's conversation started coming back to me in pieces. Things I wasn't supposed to remember. The Fed said he'd fix it so I couldn't remember, but I could. Shit. I could remember everything.

"Fine," I muttered to nobody and picked up the phone. "Hello?"

"I was beginning to think you were avoiding me, Samantha."

Of course it was The Egyptian. Who else could it be?

"This isn't my phone."

"Well, I can't call you on your burner, now can I?" I nearly dropped the phone. I nearly shit my pants.

"Burner?"

"Don't worry. I won't tell anyone if you won't." There was a silky laugh on the other end of the phone line, and I suddenly didn't know what to do or say. "Besides, Jack is with me. You can bring him his phone when you come see what I've got set up for you. You're going to love it!"

"Love it?"

"Your lab. Not as big and fancy as your father's trailer, but it will do the job for now. If I like your work ethic, we can upgrade."

I was silent. This was all moving very fast. Too fast. I needed to switch gears.

"Can I speak to Jack? Please?"

"You can speak to Jack when you get here. Your car is outside. I'll see you soon. Ciao." And he was gone.

My hand was trembling as I let the phone fall into the chair. He knew about the burner. How the fuck could he know about that? I puzzled over that as I pulled the window curtain aside and saw a black Honda Accord parked outside the house. The driver was standing by his door and waved when he saw me looking. I waved back and motioned that I'd be just a minute. He smiled and slipped back inside the car.

Great. Uber. I probably went to grade school with the guy.

I grabbed a toothbrush from a pack under the sink and quickly got as much of the puke taste and smell out of my mouth as I could. I considered calling The Fed, but if The Egyptian knew about the phone, he might be monitoring it somehow. Can you monitor a burner phone? Fuck. I needed to watch more crime movies. I don't know anything anymore.

By the time I was getting into the backseat of the Accord, I had convinced myself that The Egyptian had probably just seen the phone on my dresser when he was in my motel room. I mean, he was creepy as shit, but he wasn't psychic, right? I had probably dreamed that horrifying eye trick he did. Sure. Because my dreams weren't becoming real or anything.

I had to stop arguing with myself about what was real and what wasn't.

I hadn't gone to grade school with the driver. In fact, the driver never even spoke, no matter how I tried to start a conversation. And by *start a conversation* I mean *talk him into taking me to the bus station.* He would simply "tut tut" me and keep driving, without even glancing at me in the mirror.

We ended up on the opposite end of town from where Dad's lab had been set up, but it was just as inconveniently located in the woods. Laughing Boy's car wasn't made for off-roading, but he took a sharp turn up a dirt path that was more four-wheeler trail than actual road. We bounced and slid along for five minutes as the Accord tried to do things it had never been designed for, and then a tire blew.

But we kept going.

"Dude! You need to stop the car!" Another tire tore itself open on the rocks, and then I was pretty sure something happened underneath that nobody's car should have to go through. We were stuck. The driver, with the engine still running, got out and turned to open the door for me like a true and proper gentleman. And that was when it became clear that he wasn't just the world's most dedicated Uber driver. He wasn't in control of his body. His eyes rolled and watered as he tried desperately to do something, anything, other than simply deliver me to my destination.

I didn't know what to do, so I started walking in the direction he pointed. Looking back, I watched helplessly as he began sobbing and wandered off deeper into the darkness of the woods. At that point I was even more glad I hadn't gone to grade school with him.

"I'll be honest with you, Samantha," The Egyptian said. "I had considered closing shop here and moving solely into the heroin business." He smiled. "Less overhead, no explosions, and the buyers are more primed for the experience I'm

284

giving them than meth addicts are."

He was talking to me as though everything was normal, and it just added to the sense of unreality that was washing over me. The new lab was a small camper – one room and barely enough space to work in. The insides had been gutted, and the Mi-go were working, adding equipment, moving supplies to a secondary trailer; some were hooded, but many weren't. A few portable lights were set up, but they tended to avoid them. I couldn't believe that this was already happening. I guess The Egyptian was on a tight schedule, and what The Egyptian wants, he gets.

I couldn't decide if seeing them for real, lurching about in front of me on insect legs, was worse with the hooded robes or without. Regardless, I was now positive my dreams hadn't been dreams at all. I shuddered as this thought crossed my mind, hoping beyond hope that The Egyptian really couldn't read my mind with my new body mod in place. Every time he looked at me I felt as though my skull was tickling, and my insides turned to jelly.

But at least I was better off than Uncle Jack.

When I'd first entered the clearing, it was nearly too much for me to take in: the trailer sitting beneath a cover, the Mi-go shuffling around inside the trailer and in the trees around it, casting nightmarish shadows across the clearing as their heads shimmered and lit up in multicolored patterns; The Egyptian overseeing in his spotless suit. And then there was Uncle Jack, huddled against a tree, much like I had been at the previous lab site. He was holding his knees close and rocking back and forth, rubbing his back violently against the bark of the tree as though scratching an itch that wouldn't let up. He was crying, sobbing wordlessly, snot hanging from his nose, drool dripping from his chin.

My instinct was to run to him. To hold him like he had me. To get him out of here to safety.

But I didn't move. I simply watched it all in silence until The Egyptian turned and caught my eye, waving me over.

"Because the experience is key." He turned and held me by both shoulders, squaring me off, facing him unshielded. "Why did you smoke this garbage? What was it you were trying to achieve?"

"Achieve?" I didn't know what to say. "I wasn't trying to achieve anything. I just wanted...I don't know. I just wanted to get away." That was really it, wasn't it? Escape. That was what I'd wanted when I left Morrison and discovered that everything was shitty everywhere, sometimes magnified.

"Escape. That's the word." He smiled again and I felt tendrils probing around the edges of my consciousness. "This world is doomed. You all know it. You all sense it every day, in every interaction. It's why you go to church, start families, give to charity, steal from your bosses, cheat on your spouses. It's why you don't value anything anymore. Because you're all doomed, and you all know it."

He spun me around, put his arm around me, and walked me over to Jack, who didn't seem to even know we were there.

"Your uncle, he's a good example of this. Never amounted to anything. Never would. Between you and me, he wasn't even a very good drug dealer. Passable, I suppose. Your father was the real talent."

"Is Jack going to be all right?" I asked, despite knowing the answer.

"Don't mind Jack. He's had *too much to think*." He laughed as though it was most clever thing anyone had ever said.

"Did he ever tell you about your grandparents?"

I froze. "No. Not really. Just that they went crazy." I really didn't want to dig further into it. I was barely holding onto my sanity as it was. Finding out family secrets might send me into a freak-out worse than Jack's. But there was no stopping The Egyptian. He was on a roll.

"Oh, crazy isn't the right word. I believe you kids today call it 'woke.' They saw the secret forces behind reality, the powers that shape the world, and they saw fit to tinker with those powers. To engage them. Your father was really only a half-brother to Jack. That's why they seemed normal when Jack was young, but crazy once Billy was born."

"I don't want to hear this."

"You need to hear it. Just as Jack needed to hear it." He suddenly seemed more serious than I'd seen him. As though this information meant more than any of the meth business talk he'd shared before. He needed to see my reaction. "Your grandfather wasn't your grandfather."

I put my hands over my ears and focused on Jack. Jack focused on nothing in particular, but kept crying.

"Your grandfather was Yog-Sothoth, the Gate, the Key, and the Guardian."

"What the fuck does that even mean?"

He smiled. "Your grandparents were in contact with the Mi-go. That original Flatwoods Monster sighting was the result of their meeting. The Mi-go don't normally interact with humans. Don't care for your type at all, really. But your grandfather had an idea that intrigued them.

"Naturally, I would have put a stop to it had I known what they were planning, but this was a renegade sect. They hadn't sworn allegiance to me and, to be honest, I'd been preoccupied with other things." He waved his hand. "It was the fifties, after all. Nuclear armageddon was on everybody's minds, and I was committed to stoking that glorious fear."

"What are you talking about? This doesn't make sense."

"It makes perfect sense. The Mi-go are scientists at heart." He turned me away from Jack, toward the monsters preparing the meth lab. "They look like creatures from another world because they are, but they're not mindless monsters. They're people, like you…in a manner of speaking. Science is their true religion. They worship me to an extent, but that's only natural." I tried to pull away from him, but his arm was locked tightly around me, his hand gripping my shoulder. "I *am* something special. But science is their air, their sun, their *joie de vivre*. And your grandfather proposed an experiment that these renegades, these traitors, couldn't resist."

My knees went from under me, and I would have landed hard on the cold ground if The Egyptian hadn't been holding me up. Concern flashed briefly across his face and he gently lowered me to the grass, kneeling beside me, holding me like his own child.

"Yog-what? What does that even mean?"

"Yog-Sothoth." He rolled his eyes and bobbed his head. "My nephew, of sorts. Things were murky back then. No real records to speak of. We don't really talk."

"Stop it! Shut up!"

He jerked me around to face him again. "Mind your tone, little girl." I felt the world go dark around me, and for just an instant I was perched at the top of an immense peak. Suddenly, he was smiling and we were in the clearing again. "Sorry about that. But family is important. This is something you should know about."

"Go on, then."

"While I trudge and toil on this physical plane, doing my best to sow a little chaos and enlighten people about the true nature of reality, my nephew Yog-Sothoth exists..." He paused. "...Elsewhere and everywhere. He is co-terminous with all time and space. He knows the past, present, and future because they are all one in him, born from The Nameless Mist."

"And somehow he fucked my grandma crazy."

The Egyptian laughed again. A hearty laugh. A *real* laugh. Then he poked me in the arm.

"And he fucked your grandma crazy. Well said." He winked. "I *like* you, Samantha. I think this is going to be a positive experience for you. For both of us. We're practically family, after all."

I shuddered uncontrollably.

"You...you said 'an experiment'? What does that mean?"

"Ah, yes. The Mi-go have a gift for genetic manipulation. Tinkering with the genome and that sort of thing. Both their own and that of you lower creatures. That's why they can travel through the vacuum of space. They need no ships to travel from their home on Yoggoth to here. But it takes time, even at the speeds they can travel once gravity no longer constrains them.

"However, if they could open wormholes..."

"Yoggoth? Wormholes?"

"You know it as Pluto. And wormholes are portals through spacetime that allow instantaneous transportation to anywhere in the universe...and beyond." He paused dramatically, waiting for me look him in the eye. "Don't you watch any science fiction at all?"

I was crying. When had I started crying? "Oh god. Why are you telling me all this? What happened to my dad?"

"He's dead, isn't he? That's what you told me. You buried him." I nodded. "Which is too bad. It seemed like the experiment was a failure. The Mi-go in charge, at the instigation of your grandfather, tried to breed the gift of teleportation into a human host, which, logically, led them to invoking Yog-Sothoth and orchestrating the impregnation of your grandmother."

"Logically."

"Logically. It's not like he hasn't done that sort of thing before. Bred with human women, I mean. Horrible messes those were." He sighed a real sigh. "Sad how they all turned out. Hideous. Even by my standards. But your father was different. With the Mi-go guiding the, um, *event*, your grandfather became a vessel and everyone survived the experience, although your grandmother was never the same. Your father had issues of his own over the years, as you know. The drug addiction was mainly a coping mechanism, I'd guess. Keeping visions or madness at bay, or what have you, because the experiment, as I've said, seemed to be a failure.

"And, as I've also said, against my wishes. The sect responsible paid the price for disobedience, but I left your family alone. I thought they might come in handy someday. And lo and behold, they did!" He waved his hands around, laughing. "Without your father, we wouldn't have all this!"

He stopped laughing and leaned in close. "We wouldn't have *you*."

"A meth cook?"

"Oh, more than that, I hope."

"I don't know what you mean. I'm normal. Fucked up, but normal."

"Don't hide your light under a bushel, Samantha."

"My light?"

"Your dream. About your father. You know it wasn't just a dream, right?"

My eyes widened, and I could have sworn I felt my heart murmur. My stomach dropped and I was suddenly very cold.

That's when The Fed arrived.

He walked calmly into the clearing, as though it were the most normal thing he could be doing at the moment. The Egyptian paused, a puzzled look crossing his face for an instant before a cold calm returned. The Mi-go froze, fixated on his arrival.

"Are you okay, Samantha?" he asked casually. I had to admit, I was impressed. There was no fear about him at all. Just a cool distance that I was beginning to realize was probably not normal at all. I nodded, and he actually pulled a pack of cigarettes from his overcoat pocket, tapped out a smoke, and proceeded to light it as though The Egyptian wasn't even there.

"Ah, now it's all starting to make sense," The Egyptian said. "The Brotherhood."

The Fed nodded a greeting. The Egyptian glanced at me and then back to The Fed. What was his fucking name? That much was gone.

"Still worshipping the wrong gods, I see," The Egyptian said sarcastically.

"Depends who you ask."

"So you're not here because of me, then, but my servants?"

"We are dedicated to wiping the Mi-go from our planet." The Mi-go began communicating with one another, clicking their claws and flashing patterns of light in their heads. "Your plans are secondary."

"We both want madness and destruction, your god and I. This conflict is pointless."

"We don't see it that way."

He gave no more warning than that, and other agents opened fire from a dozen different vantage points along the tree line. The Egyptian had been so focused on The Fed, on the potential for personal confrontation, that even he hadn't noticed their approach. Either they were shielded with those fucking symbols or he was indifferent. I'll never really know. Regardless, machine gun fire tore into the Mi-go, exploding parts of them in bursts of

292

fungal body and shiny beetle-like shells.

One of the hideous things emerged from the trailer, and its glowing head exploding as a bullet pierced it. All of the Mi-go shrieked as one, but it wasn't a sound you could hear. It was a sound you felt. With their mutant lobster claws raised and clacking nightmarishly, they formed ranks and skittered toward the trees.

A dozen or so men in the same shabby, "afterthought" style of The Fed tried to concentrate their fire on the upper bodies of the Mi-go, but found targeting difficult as the alien monsters expanded and contorted, leaping toward them, gliding on fragile wings. I watched helplessly as one swooped onto an agent not ten feet from me and violently snipped his head off in a spray of arterial blood. The head landed at my feet, and I could see his eyes roll and his face contort as he tried to figure out what was happening as he died.

I had to get away. This was too much: the explosive sounds of gunfire, the smell of smoke; the screams, both human and alien. The darkness was strobed in muzzle flashes and horrors were raging all around me. The Egyptian allowed his grip to loosen as he calmly took in the chaos around him. There was a glint of a smile as he watched the battle get underway, as though satisfied with the bloodshed. The *chaos*.

The Crawling Chaos. That's what the Fed had called him. But never his real name.

Nyarlathotep.

The name sprang into being, fully formed in my head despite my never having heard it before. My breathing was suddenly difficult. My head felt cloudy, pressure closing in from around the back, over my forehead, behind my eyes. I was sobbing just like Jack. I couldn't control it.

And then, suddenly, I could.

A light went off in my mind – something popped like a flashbulb – and I felt detached from everything going on around me, from my own body. For an instant I thought that maybe I'd been shot. That I was dying. Relief flooded through me in a wave of calm, warm pleasure that was a hundred times more satisfying than cutting myself had ever been.

Nyarlathotep was still fixated on the violence surrounding us. He barely even noticed as I stood up, turned away from him, and stepped quietly through a fracture in space that had opened behind me without my even realizing.

I stand in what seems to be a vestibule of shimmering light. Behind me, the clearing fades to near-silence. I can still hear the gunfire, the death, now an explosion, but it's all very distant. I yawn to pop my ears, but the sounds are only vaguely audible. Nyarlathotep still watches the chaos, and as I turn away can feel his senses turning toward me before he does. He's about to realize I've slipped from his grasp.

So I leap, not knowing where I'm going. Not caring anymore.

I am on a crystal hillside, angled and gleaming in the sweltering light of seven suns. The slippery ground pulses rhythmically, as though strange inhuman machinery is toiling and wheezing miles beneath the surface. The air is acrid, burning my eyes, my nose, my throat. I pull my shirt up over my mouth to mitigate it somewhat.

It doesn't work.

The landscape around me is a cacophony of colors and dangerous edges; a crystalline structure that immediately reminds me of methamphetamine. There are more caverns than I can count, all opening into dark, blood-red passages, reflecting light like a universe underground, like science fair geodes cracked open and inviting.

I move toward the closest, but before I can enter, sounds of metal moving across glass echo upwards toward me. I duck back and slide down around the side of a sloping crystal wall just in time to take cover before a bizarre metallic brain clanks out into the light on spindly, steampunk legs. It stops and turns toward me, then back around the other way, searching for the thing that has invaded its world unbidden.

Suddenly it freezes – emitting a series of whirrs and clicks before skittering back underground – as something I pray I never see again appears on the horizon. It is immense, shifting itself forward on a thick conglomeration of tentacles. A humanoid body rises up from the convulsing mass, and two bat-like arms stretch out, spreading fleshy wings that help propel it toward where I crouch, hidden. *Not hidden?*

At the peak of its thick earthworm neck is a huge, three-lobed, burning eye, sending a beam of blistering light back and forth across the crystal plains, methodically covering every square inch of space, searching for me. I can feel it.

This is Nyarlathotep, following me, hunting me. Trying to bring me home.

My eyes begin to water uncontrollably and my vision blurs. There's an oppressive pressure just behind my eyes, and another portal opens up before me. I am through it before Nyarlathotep's eye alights upon me.

I am in a crimson forest, surrounded by trees, fleshy and scabrous, undulating in the warm breeze. The mere sight of them makes me gag. I turn and run toward an opening in the repulsive foliage, bursting out beneath a pale red sky. One sun is setting, throwing long shadows that confuse and conflict with the varying shadows of the two suns that remain above the horizon.

The air is sickly sweet like rot, like decay. In the distance stands a dark tower, encircled with walls and bars, locks and gates. Just looking at it makes my brain itch, and I can tell that something appalling is trapped inside. There's nothing on any world that could make me want to approach that tower, so I turn, looking for someplace to hide, only to come face to face with a hideous double-headed bat creature perched in one of the meat trees. Its countless eyes twinkle and move about on the two faces; its four fanged and dripping mouths open, and hisses escape like curses. The smell is enough to knock me to my knees. It flexes its talons, piercing the branch upon which it perches. Foul black ichor drips slowly from the wounds.

This is Nyarlathotep, following me, hunting me.

My eyes begin to water and my vision doubles. There's a painful pressure just behind my eyes and another portal opens up before me. I am through it before Nyarlathotep can swoop down from the tree.

I am on the ramparts of a high tower, overlooking an incomprehensible maze of ramshackle structures, sprawling out as far as the eye can see. Black flags snap in the wind and a charnel smell rises from the gutters and alleys below. Insects move through the city in hordes, a rush hour plague of locusts. The sky above is filled with smoke, but through breaks in the cover I can see one pale sun, barely providing enough light to see the cityscape below. It shares the sky with the spiraling apocalypse of a black hole, the event horizon stealing fire and energy from its dying partner.

Rising up out of the chaos of barely held-together shelters to the east is a seething blackness made up of innumerable mouths, snapping and screaming; a whirlwind of teeth, spittle, and tongues. Wormlike tendrils writhe and flap, squirming and spasming, shrieking my name.

This is Nyarlathotep, following me, hunting me.

My eyes close. There's a slight pressure behind my eyes and a new portal opens behind me. I lock my eyes on Nyarlathotep's hideous avatar and step calmly through before he can get anywhere near the tower.

I am back in the antechamber beneath the old lab.

Mi-go stand in all but one of the doorways surrounding me. There is no more hostility, only curiosity. I flash them a peace sign and stroll into

297

the room off the base of the stairs.

The room is just as it was in my dream. It wasn't a dream. I know that for sure now. The far wall is lined with machinery covered in lights, gauges, video screens, knobs, and switches. In the center, directly in front of me, is a glass case with brass fittings, a speaker and a camera. What appears to be a handle arcs over the top of the device. The container is filled with a dark, viscous-looking fluid. Thick bubbles rise along the right and left, making their way around the human brain suspended in its center.

"That's you in there, isn't it, Dad?"

"Hello, Sam," a metallic voice responds from the speaker, scratchy and thin. "It's good to see you again."

"You can see me?"

One of the video screens next to the container flashes to life and I see myself in grainy lo-fi. I lean in toward the brain and watch myself lean forward on the screen.

"You really shouldn't be here, Sam."

"You're one to talk." I tap the glass of his jar. "So, what the actual fuck?"

"I just wanted to get away. I really didn't think you'd come back. You were free and clear. Why did you come back?"

"Because you fucking died. Or faked your death. Or whatever this is." I kick the machinery. "Jesus *fucking* Christ, Dad. What the fuck were you thinking?"

"Language, Sam."

"Fuck you."

The speaker hisses static and we are both silent

for almost a full minute. I assume he's staring at me, trying to figure me out, as I'm doing the same thing to him. To his brain. To his fucking brain in a jar.

"Seriously, Dad. What is this? What's going on?"

"It's a little hard to explain."

"Let me just see if I can guess, then. You worked with the Mi-go to sell meth designed to make people hallucinate about the end of the world, then you freaked out and made a deal with different Mi-go to fake your death, so you could get out of it without risking the wrath of The Egyptian--"

"Um..."

"--who is not an actual Egyptian drug dealer, but is, in fact, a multi-dimensional motherfucker who craves chaos and destruction at all of our expense."

"How?"

"Yeah. I've been busy since you went underground." I kick the machinery again and his jar gurgles.

"You've met The Egyptian?"

"Aaaaaahhhh!" I kick the machine again and again until my foot hurts. "*Fuuuuuck!*"

I don't know what else to do, so I sit on the floor facing him. My image on the screen is scowling, rocking back and forth. I need a haircut. I can't tell if there are dark circles under my eyes or if it's the shitty video quality of the monitor.

"Looks like you could use an upgrade. You know there's this thing called HD, right?"

"The Mi-go are very particular about their technology."

"Right."

More silence, broken only by the low humming static of the speaker.

"Yes, I've met The Egyptian. Of course I've met The Egyptian. By the way, it looks like Jack's a drooling imbecile now. Thanks for that, too."

"Jack's what?"

"If he's not dead, that is. There was a lot of random gunfire and monsters attacking in all directions."

"What?"

"Yeah, you've missed a shit ton of story, Dad."

"Yes, a shit ton," says The Egyptian from the doorway behind me. Only he isn't The Egyptian. He's Nyarlathotep. He's wearing a humanoid body and The Egyptian's fancy suit, stained with who-knows-whose blood and gore. Some of it is green, so I guess he's been killing Mi-go, too. Of course he has been. Why wouldn't he? Why wouldn't he kill us all? His head is not a head, though. It's a swirling mass of thick smoke, spiraling like a universe being born. Four crimson eyes float freely in the weightless miasma where his head should be.

"You found me," I say, not sounding the least bit surprised.

"I did. I almost didn't, though. You're very clever." His head coalesces into the familiar face of The Egyptian as he looks around the room. "A pocket dimension. Very clever, William. I might never have found it, were it not for Samantha."

I scowl again.

"Stay away from her," bleats Dad impotently from his speaker.

"Don't worry, William. I'm not here for her."

He strolls past me, leaning in to examine the brain cylinder. "Archaic. I suppose they were going to fly you through space to their homeworld?"

Static.

"Pathetic."

"They wanted to help me. To study me."

"Of course they did." He breathes on the glass, fogging it, then wipes it clean with his sleeve. "And you wanted to get away. No more guilt. No more struggle. No more spreading my influence like a good dog. You had to look upwards and dream of the stars.

"Well, William, the stars are not for you."

I consider portaling away, but to be honest, I really want to see what's going to happen next.

"Fine then. I'm yours. Do what you want, but let Sammy go." Dad's noble final gesture. Nyarlathotep and I both snort at the same time. He glances back at me and winks.

"I'll do what I want, with no qualifiers, William. I'm tempted to let them take you. To experiment on you. They don't care about you, just your potential in the lab. You had visions, didn't you? That's why you drugged yourself into oblivion. So no one would know."

"They'd have said I was crazy." Dad's voice is soft, just barely audible above the buzz of the speaker. He is afraid.

"But you weren't crazy. You were seeing other worlds. Other times. There *was* some of Yog-Sothoth in you after all. You weren't a failure. Not entirely."

The speaker buzzes, but he refuses to respond.

"Samantha, however, is an unbridled success."

301

"Sam?"

"She has the gift you were bred for, dog. The talent the Mi-go so desperately want." Nyarlathotep turns toward me. "They'll want to cut up your brain next, girl. See what makes you tick. See what they can harvest for their own use."

The whole room seems to be moving. My breath is short. I will probably pass out if I don't brace myself against the stone floor and focus on my father's brain in its canister. How can any of this be real?

"If I hadn't killed them all, that is. Disobedience must be punished, after all."

"Sammy, you have to run," Dad says.

Nyarlathotep laughs.

"Don't worry about Samantha. She's a survivor." He turns back toward Dad's brain. "You, however, also disobeyed me. So now you must pay."

He snaps his fingers and the fluid in the cylinder begins to bubble and boil. The noise coming from the speaker makes my teeth hurt, and I'll probably hear it whenever things get quiet for the rest of my life. I suppose I should feel something more than disgust and dread, but I have a hard time identifying the brain in the jar as my Dad. I buried my Dad. This is something I never should have seen. So I disassociate like a boss.

"But what's done is done, I suppose," Nyarlathotep says as he turns and elegantly bows in my direction. "You're a different kind of chaos than I'm familiar with, Samantha, and I'm extremely curious to see what else you do with this gift of yours. I don't think you're going to be limited to

302

traveling through space."

I say nothing, expecting my head to explode, or my limbs to turn into tentacles, or for some other eldritch horror to consume and condemn me to a brief but vivid life and agonizing death. I welcome it. I want this to end. I don't want to be afraid any more. I want to escape the only way I can at this point.

"What are you doing? What's that look on your face? Get up." He extends his hand to help me to my feet. "The Brotherhood will likely have dispatched the Mi-go by now. They're notoriously dogmatic like that." He smirked. "They won't like what you are, that's for sure. No, indeed. You'll be something of an abomination in their eyes."

I frown, confused.

"Once they know, of course. Let's go introduce ourselves, shall we?"

Before I can respond, Nyarlathotep and I are back in the clearing. There are bodies everywhere, both human and Mi-go. Jack is dead, riddled with bullets, bled out at the foot of the tree where he had been huddled, crying. I disassociate again. I might feel all of this later, if I live through it. Is this normal? Should I be able to do this?

"Samantha!" The Fed steps out from behind the ruined meth lab trailer - guess I can forget about adding "cook" to my resume - but stops short when he sees Nyarlathotep at my side. "Are you okay?" he asks hesitantly.

"I'm fucking great." He's covered in blood and gore. He's a walking Jackson Pollack in Christmassy red and green. His eyes are locked on

Nyarlathotep, so he doesn't even acknowledge me walking up to him, rearing back, and punching him in the chest.

"Ow! What?"

"I was *bait*?"

"You were safe." I hit him again. "Mostly." Nyarlathotep laughs. The Fed steps past me, putting himself between me and the Crawling Chaos. "Your operation here is finished, Horror. Leave Samantha with us."

Nyarlathotep and I snort simultaneously again. This is getting embarrassing.

A handful of wounded cultists in shabby suits emerge from the darkness, leveling guns at Nyarlathotep.

"I was finished here, anyway. As I told Samantha earlier, meth is so tedious. Heroin is much more expedient and is doing wonders in other parts of this sad, existential petri dish of a state.

"She's yours." He turned to me and smiled his most charming smile. "But I do require a finder's fee." He vanishes, and the rest of the surviving Brothers collapse in writhing agony, clawing their eyes in hideous pain. The Fed whimpers, watching helplessly as they fall all around him, powerless to do anything to stop it. It's endearing, really. Like a child watching his parents take his puppy away. I have to restrain myself from laughing and telling him it will be all right. That they're just going to live on a farm.

Something is wrong with me.

I reach up and place my hand on his temple. Suddenly he has a seizure as I show him other worlds, other times. Shambling, shapeless beasts rising up against their masters in the Antarctic. Foul-smelling fish-men breeding with human women in New England coastal towns. A great dark mass in the deepest ocean, sleeping, waiting, madness seeping from it like a toxic spill. The Fed gets it all at once. His nose and eyes start to bleed. He foams at the mouth, collapsing at my feet. *Agent Chambers*, that was it. I remember it all now. All the times he'd told me horrible things, abusive things, bullying me into service. Then he'd wipe my mind and try again, until finally I agreed to come here. I kneel down next to him and pat his cheek. He helped awaken my gifts with all that tinkering. He broke down whatever natural barriers my mind had built, and now I was free.

As a final parting gift from Nyarlathotep, I suddenly begin receiving visions of junkies all over the county convulsing, mouths foaming, eyes bleeding, noses bleeding, very much like Chambers here. We share the same style, it appears. I watch dispassionately as the snaggletooth vampire junkies writhe and scream, dying alone, needles in their arms. He really is cleaning house. In Braxton County, anyway. Almost before I realize what it is I'm seeing, the visions stop. The death, the horror – all of it over in an instant. For the users, at least. Now the horror starts for their families and friends. It's all horror, all the time, in this place. There's got to be someplace better.

When I turn my back to The Fed, I see a multitude of pathways extending outward in all directions, like hundreds of silver strings flung into a weightless void and superimposed over the carnage of the clearing. Instinctively, I know what

305

to do. I know that I am safe. When I travel, it will not be random, even if I don't consciously choose a destination. I won't step out into the heart of a sun, or into an airless abyss. I will travel to places that, if they won't welcome me, at least won't kill me before I know what's happening. Or perhaps I will change, adapting to new environments, surviving whatever the multiverse throws at me.

I have a heart of chaos, but I know now that chaos is not evil. Chaos is essential for life. And I want to live.

So that's what I choose to do.

Elsewhere.

Who We Be

R. Mike Burr

Mike Burr is a dedicated social democrat, handyman, and physical science teacher who currently resides in the Deep South. He can often be found prowling the streets of his neighborhood with his canine companion, wreaking havoc on property values. A recent addition to his family has necessitated doing most of his movie viewing online. Some current picks from his queue include *Out of the Furnace*, *Blue Ruin*, *Prince Avalanche,* and *This Must Be the Place*. Mike has written mostly about music, and has interviewed everyone from Bootsy Collins to Josh T. Pearson, Jay Reatard and Katy Perry.

Dan Gorman

Dan began working as a Sketch Card Artist in 2010 and has since worked on over 120 Licensed Trading Card sets featuring properties that include, but are not limited to: Marvel, DC, *Star Wars*, *Star Trek*, *Game of Thrones*, *Alien*, *The Lord of the Rings*, and AMC's *The Walking Dead*. In 2012, Dan began penciling stories for *AC Comics: FemForce* and continues to do so. Dan's work can also be seen in two issues of the *Grindhouse* mini-series published by Dark Horse Comics. In 2015, Dan launched his first free weekly webcomic called *The Atomic*

Blonde. Each week's installment is an homage to the Golden Age of comics with a retro sci-fi flare. The webcomic caught the eye of AC Comics and is now a recurring character in the pages of *FemForce.* Also in 2015, Dan launched a weekly internet radio show about comics and pop culture called "The Altered Realm," which he co-hosts on krmaradio.com every Saturday night from 8pm-midnight. In 2016, Dan launched another webcomic, *The Akron Knight,* which appears in *The Akron Devil Strip* magazine as well as online at AkronKnightComic.com, and has been optioned by Empire Comics Lab to run as one of their featured webcomics. Dan is a regular contributor to Empire Comics Lab's flagship title, *Cemetery Plots,* starting with issue #2. Dan also contributes artwork to another comic strip appearing in *The Akron Devil Strip* called *The Altered Realm.* You can see more of Dan's work at dangormanart.com, and be sure to follow him @GDanArtist on Twitter!

Dan Johnson

Dan Johnson is a North Carolina-based writer. At this time, he is the editor and head writer for Empire Comics Lab's horror anthology, *Cemetery Plots.* Dan has also worked for Antarctic Press, Campfire Graphic Novels and the *Dennis the Menace* comic strip. Besides his work in the comics industry, he has also written for *Alter Ego, Back Issue, Comic Book Marketplace, Filmfax, Hogan's Alley, Monster Memories, Monster News* and *Scary Monsters Magazine.*

310

Dan Lee

Dan Lee is a horror fiction fiend and freelance writer living in the outer edge of a large, southern metropolis. His stories and articles have been featured in several 'zines and online publications, including *Psycho Drive-In* and *52 Weeks of Horror,* and his fiction continues to be developed through his blog at *dannoofthedeadblog.wordpress.com* and on Twitter and Instagram as @dotdblog.

Paul Brian McCoy

Paul Brian McCoy is the Editor-in-Chief of both Psycho Drive-In and PDI Press. In 2011 he published his first novel, *The Unraveling: Damaged Inc., Book One,* followed shortly by his collection of short stories, *Coffee, Sex, & Creation.* He recently contributed the "1989" chapter to *The American Comic Book Chronicles: The 1980s,* and also kicked off Comics Bulletin Books with *Mondo Marvel*: *Volumes One-Four* and PDI Press with *Marvel at the Movies (1977-1998), Marvel at the Movies: Marvel Studio:, From Iron Man to Ultron,* and *Spoiler Alert: Hannibal Season One: An Unauthorized Critical Guide.* Paul is also unnaturally preoccupied with zombie films and sci-fi television. He can be found babbling on Twitter at @PBMcCoy.

John E. Meredith

J. Meredith is a freelance writer from the American Midwest. He will go on about damn-near anything if you let him, from movies and music to the world and himself. A Halloween baby, he has a natural tendency toward things dark and awful, or at least shot in black-and-white, and he should probably be on some kind of medication. Feel free to haunt him on his Facebook page /John E. Meredith, or contact him at scribe6903@yahoo.com.

Rick Shingler

Rick Shingler very often catches himself in the act of writing, but hopes one day to find the right support group to help relieve him of this tendency. In the meantime, he has published two e-books and is scripting forthcoming online comics with Empire Comics Lab. An Ohio exile living in New Jersey, he is consistently puzzled by the native Jerseyan reverence for Bon Jovi, disdain for Springsteen, and lack of awareness when it comes to the Swingin' Neckbreakers. He recently published his space opera, *The Perilous Journeys of Pericles, Prince of Tyre.*

Alex Wolfe

Alex Wolfe is a writer, dungeon master, and part-time critic with an addiction to the macabre and an intense love for well-spun characters. Their quest for world domination currently remains on a back burner, so enjoy this grace period of freedom and comfort before that becomes a thing.